"MRS. HAWKINS, LOOK AT ME."

Logan's gray eyes were intense, like storm clouds when lightning flashes through them. "This looks bad, but I've been in worse situations and lived to tell. Stand with your back to mine. Have your gun ready, but by God, don't shoot until I tell you."

"I won't be taken again. I won't go alive into that hell."

He didn't respond. He pulled her revolver and checked the chamber, rotated it once, then closed it and put it in her shaking hands. "We don't know it's gonna come to that. If there's one thing an Indian hates, it's unexpected behavior. Our standing here is sure as hell unexpected. Let's just see where this goes."

She pressed her back to the man who had been her salvation since he'd joined the small group of travelers. She could feel the heated leather of his vest against her shoulders. He was tall. Brave beyond reason.

And about to die because of her.

Also Available by Elaine Levine

RACHEL AND THE HIRED GUN

AUDREY AND THE MAVERICK

LEAH AND THE BOUNTY HUNTER

Published by Kensington Publishing Corporation

LOGAN'S OUTLAW

Men of Defiance

ELAINE LEVINE

ZEBRA BOOKS
KENSINGTON PUBLISHING CORP.
http://www.kensingtonbooks.com

ZEBRA BOOKS are published by

Kensington Publishing Corp.
119 West 40th Street
New York, NY 10018

All Kensington titles, imprints and distributed lines are available at special quantity discounts for bulk purchases for sales
promotion, premiums, fund-raising, educational or institu-
tional use.

Special book excerpts or customized printings can also be cre-
ated to fit specific needs. For details, write or phone the office
of the Kensington Special Sales Manager: Attn. Special Sales
Department. Kensington Publishing Corp., 119 West 40th
Street, New York, NY 10018. Phone: 1-800-221-2647.

Zebra and the Z logo Reg. U.S. Pat. & TM Off.

ISBN-13: 978-1-4201-1867-4
ISBN-10: 1-4201-1867-6

First Printing: March 2012
10 9 8 7 6 5 4 3 2 1

Printed in the United States of America

To Barb,
for hugs after nightmares and believing when I didn't.
You are the best sister ever.

And to Barry,
my everything.

Chapter 1

The cold steel of the Peacemaker gave Sarah Hawkins an artificial sense of security. Had she owned this gun a year ago, the Sioux would never have taken her alive.

"You're too little for that piece," the shopkeeper said as he frowned down at the revolver she was examining. "That's a seven-and-a-half-inch barrel, almost three pounds fully loaded. And begging your pardon, ma'am, but after you fire it, you'll be sitting on your backside."

"I have to agree, Mrs. Hawkins," Captain Frasier spoke up. "A derringer is just as deadly and would be easier for you to handle. You don't have the strength a man has in his hands and shoulders to use a Colt effectively."

Sarah checked the cylinders of both guns. They were empty. She pointed the derringer at the shopkeeper, practicing her aim, familiarizing herself with the weapon. He barely registered concern. When she lifted the Peacemaker, he stepped back quickly—even knowing it wasn't loaded.

A gun was for killing. The bigger, the better.

The fear she'd felt when the war party raided their cabin had been crippling. She doubted her ability to kill herself with the little derringer, should the situation arise again. And she knew, sometime in the next fortnight, it would.

"How much for the Colt?" she asked the shop-keeper.

"Twenty-five dollars."

Sarah gasped, shocked. "The catalog price is just seventeen dollars! Shame on you for taking advantage of a widow."

"I got a strong market for that gun, ma'am. Ain't a man on the post who wouldn't sign over two months' wages for it. None of 'em want to be caught out on the plains without a piece of iron at their side. But if you want the catalog price, then I'll place that order for you. In three months or so you'll have your gun."

Waiting was not possible. She was leaving for Cheyenne tomorrow. "I'll pay twenty dollars for the gun and five boxes of cartridges."

The shopkeeper's eyes bulged. "You want me to give it away? I told you I got buyers standing in line for it."

The captain cleared his throat, catching the shop-keeper's eye. A look or signal passed between the men that made Sarah grit her teeth. She was a sup-plicant, in need of anyone and everyone's help.

The women at the fort had taken up a collection for her, which was the source of the funds she planned to use for the gun—and the very clothes she wore. She hated being needy, even as she was grateful so many were willing to help.

After paying for her stage ticket and food supplies for the journey, she had only thirty dollars to her name. This purchase would leave her with ten dollars once she reached Cheyenne, enough to live on for two weeks if she found affordable lodging and ate only once a day. Two weeks was enough time for her to find a job, to begin over—or at least, to find a way to support herself until she felt it was safe enough to leave Cheyenne.

It was the only plan she had, and she was sticking to it.

"What I expect, sir, is for you to sell the gun to me for a fair price."

The shopkeeper glared at her, his mouth compressed into a thin line. He exchanged another look with the captain. "The gun and three boxes of cartridges."

"Done," she said.

"And throw in a holster and a gun belt," the captain added. "And a kit for cleaning the pistol."

"No!" Sarah turned to look at him. "I haven't the funds for those things. The gun and cartridges are all I need."

"Then the others will be my gift to you, Mrs. Hawkins. It is the least I can do, as an officer of the United States Army."

The shopkeeper eyed her waist. "Don't have a gun belt that'll fit a tiny thing like her."

"Then get a large one we can wrap twice around her," the captain said.

A short while later, at an area designated for shooting practice, Sarah took the gun out of the holster and put it back, twice, getting a feel for the revolver, making sure she could handle it even with the tight fit of her gloves. The weapon's heavy weight made her feel less a victim. The Sioux might come for her again, but if they did, she wouldn't be taken alive—and she wouldn't die alone.

She nodded at Captain Frasier, ready to begin learning some rudimentary things about loading and handling her gun. "Have you ever known a gun-fighter, Captain?"

He frowned. "Why do you ask that?"

Sarah smiled as she holstered her Colt and spread her hands wide. "Because I feel like one right now. Don't I look rather fearsome?" She laughed, softening the intense curiosity behind her question.

"I did know one once. Red McGuire. He's in jail now. Heard there was another one up in Defiance, but I think he's retired."

"What's his name? Where's Defiance?"

"Jace Gage. Wyoming." Captain Frasier crossed his arms. "You seem intent on finding a gunfighter. Why?"

Sarah sighed. "I'll only have this afternoon to practice with you. Surely it takes much longer to become an expert shootist."

The captain's brows lifted. "Mrs. Hawkins, please forgive my curiosity, but why in God's name would you want to become a shootist?"

"Because, Captain, I am a widow. I need to be able to protect myself."

The captain glared down at her. A red flush slowly rose up his neck. "None of that is necessary. You could marry me. I would protect you. You would have my name. No one would dare whisper even a hint about what happened to you. You wouldn't have to leave the fort, except with me when I'm re-assigned to a new post." He took hold of her free hand as his words spilled out in an impassioned fervor.

At the contact, a buzzing started in Sarah's head. She tried to pull free, but he wouldn't release her. She tried again with no better results. Her lungs ceased pulling air.

"Please tell me you'll consider my proposal." Sarah went very still, neither resisting nor encouraging him. "I know what you've been through, what those red monsters did to you. You must know by now that I would not hold it against you."

He paused, releasing her hand as he became aware of her stillness. Anger broke the panic crippling her lungs, letting her take little gasps of air. Her wounds were still raw, her scars permanent. If he married her, she doubted he would ever be able to forget—or let her forget—what had been done to her.

It didn't help any to know the captain was right. Few men would take her to wife once they learned what had happened to her. She had no money, no skills, and no family. Though she was fairly well educated and could perhaps find a teaching job, that would only last until her students' parents learned she had been a captive. Everything was lost to her. Perhaps, when she had completed the task she'd set for herself, his offer would still be open.

Marriage—to anyone—was her best chance for survival.

She had only to get to Cheyenne and give the sheriff the papers, correct a wrong she needed to see put right. What happened after that mattered very little.

"Captain, I am not ready to be a wife again." She could not bring herself to look at his eyes. The very thought of letting a man near her body made her physically ill. "Though it is kind of you to offer. Let's just focus on the lesson, shall we?"

Unfortunately, before they could get beyond loading and unloading her gun, Captain Frasier was summoned back to the office to attend to a military matter. He escorted Sarah to the little cabin she'd been provided as lodging among the laundresses' quarters. Several cots filled the small, one-room space. During the time she'd been at Fort Buford, other women had occasionally stayed there with her, but it had been hers alone for the past week.

The captain took her key from her and was just fitting it into the lock when the door swung open.

"Mrs. Hawkins, you must pay attention to securing your quarters. We're a small, close-knit group of people here at the fort, but there's no need to put temptation in front of anyone. We do have many transients come through, begging for handouts— Indians and such. It isn't safe to assume—"

"I did lock it." Panic made her bold enough to interrupt his lecture. She slipped past him into a space that looked as if a buffalo had been let loose in it. Furniture was overturned. Bedding was slashed and shredded. The supplies she'd bought for the trip littered every surface. Straw and feathers were spread about. Her fine linens—the only mementos left of her family's Philadelphia home—were cut into scraps. Even the clothes that had been donated to her by the fort's women were sliced and ripped.

She couldn't breathe, couldn't move. Her heart-beat sounded in her ears, pounded her brain, drowned out whatever it was that the captain was saying. He stepped to the door and shouted an order. In the midst of the debris, she sighted her carpetbag turned upside down. It lay discarded next to her empty trunk, whose false bottom had been dislodged.

She stepped woodenly toward the satchel, look-ing for its support board, the one she'd sewn her husband's papers into. She sifted through the pile of shredded clothes and spilled foodstuffs.

It was gone. . . . Fear made her knees weaken. The room started to spin. It was gone.

Men hurried into the room. There were angry voices behind her. Someone pulled on her arm, but she jerked free. She pushed aside more debris, digging to the left, to the right. Her frantic motions stirred up a fog of flour from a ripped sack. Someone pulled at her again, but as he started to draw her to her feet, she found the support board. Crying out, she lunged for it, clasped it to her breast. The stitches were untouched.

Whoever had done this had left empty-handed. The papers were safe.

Logan Taggert pulled his saddle off his lathered mount and set it on the corral fence. Even at this early hour, the hostlers were rushing about the livery, taking care of the livestock.

"Taggert!" the stable master shouted as he trotted over. "What in the blazes are you doin' out here?"

Logan shook hands with the old cowpoke. "I could ask the same of you. Thought you retired to a life of luxury."

"I'm too old for running cattle, but not too old to clean a hoof or two. Need a fresh mount?"

"I do. I'm headin' over for some grub. You think Bella's kitchen is open?"

"Today it is. There's a stage leaving for Cheyenne. You ridin' shotgun? Heard they were looking for a couple of men."

"Hell no. I value my scalp too highly for a leisurely coach ride across open country while the Sioux are on the warpath." He looked over at the black stage where six horses were being hitched up. "Who in his right mind would run stages between here and Cheyenne, anyway?"

"It ain't no more crazy than opening trading

posts in Indian country, I reckon," the grizzled old man said, shooting Logan a meaningful look. "Martin Chandler, the man who owns that coach and a dozen others, is figurin' on beating out the competition, getting the first start carrying folks between Deadwood and Cheyenne, what with all the gold being found in the Black Hills."

Logan whistled. "He's got no business up there. That land belongs to the Sioux."

"Since when has that ever mattered? There's gold up there. I, for one, am glad for the business it's bringing us. The hell with them red savages. I may actually retire and go panning myself."

Logan's mood darkened. The hostler's attitude was exactly why no white man, woman, or child was safe here anymore. He strode over to the trading post, wanting to eat and ride out, well ahead of that stage and any trouble gunning for it. He hoped the storekeeper's wife could be talked into making him one of her famous breakfasts. His stomach grumbled in anticipation.

He crossed the dusty road, passing fort buildings that cast long, angular shadows of the morning sun across the ground. As brisk as the morning was, the day promised to be brutally hot. He stepped up on the boardwalk that fronted the trading post. A couple was strolling his way. The man wore an officer's uniform bearing a captain's insignia. The woman, far too thin, wore an ill-fitting dress of brown homespun. The captain carried her carpetbag and held her coat draped over his arm. The woman looked up at Logan as they went past.

Their eyes connected. Locked. He sucked in a breath. All rational thought fled his mind, as did his manners. He didn't lift his hat or nod or even move aside to give them room to pass. He just stared. Her hair was of the palest blond he'd ever seen, paler even than his own. Her nose was straight and little. Her chin came to a delicate point. Her eyes were big and brown. And utterly, devastatingly, haunted.

He caught the tail end of their conversation as they passed him. "You'll be safe on Chandler's stage, ma'am," the captain assured her. "He's hired a professional guard to ride shotgun. Chandler's setting up roadhouses along the way, so there will be a few overnight stops that don't involve camping outdoors. He can make the trip to Cheyenne in a little less than two weeks from here."

Logan propped himself up against a corner of the trading post and continued listening to their conversation, intrigued that the woman was not the soldier's wife.

"Thank you, Captain. How far did you say Defiance is from Cheyenne?"

"About three days ride."

What did she want in Defiance? No one ever went there intentionally. Not unless they were looking for trouble or heading up to the lumber camps. She followed the captain out into the sunshine. Light poured over her pale features, making the braids that circled her hair look as if they were woven from gossamer strands of white-gold. She pulled her bonnet on and tied it beneath her chin.

"I think I'll get to Cheyenne myself in a couple of months." The captain stopped and faced the woman. "Would it be terribly forward of me to think that I might call on you, Mrs. Hawkins?"

Logan ground his teeth. *Mrs.* Hawkins. She wasn't the captain's wife, but she was married. Still, he held his breath, waiting for her response. She lowered her head, letting her bonnet block her face from both him and the captain. "You have been the very soul of kindness, Captain. I shall not forget that. I regret, however, that I'll not be in a position to entertain gentleman callers. It is too soon."

The captain did not take that as a no. Or perhaps he'd stopped listening after her first sentence. Logan almost had. Her voice was husky yet sweet and feminine, the kind of voice that set all the wrong sort of images floating around a man's head. The captain hooked a finger beneath the woman's chin, forcing her to look up. Logan felt the shock of that contact through his entire body. He started forward, intending to teach the bastard to keep his distance, but Bella, the sutler's wife and a sublimely talented cook, came out to stand with him.

Logan didn't waste time exchanging greetings. "Who is she?"

"Poor Sarah Hawkins. Bless her heart. She and her husband were attacked by a Sioux war party about a year ago. Her husband was killed and she was taken captive. She showed up here at the end of April, a ghost of a woman, near frozen and half starved. It's taken the women of the fort all this time just to feed her up to the puny thing she is now.

"And as if that wasn't enough, someone vandalized her room yesterday. Shredded everything she owned, including all of the clothes that had been donated by those of us with something to spare." The matronly woman shook her head, anger darkening her features.

"She's a kind soul, that one." She shoved an elbow into Logan's side, giving him a meaningful look. "All the single men—and even some that ain't—are plumb crazy about her. Heard that red devil who married her still wants her back. I hate to see her leave. She would be safer if she stayed here." Bella looked at Logan. "What kind of world do we live in where Indians can do that to a family? When are we ever gonna be safe out here?"

Logan didn't offer a comment. How many Sioux, Cheyenne, and Arapaho warriors had asked him the same thing—but about the soldiers that dogged them?

"Bella, I'd be forever in your debt if you'd pack up as much of that fine corn bread as you can spare. I'm gonna get some supplies from your husband and retrieve my saddle."

"Logan Taggert! You ain't even stopped for a real visit yet. Where are you running off to?"

Logan grinned as he kissed her cheek. "I got a stagecoach to catch!"

Chapter 2

The leather curtains did little to keep the dust out of the tight stagecoach cabin. It settled like a fine powder on every surface. It was in Sarah's hair, her teeth, her eyes. After four long days, the terrain was little changed, and they were still more than a week from Cheyenne.

Though her fellow traveling companions were generally disinclined to chat, she'd discovered the middle-aged matron, Mrs. Powell, was recently widowed and traveling to her son's home in Cheyenne. Mr. Reimer was a man whose occupation was unknown to her. His clothes were not elegant enough for a gambler, or plain enough for a rancher, but he wore a pistol as comfortably as a seasoned gunfighter. The remaining passenger, Mr. Taggert, was the gray-eyed stranger she'd seen at the fort the morning they'd left. A trader of some sort. She still felt the chill of his eyes, the way he'd probed into her mind through the single glance they'd shared, as if he could see her secrets. As if he knew her shame.

She wondered if either of the men had known her husband. They both had a look of violence about them. Had one of them ransacked her room? How could her husband's associates have found her at the fort? Her hand shook as she held the curtain.

The trunk.

She'd asked a neighbor to keep it for her. She'd hidden the papers she'd stolen from her husband in the false bottom. When she arrived at the fort and was able to draft a letter, she'd sent word to have the trunk delivered to her. Her husband, Eugene, hadn't had time to discover his papers were missing before Swift Elk raided their ranch, but someone knew they still existed and wanted them back.

She shivered despite the heat. Her hands were sweaty, but she had no intention of removing her gloves and exposing her scars for all to see. Lifting the corner of the leather curtain, she forced herself to watch the countryside slowly rolling by. It would be over soon. Once she'd given the papers to the sheriff in Cheyenne, she would cease being a threat to her husband's enemies.

Sarah could feel the weight of Mr. Reimer's gaze. She'd managed to avoid conversing with him so far on the journey, but his interest in her had intensified over the last few days. Now he leaned back in his corner seat and watched her. "Is it true you married one of them Injun chiefs?" he asked, breaking the cabin's comfortable silence.

The matron gasped, settling her shocked gaze on Sarah. "I thought Mr. Chandler was more selective about whom he allowed on this stage," Mrs. Powell complained.

Sarah made no comment, silence being the best answer to such observations. She studied the edge of the curtain she held.

"The government mollycoddles those savages on huge reservations, feeding them, teaching their children, training the few who are willing to work, and yet they still go raiding, terrorizing honest citizens," the woman continued.

Hearing a kindred spirit, the man spoke directly to Mrs. Powell. "They're still crawling around everywhere. Ain't nowhere a person can go that's safe from them."

Sarah's stomach clenched at Mr. Reimer's chilling reminder. They traveled across open prairie, a lone coach protected only by a single gunman. She sent Mr. Taggert a sideways glance. He had yet to join this or any conversation in the cab. He was sprawled in his corner, his hat pulled down over his face, his arms crossed over his chest. Perhaps he was asleep.

"Your husband is Sioux? Cheyenne?" Mr. Reimer asked. The matron's gaze flew to Sarah's face with a look of unmitigated disgust.

"My husband is dead. He was murdered," Sarah quietly announced. She looked at Mr. Reimer, then at Mrs. Powell. "I will thank you to find another topic of discussion." She gritted her teeth, feeling the crunch of dust in them.

"Don't think I ever met a gen-u-ine squaw before,"

the man in the corner persisted, drawing out the vowels of "genuine."

Before she could respond, before she could even sigh, Mr. Taggert kicked the opposite seat, his boot landing midway between Mr. Reimer's spread legs.

"The lady said drop it," he growled, pushing his hat back far enough to glare at the man.

"You her squaw-man?"

Fast as lightning, the stranger next to her had Mr. Reimer's collar in his fist and the stage door open. He held him out over the ground as it passed in a blur. The swift change in positions made the cabin sway. The woman issued a shrill sound as wind, road noise, and dust filled the cabin.

"Whoa! Hold on there!" the man pleaded, grabbing for a handhold on the sides of the coach.

"You got something else to talk about?" Mr. Taggert asked between clenched teeth. He leaned closer to her detractor, pushing him farther out the door. "'Cause I'm done listening to your Indian prattle and the lady doesn't need your prying questions." Mr. Reimer nodded vigorously. "Good. In fact, how about you just keep your trap shut?" Mr. Taggert suggested as he pulled the man back inside the cabin and shoved him roughly into his seat.

Sarah wrapped her arms about herself. Her heart was hammering. She was alone in the world—a pariah, as the conversation of this little gathering showed. She didn't know what to do or where to go, and she had only until Cheyenne to decide. She blinked the grit from her eyes and drew a long breath from the open window. She wished it had all turned out differently. She wished her husband had been the man of her dreams, the man he'd appeared to be during their brief, whirlwind courtship.

A few hours later, they stopped for the night at a stage station, the first along their journey that provided overnight accommodations. It was past eight in the evening. The sun had dipped close to the horizon, coloring the sky in the soft pastels of a prairie sunset.

Sarah waited for the two passengers on the opposite seat to disembark before climbing down, assisted by the driver. The man who had ridden shotgun tossed down her satchel.

Mr. Taggert stepped out of the coach. He paused, looking down at her. He was easily a head taller than Sarah and broad-shouldered. His eyes were a light gray, so pale they were hard to look at. They seemed to see far more than she wished. His skin was weathered, darkened by the sun. It was impossible to tell his age. His nose was narrow and straight. His brows were a dark blond. His hair was shaggy, and what she could see of it was bleached white by the sun. His cheeks were lean. All of him was lean, like a long, sharp knife.

"Thank you, sir, for your assistance earlier."

His cold gaze dropped to her face. "They were like dogs with a bone. Made it hard to sleep." He looked beyond her, scanning the land surrounding the station. He reached back inside the cab for the rifle he'd stowed on the floor by their seat. He sent another look around them.

Feeling his tension, she cast a look around as well. There was only sagebrush, paintbrush, and short grass as far as the eye could see, green with recent rains, washed orange with the sunset. It was an evening like this when the Sioux had come down the hills surrounding the small settlement where she and Eugene had lived, a silent tide of raging violence.

"Best get inside." The stranger's voice broke into her thoughts.

Agreeing with that directive, she stepped into the small mud-brick building. The stationmaster's wife was lighting lanterns as she directed the passengers to a back room where cots were set out, one for each passenger, both men and women to sleep in the same room. Mrs. Powell had taken a cot on one side. Sarah selected the one next to it and set her satchel, coat, and bonnet down on it. In her turn, she made use of the outhouse, then freshened up at the wash station.

The mouthwatering smell of biscuits and stew drew her to the common room. She was the last to come to the table as the stationmaster and his wife filled bowls with hot stew. Her stomach grumbled. She took the open seat across from Mr. Taggert. Mrs. Powell set her spoon down rather loudly, but Sarah paid it no heed. The woman made a loud huffing sound. The men at the table grew tense. Sarah did look up then. The driver, the guard, and Mr. Taggert kept eating, but Mr. Reimer and Mrs. Powell were glaring at each other in silent communication.

"I will not sit at a table with a woman who has been used by savages like a common trollop."

Sarah felt her cheeks color. Memories she'd fought to bury deep rose to the surface. Horrific images popped through her mind. *God, the pain.*

The driver and the stage's hired gun looked at each other. "Now, there's no call for that kind of talk. We're all just passing through, ma'am."

Mrs. Powell huffed again. Sarah started to rise, but Mr. Taggert's hand grabbed her wrist, forcing her back to her seat. The touch was fast—he released her almost immediately.

"There's plenty of space on the floor, lady," the gray-eyed stranger told the matron. "Sit where you like."

"Well! I never!" Mrs. Powell pressed a hand to her chest; her mouth hung open in mortification.

"Then I reckon it's high time you did," Mr. Taggert added.

Mr. Reimer stood up. "Never mind them, ma'am. We can use the bench on the porch." He lifted up his bowl and utensils and went to stand near the offended woman while she got up from the table and gathered her things. They went out front, leaving Sarah alone with the cold-eyed stranger and the stage's men.

"I don't need you to fight my battles, sir." Her statement would have carried a great deal more impact had her voice not wavered. She lifted her head, glaring at her defender.

Mr. Taggert paused, his spoon midair. His gray eyes met hers. She fought the chill his look caused.

"I wasn't fighting your battles, lady. Just keeping the stink from my table."

Sarah looked at her bowl and wondered if this was what her life would be like from now on. Having to hide who and what she was, afraid her husband's associates would find her. Afraid some nosy matron would discover she'd been a Sioux captive. Would she be able to lose herself in the busy town of Cheyenne?

Maybe she shouldn't stay in Cheyenne. But she couldn't go south into Texas; Apache and Comanche raids still ravaged the settlements. There would be no place for her in the rigid social structure of the East. And she feared making the trip to Oregon without the protection of a husband.

The bowl of stew blurred as she stared down at it. She forced herself to finish her portion though her ever-present tension had stolen its flavor. When the Sioux had first taken her, she'd gone three days without being fed. She knew better than to not eat when food was available. She brought a spoonful to her mouth, consuming it for survival alone. If the stage were attacked somewhere on the trail still ahead of them, there was no telling how soon she would have an opportunity to eat again.

After supper, she took advantage of the laundry facilities the station offered and washed her kerchiefs, linens, stockings, and shirts. She'd just hung the last of her things to dry when Mr. Reimer stepped outside. She was in the side yard by the laundry lines, out of sight of any window or doorway. She stood still, hoping he would step away and not block her access to the station.

Her luck didn't hold. He headed straight for her. Sarah retrieved the wash basket and started for the porch, moving as briskly as she dared without revealing her fear. How many times among the Sioux had she been ordered to see to one task or another that took her away from the women, making her easy prey for the warriors in the village?

And now it was happening again, here, among her own people. The moonlight was too bright for her to mistake his expression. She hurried past him in a wide arc. He lunged and caught her, causing her to drop her basket.

"Where are you hurrying off to? Thought we'd have a little friendly visit, just you an' me." He nuzzled her hair. The scent of him hit her face. Whiskey and sweat.

Fight.

Don't fight.

Scream.

Don't scream.

Nearly a year in the hostile care of warriors who used her and their other white captives as whores had taught her the hard way to suffer their outrages in silence. But she wasn't among the Sioux now. And only a few yards away was a station full of people. She felt the weight of her gun belt. Could she draw her pistol? Could she really shoot someone?

Mr. Reimer pulled her close. He kissed her cheek, his lips wet against her face. He took her silence as acquiescence. He tried to kiss her mouth but she turned away, pushing against him. Bile rose in her throat. His hand pinched her breast. Memories of the black, terrible days of her early captivity boiled to the surface of her mind. She began shaking and was only dimly aware when Mr. Reimer pulled back and muttered a curse.

Another man had come outside. Mr. Taggert. He leaned against the side wall of the station house, a knee bent as he withdrew cigarette papers from his jacket pocket. He selected one and set it on his bent knee. He returned the papers to his pocket and retrieved a pouch of tobacco. God, had he come to watch her be outraged?

"We're a little busy here, friend. Wanna find a different spot for your smoke?"

"Nope." The man put a pinch of tobacco on the paper, then put the pouch away. He took his time rolling the paper over the tobacco.

"Look, you can have her when I'm done with her, so get lost."

The man put the cigarette in the corner of his mouth, then patted his pockets, looking for his matches. He found them in the fourth pocket he searched. Striking a match on the side of the house, he cupped his hand from the wind and lit the end of his cigarette.

Mr. Reimer cursed and stomped over to him, dragging her forward. "This ain't your affair, Taggert. She ain't your woman. She's a squaw. You know how they treat captives. She's used to servicing men; it ain't no big deal to her. Might as well have some fun with her while we can."

A slow stream of smoke left one corner of Mr. Taggert's mouth. He shook his head as he straightened and pushed off the wall. "That ain't my idea of fun." He shoved a fist into Mr. Reimer's stomach, doubling him over, then dragged him up by the shoulders and kneed him in the groin. Mr. Reimer buckled over, cupping himself, moaning into the dirt. "How about *you* take it somewhere else?"

The stage driver and the stationmaster came out. "What's goin' on here?" the latter demanded.

Mr. Taggert dropped his cigarette butt and crushed it with his heel. "Just showin' Mr. Reimer what happens when a man forgets how to treat a lady."

The men looked at her, then at Mr. Taggert before lifting Mr. Reimer to his feet. "Ma'am, are you hurt?"

Sarah clutched the edges of her collar together and shook her head. They dragged Mr. Reimer inside, and she drew the first full breath she'd taken in several minutes. She was shaking. Disgust and rage chased around in her gut until she felt ill. She wrapped her arms around her waist.

"Want a smoke?" the gray-eyed man asked her.

Sarah choked on her response. A smoke? "No. No, I don't want a smoke. I want to kill something," she hissed, her voice thin with rage.

"Got a knife?"

Now she wondered if the man had just plain lost his senses. "No, I don't have a knife."

He took his out of its sheath and handed it to her hilt first. She took the long blade, her hand slipping firmly around the grip.

"Throw it."

She drew her arm back behind her, her fist wrapped around the handle.

"Hold on, there." He stopped her mid-swing. "You don't throw it like that. You got no control over it that way." He held his hand out for the knife. She handed it back to him and felt the shift in power its surrender caused.

"You can hold it either by the blade or the handle. For you, I recommend holding by the handle, like this, with your index finger just touching the base of the metal on the flat side. Pull your arm straight back. Look at the place where you want it to land." He pointed to one of the posts supporting the laundry lines. "Then send it on its way." He drew the knife up and whipped it through the air. It landed precisely in the center of the post, where the heart of a six-foot-tall man might be.

"You try."

She pulled it out of the post and returned to her spot. Holding it as he suggested, she threw it. It hit the ground near the post, blade first. She retrieved it and threw it twice more, with little better success.

"Don't look at your hand, Mrs. Hawkins. Your brain and your hand have already agreed on an outcome. Just look where you want it to go—see it already there." She closed her eyes, forced herself to relax. Then she sighted the post, drew back her arm, and sent the knife flying. It hit the post and stuck. Low, but hard. It would have hobbled a running attacker.

She looked at the reverberating hilt, surprised.

"Good. That's good." He retrieved his knife and sheathed it. When he looked up, he studied her. "How much more were you gonna take before you fought back?" His voice was a quiet, raw whisper.

She had no answer for him. Confronted with actually needing to use her gun to defend herself, she found she hadn't the courage to do it.

Mr. Taggert sighed. "A weapon's only useful if you use it. The world will not mourn the loss of a lowlife like Jeremy Reimer. May I see your gun?"

She drew her Colt from its holster and handed it to him. He shifted so that the moonlight filtered down on his hands, illuminating the cylinder. "You got six cartridges loaded." He removed one of them, then closed the cylinder. "Your revolver looks new, so it's likely not a problem. The safety notch can be brittle. Let the hammer down on the empty chamber just to be safe. Have you oiled your piece yet?" He handed her the extra cartridge.

"No." Captain Frasier hadn't gotten to the cleaning part of gun handling.

He handed her the Colt. "When we go back in, I'll clean it for you." He unbuckled his gun belt. Fear sheared through her. Why was he stripping? She stepped back. "Whoaa, there. I got no plans to hurt you, Mrs. Hawkins. I'm just taking the knife sheath off so you can put it on your gun belt."

Sarah looked at Mr. Taggert. He had the coldest eyes she'd ever seen, eyes like a warrior angel. In the shadows of the moonlight, his face was all planes and angles. His movements were precise, controlled. If Eugene's associates had sent him, they'd picked an excellent killer. It occurred to her he might be helping her as a means of lulling her into trusting him, to get beneath her defenses so that he could learn where she'd hidden the papers. She straightened her spine.

"Thank you for your help." He held the sheathed

knife out to her. She shook her head. "I don't need your knife."

He gave a dry laugh. "The hell you don't. Take it. Keep it under your pillow at night." He frowned down at her for a long moment. "You got a rough road ahead of you. This ain't a safe place for a woman to be traveling alone. Where are you headed?"

Why did he want to know that? Her fingers closed around the hard leather of the knife sheath. "Cheyenne," she replied, purposely vague.

"The whole stage is heading for Cheyenne, but few people stay there. You got family in the area?"

"No."

"You got family you can go to?"

"No."

"What about your husband's people?"

"He never mentioned anyone."

Logan frowned. He was butting up against her secrets. He didn't like women who were enigmas. And most women were, which was why he steered clear of them—except for occasional short encounters that held no meaning or permanence. Why was it that he wanted to discover what this woman was hiding? Why, with her and no other before her, did he feel compelled to help and protect her, secrets and all?

"You done out here?" He lifted the laundry basket and handed it to her. She nodded. "Then let's go inside."

Chapter 3

Sarah had retrieved her wash the next morning without any incident. And she'd met with no resistance when she joined the others for breakfast. Though the hour was early, the sky was already bright. Her fellow passengers were dressed and ready to leave, as was she. Their luggage was assembled by the front door of the station house. The driver was finishing his breakfast, but he kept sending his guard a measuring look. Sarah did the same, noticing the man was strangely pale and yet his cheeks were flushed.

"Are you feeling well, sir?" she asked him. His breakfast plate had been untouched. His arms were folded, his hands tucked close at his sides.

"No, I ain't." He looked at the driver. His face tightened into a grimace. "This fever's settin' in good. I'm not going to be any help to you. I got to stay here and wait this thing out."

Mr. Reimer looked at the guard. "You must come with us. We can't leave without you."

Mr. Taggert stood by the open window. A gentle

breeze blew in, circling the room. He had looked at her when she entered the room, but not again since. He took his revolver from its holster and checked the cylinder. It spun. He clicked it once more, then snapped it shut and holstered it. He slipped a cartridge belt over his shoulder, then picked up his rifle and checked the cartridges in it. "We may not want to leave at all."

"What are you talking about?" Mr. Reimer complained as he joined Mr. Taggert at the window. He pushed aside the curtain and looked outside. Sarah saw him tense and bend closer.

"Holy Mother of God. There are Indians out there!"

"Yep. Been following us since yesterday."

Mrs. Powell gasped. Sarah felt fear twist like a knife in her gut.

"What do we do?" Mr. Reimer asked Mr. Taggert.

He shrugged. "Make a decision. Stay or go. Either way, we may have to fight. They may not be here to make trouble—they could have hit us anytime yesterday afternoon, but they didn't."

The stationmaster, a short, stocky man, looked out another window. He wrung his hands as he faced the men. "Don't fight them. Don't make trouble for me. I have a good understanding with them. I trade with them—fairly. If you start shooting, they will come back and kill me and the missus."

"We could wait them out," Mr. Reimer suggested.

Mr. Taggert looked at him and slowly grinned. "Ain't a man alive who's got more patience than a Sioux warrior."

"We could go out and talk to them," Mr. Reimer suggested.

"You could." Mr. Taggert sat on a worn chair and leaned it back against the wall, away from the window.

"You go," Mr. Reimer said to him. "You seem familiar with their ways."

Mr. Taggert laid his rifle across his lap and folded his arms, giving Mr. Reimer a wry look. "Sure enough, but I'm too fond of my scalp to do something so foolish."

Sarah watched the proceedings with a cold heart. She knew how merciless the Sioux could be. The travelers were no safer here than on the road. Their supplies would give out in a few days, then they would have to venture out anyway. They would be picked off one by one when they went for water, while the warriors stayed out of firing range.

It was possible the band watching them was just curious. The station house was fairly new. They might be reconnoitering for their village, observing the traffic that moved through the station, gauging the threat of leaving the station undisturbed.

"Well, what do we do?" Mr. Reimer asked the room at large.

"You leave," the stationmaster said. "They won't make trouble. There have been no Indian attacks on this road since the sixty-eight treaty. It's safe. I would go if I were you."

"We can't leave without someone to ride shotgun," Mr. Reimer complained. The men were debating among themselves. She had a bad feeling that they would regret whatever they decided. They consulted Mrs. Powell, who was in favor of getting as close to Fort Laramie as they could as fast as possible. Fort Laramie was still a three-day journey from the station house. Even if this band of warriors let them pass, the next might not, Sarah knew. No one asked her opinion, however, and Mr. Taggert left the decision to the others.

"We'll go," Mr. Reimer announced.

"I got her all loaded," the driver said. "Let's get aboard and hit the trail." He looked at Mr. Taggert. "You'll ride shotgun?"

"Sure."

Sarah hurried in the wake of Mr. Reimer and Mrs. Powell, both of whom climbed into the stage before she did. When it was her turn to board, a strong hand took her arm and helped her up the steps. She looked into Mr. Taggert's cool gaze, feeling it blow over her like an icy wind on a hot, summer day. He turned from her to climb up to the driver's bench, his rifle in hand. The coach lurched forward.

Sarah glanced at her fellow occupants. Fear tightened their features. She shoved the leather curtain open, straining to see any signs of the Indians. The stage was heading into the wind, so no dust clouds announced their followers, if there were any. She couldn't see much out of the opposite window. There was nothing for it but to wait. They would ultimately make it to Fort Laramie, or they wouldn't. She could do nothing to affect the outcome.

Five minutes eased into a quarter of an hour. When a half hour had passed, Sarah cautiously began to be hopeful they weren't being followed. The driver slowed the coach, keeping the horses to a comfortable trot. A few more hours passed, still with no sign of the warriors. Perhaps they had been more interested in the station house after all.

"Look! They're coming!" Mr. Reimer shouted. He leaned out the central window and began firing at their pursuers. Mrs. Powell clutched the passenger strap for support as the coach lurched into a fast speed. Sarah closed her eyes and offered up a silent prayer. Even above the road noise in the cabin, she could hear the thunderous approach of several riders. And then the scream of their battle cry—a sound that still tortured her dreams.

The warriors advanced until they were riding parallel with the coach, their ponies leaping over sagebrush with the grace of antelopes. They waved their guns, bows and arrows, keeping their shields toward the coach. Mrs. Powell began crying and chanting a string of unintelligible words. The driver lashed his team to a full gallop. The coach lurched wildly as it careened down the rutted dirt road. Sarah's hand slipped to the holster on her hip. Mr. Reimer reloaded and continued firing. Sarah couldn't see if he'd hit his mark, but the band of warriors fell back.

The driver rode the team hard for another few minutes, then let them slow up. Sarah looked out the window, but could see no sign of the Indians. They drove for another hour. Sarah was sure each breath was her last. The Indians were playing with them. Advancing and retreating. Tormenting their prey.

"If they come up again, Mrs. Powell, you get

yourself down on the floor and keep your head low," Mr. Reimer ordered solicitously.

"What do they want? Why are they doing this?" the matron asked. "They are going to kill us all. They will kill us and take our scalps. Oh, merciful heaven, we are dead."

Sarah felt a cold sweat dampen her skin. Fear moved like ice through her veins. She knew death was a far more merciful outcome than surviving an attack. Bile rose in her throat as she remembered warriors pushing her to the ground while her husband fought with other warriors. They ravaged her there, in her front yard, while her husband watched. Then a warrior's tomahawk made short work of his resistance. They'd looted her house, taking whatever they could carry easily. She'd been tossed over the back of one of the ponies, tied so she couldn't fight or run. They'd set out at a full gallop, but they didn't outride the smell of her burning home. It couldn't happen again. Not again.

The temporary calm in the cab was broken by a war yell the likes of which only a Sioux could issue. A warrior came even with Sarah's window and rode beside the stage for the length of a heartbeat. He looked into the stage, locked eyes with Sarah. His face was painted a fearsome black and red. The hawk feathers tied in his hair jumped and flipped in the wind. The driver whipped the horses into a run.

The warrior slipped away, joining the band that was riding parallel to the stage, out of the range of gunshot. Then once again, they fell back, disappearing in the gently rolling prairie. Sarah's insides writhed like snakes awakening from a winter sleep.

"It's her." Mr. Reimer's shrill voice broke into the stunned silence in the cab. He waved his gun at her. "They want her back."

Sarah looked at their pale faces, their eyes white-rimmed with fear. "No," she whispered.

"We should put her out," he shouted. "They'll leave us alone then."

"No!" Sarah said again, louder.

Mr. Reimer looked at Mrs. Powell. "Would you give your life for hers? If she stays, we'll all be killed. If we put her out, we'll live."

"No. No. Please," Sarah begged. "Don't do this. Who can know what they want? I didn't recognize the warrior who was just next to us. I don't know them. They don't know me. Please, don't do this."

Mr. Reimer and Mrs. Powell looked at each other. The matron's expression calmed as her back stiffened. The hand that clutched a kerchief to her face lowered to her lap. "I'm a widow in possession of a significant fortune, Mr. Reimer. I would pay you a substantial reward for ensuring my safe arrival in Cheyenne."

Mr. Reimer studied Mrs. Powell. He cautiously looked out his window. Seeing the way was clear, he poked his head out farther, checking for the dust trail of the Sioux. He shouted up to the men riding on the driver's seat. "Stop the coach! Stop it now!"

"What is it? Anyone hit?" Mr. Taggert shouted back.

"No. Stop the coach!"

"Ain't gonna happen," Mr. Taggert scoffed.

Mr. Reimer pointed his pistol at the shotgun rider. "I said stop the coach."

Sarah was breathing in short gasps, her stomach in her teeth. Her only hope was that Mr. Taggert could convince the passengers not to do this terrible thing.

The coach pulled up, shifting as Mr. Taggert jumped to the ground. He yanked the door open and dragged Mr. Reimer outside. "You better have a goddamned good reason for stopping."

Mr. Reimer looked at her. "Get out."

"She stays put."

"We want her out. The Indians are after her, not us. We give her to them, they'll leave us alone. We live. You live. The driver lives. If she stays, we all die."

"And if we leave her here, she'll die." He shook his head. A dust cloud was rising again on the horizon. "Get in the coach. We're not leaving anyone behind."

"I'm afraid you are, Mr. Taggert," Mr. Reimer said, his silver-handled Colt pointed at him. The two men glared at each other for precious seconds. Mrs. Powell whimpered. Mr. Taggert shouted up to the driver to toss down his gear and Mrs. Hawkins's satchel and bedroll. Fast as anything, several parcels fell from the top of the coach. Mr. Reimer shrugged free and scrambled into the cab. He turned the gun on Sarah. "Get out."

"No. Please. I beg you, don't do this. Please. You don't know what they will do. I do."

"Get out," Mr. Reimer snarled. He cocked his gun, then waved it at her.

A sob caught Sarah's breath as Mr. Taggert pulled her from the wagon. He slammed the coach door shut and shouted up to the driver. The coach lurched forward.

Sarah glanced around, searching for a boulder, a dip in the ground, something to give them a little bit of cover. There was nothing. They were a mile from the tree line that bordered a narrow creek. There was nowhere to hide on the high, flat prairie.

She wanted to vomit. She wanted to run. She couldn't breathe. Her hands were like ice. She doubted her ability to even shoot herself, now that the moment was at hand.

Mr. Taggert gripped her arms and lifted her to her toes as he bent toward her. "Mrs. Hawkins, look at me." His gray eyes were intense, like storm clouds when lightning flashes through them. "This looks bad, but I've been in worse situations and lived to tell. Stand with your back to mine. Have your gun ready, but by God, don't shoot until I tell you."

"I won't be taken again. I won't go alive into that hell."

He didn't respond. He pulled her revolver and checked the chamber, rotated it once, then closed it and put it in her shaking hands. "We don't know it's gonna come to that. If there's one thing an Indian hates, it's unexpected behavior. Our standing here is sure as hell unexpected. Let's just see where this goes."

She pressed her back to the man who had been her salvation since he'd joined the small group of travelers.

She could feel the heated leather of his vest against her shoulders. He was tall. Brave beyond reason.

And about to die because of her.

"Easy, Mrs. Hawkins. Easy. Hold steady."

The dust cloud thickened. The Sioux were returning. Their battle screams ripped through her nerves. She pushed harder against his back, needing the contact to keep her legs from buckling.

Mr. Taggert had his rifle ready, but not up in a firing position. The fierce warriors rode in a wide circle about them, waving their weapons. Ten of them, every one of them bent on death and violence. Sarah knew the joy they took in terrorizing their enemies. It fed their souls more completely than any physical sustenance.

The circle of riders tightened, a lariat of horses and warriors, closing in around them in a blur of dirt. Black-and-white ponies. Bodies painted with war colors, red, black, yellow. Feathers and shields. Sarah tried to focus on one, then another, but they moved too fast, swirling and tightening.

Suddenly, the riders stopped. They formed a half circle around the two of them, facing Mr. Taggert. Every breath Sarah drew was filled with the pale dirt of the arid prairie, clogging her nose and throat, making her eyes water, filling her lungs with grit.

Silence. The quiet was more alarming than the battle screams had been.

Chapter 4

Sarah twisted around to watch what was happening, standing shoulder to ribs with Mr. Taggert. No one moved. No one spoke. A horse flinched now and then when bitten by a fly. Only the dust dared swirl on the remnants of the air currents kicked up by the crazy, circling ride of the warriors.

One of the warriors moved his horse forward, stopping several yards in front of Mr. Taggert. "You trespass on our hunting grounds."

Sarah had thought she had forgotten the Sioux language she'd learned while a captive, but the first words from the warrior's mouth brought it all slamming back to her. She started to translate for Mr. Taggert, but he cut her off, answering the warrior himself.

"You aren't hunting today. You haven't been hunting for several days," he said in Sioux. "You've been following us."

Mr. Taggert, she'd learned from bits of conversation over the last few days, had a series of trading posts from the Dakotas west through Wyoming and south to Texas. She wasn't surprised he could understand Sioux, but he spoke it like a native.

Sarah studied the warrior as she tensed for action. Her hands settled and resettled around the butt of her pistol. He showed no reaction to Mr. Taggert's ability to speak his language, which in itself was proof he was shocked. She wondered if Mr. Taggert knew how sneaky warriors like these could be. If his trading posts were in garrisoned forts, he might have no idea of the Sioux's natural perfidy, especially when dealing with whites.

"I am Cloud Walker." He nodded his chin toward Sarah. "You have Yellow Moon, a woman of our people. I come to claim her. She is wife to one of our chiefs. I will return her to him."

How did he know her? She looked at Cloud Walker more closely, but could not remember having met him.

"She belongs to me."

The warrior regarded Mr. Taggert in a steely gaze. "How is it you speak our tongue?"

"I am Logan Taggert, known as Shadow Wolf among your people." Mr. Taggert held his rifle across his left forearm and gestured with his right hand, conveying his message as much in words as sign language. "I have trading posts at Bad River and the Big Muddy and other rivers. I trade fairly with your people and have joined many a hunt with Gray Bear. I have smoked many a pipe with Standing Antelope. I am a friend to your people."

"Then you will know you cannot take a man's wife without paying for her."

"I didn't take her. She left the Sioux."

"That was not her choice to make. Her husband, Swift Elk, will be glad we found her."

Standing with her shoulder against Mr. Taggert's side, Sarah felt the tension that washed through him at the mention of Swift Elk.

"What is done, is done. I claim her. I am willing to meet a bride price equal to her value," he offered in a calm voice.

"She belongs to our people."

Mr. Taggert made a dismissive gesture. "She is a white woman. She can't be owned by your people if it isn't her choice."

The warrior leveled a hard stare at Mr. Taggert. "Why are you alone here with the woman and not in the black coach with the others?"

"They feared you. They sent us to speak to you."

The warrior studied Mr. Taggert a long moment, then shouted an order to the other warriors. As one, they wheeled their horses and rode after the coach. War cries filled the air.

Silence slowly settled around them. Sarah's knees gave out. She crumpled to the hard ground. Her hands shook as she uncocked her gun and holstered it. "Will they be back?"

"Depends." Mr. Taggert shrugged.

"On what?"

"On how you left them." He watched the fading dust cloud. "Did you escape, or were you ransomed?"

"I ran away."

"Then they'll be back. You still belong to your husband."

"I never consented to marry Swift Elk. That was no marriage."

"Your beliefs have no bearing on the facts, Mrs. Hawkins. It's a terrible disgrace for a wife to run away. You will be returned to the tribe and punished for leaving."

Sarah jumped to her feet. "I was a captive, Mr. Taggert. All of the men in Swift Elk's band used me most cruelly. I won't go back. I don't belong to the tribe."

Mr. Taggert lifted her satchel and put his arms through each strap so that he could carry it on his back. He tossed his saddlebag over the satchel. "They think you do. A white wife is of great value— for ransoming, if nothing else. When you left, you cheated Swift Elk of his valuable property—you."

He started off down the faint tracks that the stage had followed. Sarah grabbed their bedrolls and hurried after him, her mind sifting through everything that had been said. "You told him I belong to you."

"You do."

That wasn't the answer she was expecting. "You have no idea how grateful I am for all you've done for me in the last several days."

She sent a quick look at Mr. Taggert's hard profile. He seemed either to not be listening or not comprehending what she was saying. "I do need your help to get to Fort Laramie. It's true. But I'll be fine from there to Cheyenne. There's no need for you to commit more of your time on my behalf."

He shrugged. "I've claimed you. So I am responsible for you. That's how it works."

"That was only survival negotiations. No one will hold you to it."

"*I* will hold myself to it." His pale gaze slashed her way. "My word's all I got at the moment, Mrs. Hawkins. And in case you didn't notice, my word just saved your hide."

"Mr. Taggert—" Sarah adopted a stern tone. "I know nothing about you. You know nothing about me. Strangers don't claim each other."

"You know I own some trading posts in the region. I am comfortably fixed for money. You're a widow. You got no family to protect you. And you're running from something. What else do we need to know?"

Sarah stopped to glare at him, but his long strides swiftly carried him away. She jogged a bit to catch up to him. "What makes you think I'm running from anything?"

"Besides the sidearm you're packing that you don't know how to use? Or the fact that you're going to Cheyenne—deeper into the same troubled country that's treated you so bad? A sane woman would be heading back East."

"I-I have friends in Cheyenne."

Mr. Taggert stopped walking. "Let's get something straight right now. I don't like liars. I won't lie to you, and you don't lie to me."

She drew herself up to her full height. "I appreciate your help. I *need* your help. But I am not going to exchange my life for it. You cannot claim me."

He shrugged. "It's your decision." He looked up at the sky and squinted. "I figure you got between now and when that war party comes back to decide. Me. Or them."

The wool blankets of the bedrolls she carried were making her arms itch in the afternoon heat. "I will not marry you."

"I haven't asked you."

She frowned at him. She was beginning to wonder if the sun and the stress of their situation hadn't gotten to him. "Are you quite sure all your faculties are intact, Mr. Taggert?"

He grinned and flashed a look her way. "You think I'm loco? Because I left a perfectly sound coach to escort a stunningly beautiful woman—who happens to be the runaway wife of one of the fiercest Sioux chiefs alive—across hostile Sioux country on foot?"

"No." She scratched at her forearm. "Because you got on the stage in the first place. You had your saddle. You could have hired a horse for the price of a seat on the stage. Why would you do that?"

He pulled her satchel off his shoulders and took the bedrolls from her, kneeling to tie them to her bag. He looked up at her, a casual slice of his gray gaze. "Are you so wounded that you think every man is out to harm you?"

She stared down at him. "Yes."

He stood up and slipped his arms through the handles of her satchel and slung his saddlebag over the top again. He stared at her for an uncomfortable moment. "That, Mrs. Hawkins, is the most honest thing you've said to me yet. I have never hurt a woman, and I don't intend to start now." He took her hand and started forward again.

"I don't know what you mean when you say you 'claim' me."

"Neither do I." He grinned at her. His smile crinkled the corners of his eyes, curved the hard edges of his mouth. "I've never claimed a woman before."

"Mr. Taggert—"

"Logan," he interrupted her.

"If it's all the same to you, I'd rather we weren't on such a familiar basis with each other as to use each other's given names."

"It isn't all the same to me."

She pressed her lips together, terribly confused by the man holding her hand. She looked at his hard profile as he scanned the horizon. A shadow from the brim of his hat slashed across his face. Best just say what needed to be said. She'd long since lost her modesty. "I am not prepared to share my body with you or anyone." *Ever again.*

His hand tightened marginally. This time when his gaze met her eyes, there was no humor in it. "I haven't asked you to. When I do, you'll know it, so there's no use worrying about when I'm going to ask. And you'll want it, too, or not a damn thing will happen between us."

"Then why are you holding my hand?"

"Because you're scared. And I'm not. You can let go anytime you want, honey."

Sarah gritted her teeth. Why did he have to say that? And sound so nice saying it? He was carrying

her satchel, their bedrolls, and his saddlebag—
everything they owned, a burden that, among the
Sioux, she would have been expected to carry. And
it felt good to hold his hand.

She let go of him.

"Why don't you tell me what trouble it is you're
running from? Maybe there's something I can do.
At the very least, I'll have a better idea about how
to keep you safe."

Sarah said nothing for several moments as she
tried to figure out how much she could reveal without telling him anything significant. In the end, she
decided to tell him the story her husband had told
her. "My husband was investigating corruption at
several of the Indian agencies in the Dakota Territory. He made some powerful enemies. They didn't
want him to publish what he'd discovered." How
easily she'd fallen for that tale. Until Eugene had
asked her to forge several land deeds.

Mr. Taggert whistled low and shook his head.
"That's it? That's all you're gonna tell me? There's
gotta be more to it than that."

"That's all I can tell you."

"Sooner or later, I'm gonna need the whole
story."

She said nothing more, and he didn't press her.
"Where do you think we are?" she asked, changing
the subject.

"By foot, about a week northeast of Fort Laramie. Let's move closer to the tree line. We'll be
less obvious."

* * *

It was well into the evening before they saw the smoke rising on the distant horizon. Sarah cried out and started forward at a quick pace.

"Whoaa—hold up there," Logan grabbed her arm, keeping her at his side.

"That's the stage, isn't it?"

"Can't know for sure. But it's likely." He pulled the pack off his shoulders and set it on the ground. They would stop here for the night. Both of them were exhausted. And this spot was somewhat defensible, should they need cover.

"We've got to go help them!"

"You'll never make it before dark. That fire's at least three miles away. And you don't know what's between us and them."

Sarah shook her head, the blood rapidly leaving her face. Her eyes went big and dilated so that the warm brown of her irises looked black. Her gaze became unfocused. It was as if she'd gone somewhere inside herself, Logan thought. A place of terror.

"The warriors are coming back, aren't they?"

He didn't answer her. He didn't need to answer her.

"Oh, God. No," she mumbled, over and over as she snatched up her satchel and the attached bedrolls. She backed a few steps away from him, then pivoted and ran for the thin line of trees that bordered the river.

"What are you doing?" Logan followed her. She

stuffed the pack into a hollow at the cavernous base of an old cottonwood, then covered it with branches and leaves.

"Hurry! We have to hide." She ran frantically along the bank, searching for something. He followed her.

"We don't have to hide. I won't let them harm you."

She found the perfect hiding place inside a thick stand of cottonwoods where saplings grew from the roots of the older trees. Holding her skirts tight to her body, she pushed her way inside the screening, careful not to break any branches.

"Mrs. Hawkins, please. There is no need for this panic." He reached out and snagged her arm as the wide, green leaves slipped over her body. Even if she did nothing more than that, it would have been hard to spot her, standing as she was in her brown homespun dress amid the dense foliage of the lower brush.

"They're coming. They will do to us what they did to the passengers," she hissed. "I don't want to die, not that way. And I won't be taken again. Hide with me. Hide now." She withdrew into the arms of the saplings, disappearing into the bank, perfectly camouflaged. In seconds flat there was no sign that anyone had been there. He'd seen native women take longer to hide themselves and their young from soldiers and bounty men hunting the tribe than it had taken Sarah to disappear.

Logan lifted his hat and shoved his hand through his hair. The woman was scared through and through. There was no convincing her that he would protect her. He made his way back up the bank and walked a few yards away, haunted by the terror in her eyes.

He wasn't sure what he became aware of first— the percussion of hooves against the hard ground or the noise of galloping horses. The band of warriors they had met earlier thundered to a stop in a semi-circle around him. Two of the warriors rode Morgans from the coach, leading their paints and the other two horses from the coach. One of them used Logan's expensive Spanish saddle. Loot from the wagon was tied in bundles behind them. Three of the warriors had bloody scalps fixed to their shields.

Christ. There was nothing he could do about the other passengers. Had they not put Sarah out, he would have gladly negotiated on their behalf. No matter what his feelings for them were, no one deserved deaths such as they'd likely met. None of that mattered now. Making an issue of the attack would serve no purpose in the bartering he was going to have to do to obtain Sarah's release from her Sioux husband.

Logan could feel the burn of Sarah's gaze from her hiding spot. He hoped like hell she held her fire.

Cloud Walker ordered the man leading the two spare ponies to bring them forward. An antelope was draped over the back of one of them. "We bring you horses so that you don't have to walk."

Logan did not spare a glance for the horses. "I have nothing to trade for them. I cannot accept them."

Cloud Walker looked around them. "Where is Swift Elk's wife?"

"*My* wife is preparing our camp."

Cloud Walker had one of his men cut the antelope off the pony. He dropped it at Logan's feet. "We have brought an antelope for Yellow Moon to prepare for us. We will smoke and talk about the ponies while she cooks."

"I will summon her."

Logan went down the embankment, putting the trees between him and Cloud Walker's band to obscure Sarah's hiding spot. Even knowing where she was, he had to search for her. "Mrs. Hawkins, you were right. They have come back." Her head lifted up. Leaves were stuck in her hair. "They've brought us an antelope and requested that you prepare it for them. Do you know how to do the butchering?"

She nodded.

"Could you please join us?"

She violently shook her head.

"It is best that we don't anger them by rejecting their gift. They have also brought us ponies to ride." He reached over and pulled a leaf out of her hair. "I will negotiate for your freedom. Do you think you can trust me?"

"You, maybe. Not them. They will dine with us, then kill us. They turn in a flash. You don't know them like I do."

"I do know them, but I know them differently."

"What of the stage passengers?"

Logan sighed. "They have the horses from the stage, my saddle, and three fresh scalps."

"Oh, God. Oh, God." She covered her mouth and immediately ceased all sound. She shook her head.

Her eyes pleaded with him, terror drawing the blood from her face.

"Never mind. I shouldn't have asked. I'll tell them you're sick and cannot prepare their meal."

"No! It won't matter to them. They won't accept that answer. They killed our fellow travelers, Mr. Taggert. It's wrong that you would have me cook for them. It's wrong. They are evil. They will kill us, too."

Logan sighed. "Their people are at war with ours. What they did, against your settlement, against the coach, was an act of war. You and I are fortunate that they don't see us as enemies at the moment. I'm asking you to cook for them because they are hungry, and I am hungry, and because it will make our negotiations go better."

Sarah pushed up from her leaf cover. For a long moment, she studied his eyes. At last, she nodded and smoothed debris from her hair. Logan could see the tremor in her hands. "I need to gather firewood."

He lifted her chin, forcing her eyes to meet his. "Running would not be a good choice, sweetheart. I need you to trust me on this."

"I won't run."

When she approached the camp a short while later, she made a pile of thin sticks near the antelope and left some items she'd taken from her satchel, seasonings and such that she'd brought for the trip. She collected kindling and larger pieces of firewood, which she laid out in a circle near where the men sat in a circle. She propped a few tall rocks on either side of the fire to brace the skewers upon. Logan handed her his matches to light the kindling. When the fire was started, he watched as she set to work on the antelope. It had already been gutted, Logan knew. The warriors would have eaten the liver and heart immediately after the kill, and would have emptied the intestines of any foodstuffs the animal had grazed on recently. The rest of the innards they'd have left at the kill site for the carrion to take.

She skinned one side of the animal, then carved out several thin strips of meat. She pounded these between large river rocks to tenderize the tough antelope meat, then seasoned and skewered them. Logan watched her make short work of the carcass, lining up dozens of skewers to cook.

Sarah Hawkins was an enigma. Sometimes frightened and fragile, sometimes brave and resourceful. She could walk all day without complaining, though he knew she had to be as tired as he was. She could hide in an instant like a native and prepare an antelope like an experienced butcher—all things few white women were able or willing to do. He wondered if she was aware of her very considerable strengths.

Cloud Walker started a pipe, drawing and releasing smoke as an offering to the four directions, the Earth, and the sky before taking a smoke of his own. When the pipe was passed to him, Logan drew the smoke into his lungs, held it until it burned. He passed the pipe to the man next to him and slowly released the smoke.

"Shadow Wolf, what have you to trade for the two horses we offer?" Cloud Walker asked once every man in the circle had smoked from the pipe.

"I have a very fine saddle that I would consider trading in exchange for the two horses and a knife."

"Where is that saddle? I do not see it among your things."

"I left it with the black coach. They were to deliver it to Fort Laramie, where it would be held for my arrival."

"That is my saddle," one of the braves asserted. "I took it in the raid on the coach. It is not yours to trade with," he claimed.

Logan made no comment, but looked at Cloud Walker. If ownership was determined by possession, then they could not claim Swift Elk still owned Mrs. Hawkins. The crafty old Indian caught the implication.

"We did not know the saddle was yours, Shadow Wolf. We will take it in trade for the ponies."

"And a knife. That saddle is valued, in my world, at a man's work for half a year. Ponies are but a day's work for a man in your world."

"Ponies cannot be acquired as easily as in days past. And each pony is of no value until someone has spent many weeks training him. As you know, owning one could be the difference between traveling across this land and dying within it. You don't value horses as you should."

Logan nodded his head. "It is true that the ponies are of significant importance. I will be pleased to exchange my saddle for the two ponies and a knife."

Cloud Walker ordered Many Deer, the warrior who had claimed the saddle, to give his knife to Shadow Wolf. The warrior was not pleased with the decision, but he complied. He withdrew the knife from the sheath at his belt and threw it with lethal precision so that it landed in the space between Logan's crossed legs and his crotch, embedding itself in the hard dirt.

"It is done," Cloud Walker said as he motioned that the negotiation for the horses was completed. The pipe was again passed around the group.

Sarah brought the skewered cuts of meat over to the campfire and braced them across the rocks she had placed strategically in a ring about the fire. She'd rolled up the sleeves of her dress to tend to her work, and now the firelight danced over scars that marred her pale skin. Logan tore his gaze away, but his mind snagged on what he'd seen. Did such scars cover her body? He'd heard horror stories of women taken captive, some reports sensationalized, some understated. Her experience had left her frightened and scarred, yet here she was using the skills she'd learned as a captive on behalf of warriors like those who'd captured her, all because he'd asked her to.

"It has been decided, Shadow Wolf, on the matter of Yellow Moon, that you will be allowed to fight one of our men. If you win, we will negotiate a price for her. If you lose, we will take her back to Swift Elk."

Logan released a breath of blue smoke, watching it writhe and swirl as it merged with the evening air, rising to the Great Spirit, carrying his silent prayer to be victorious. "I accept that challenge."

When the meat was cooked, the warriors hungrily dug into their portions. Sarah replenished skewers over the fire, keeping the food coming. When she set a fourth round to cook, Logan caught her wrist, stopping her quick retreat from the circle of men. She froze, her face pale in the failing light of the evening.

"Have you eaten?"

She shook her head. Logan gave her the last skewer he'd taken from the fire. "Sit behind me and eat this."

Sarah did as he directed, though fear made it difficult to eat. She'd heard Mr. Taggert's calm acceptance of the fight challenge. He did not seem afraid. Nothing fouled his inner tranquility. She took a bite of the roasted meat. If Mr. Taggert was not successful in his bid to win her, he would be killed, and she would be left to the mercy of Cloud Walker and his men. She had no doubt they would return her to Swift Elk. Once they were finished with her.

Cloud Walker stood up to make a pronouncement.

"Shadow Wolf and Many Deer will now fight. You will both pick your weapons. Guns are not an acceptable choice."

Many Deer's eyes were lit with a vengeful fury. He borrowed a knife from another of the men and walked a ways off from the fire. Mr. Taggert went to his saddle and untied his rope. He coiled it into wide loops that he draped over his head to lie across his shoulder, keeping the noose end in easy reach. Bare-handed, Mr. Taggert followed Many Deer.

Sarah felt like crying. Fear clung to her like a shadow. She couldn't shame Mr. Taggert by weeping over him in front of his opponent. They would think she lamented his lack of prowess. She turned away, intending to retreat to the riverbed while the warriors were focused on the fight. If she could get back to her hiding spot, she might be able to elude the warriors by slipping down the river if things went bad.

Cloud Walker stepped in front of her. She resisted looking up at him, but she couldn't avoid his hissed comment. "This is what you, a faithless woman, have brought upon two brave men. One will die tonight. Because of you."

She stood frozen in place, crippled by the warring forces of guilt, fear, and a desperate need to live. She looked back at the men facing off. Cloud Walker was about to start their competition.

"Stop this!" Her words were spoken in English. "Stop!" she repeated in Sioux. "It is not right that harm come to anyone because of me. Mr. Taggert, I will go with them."

Many Deer straightened, a look of disgust on his face—whether for her or for the loss of a fight, she couldn't tell. Neither one boded well.

"Shadow Wolf, Swift Elk's woman has decided the outcome. There is no need to fight. We will take her and go," Cloud Walker declared.

"She is my woman. She has no say in the matter. You will have to fight me to take her. I am not tired of her and have no wish to sell her."

Many Deer grinned. "Then begin," Cloud Walker said as he stepped away from the men.

They circled each other. To Sarah's shock, Mr. Taggert appeared to be enjoying the confrontation.

Many Deer charged at him. Mr. Taggert held still until the last minute, when he turned to the side and tripped Many Deer. The warrior reacted quickly, falling into a fluid roll and jumping to his feet again. They grinned at each other.

The next time Many Deer approached more slowly, his knife swiping the air around Mr. Taggert. Sarah watched as he walked backward, ducking, leaning, dancing with the knife, his movements mesmerizing. He grabbed Many Deer's hand, blocking the knife as he swung a fist at the warrior's chin, connecting with his jaw. Many Deer stumbled back.

The warrior took aim and let loose his knife. Mr. Taggert reacted instinctively, leaping out of the way. When he came to his feet, he was already working his lasso, letting the rope out. Many Deer watched his movements with little concern. He started to circle around Mr. Taggert, who threw the rope in a blinding movement, slipping it beneath the warrior's feet. He yanked on the rope, pulling it tight. No sooner had Many Deer fallen than Mr. Taggert was upon him, flipping him to his back, tying his hands to his feet. He stood up and raised his arms, laughing with victory.

Cloud Walker handed him a knife. "It is a fight to the death, Shadow Wolf."

Mr. Taggert stared at the knife a moment. Many Deer ceased his struggles. He simply watched Mr. Taggert, his eyes alive with hatred. Mr. Taggert tossed the knife into the dirt at Cloud Walker's feet. "I will not kill a friend. This fight is ended."

Cloud Walker's face showed no emotion. He

nodded. "It is ended. We will smoke a pipe and discuss the bride price for Yellow Moon." He looked at Many Deer struggling with his bonds and chuckled. "Release him."

Mr. Taggert set him free, then gave him a hand up. Many Deer rubbed his wrists. "You are a cruel man, Shadow Wolf. I was the best fighter in our band until that trick. See how they laugh at me now. When we meet next, I will know how to do that trick, and then they will not make a joke of me."

Mr. Taggert laughed and clapped him on the back. "I look forward to that moment."

He glanced at Sarah as she stood in petrified stillness. Changing direction, he walked over to her, pausing only a moment. She thought he might pull her into a hug. And right then, more than anything, she wished he would. "Breathe, Mrs. Hawkins," he whispered against her temple. "This is almost over. I will get you to Cheyenne."

Before she could do as he suggested, he'd moved on, joining the warriors around the fire again. They were joking about the way Many Deer had been bested. A pipe was started and sent around the circle. She turned woodenly, resuming cutting slices of meat to skewer. There was plenty of meat left—she could cook ahead for breakfast. Talk in the circle turned to her worth. Her ears burned. She tried to listen, but they had lowered their voices until the drumming of her heart drowned out all but a few words. She prepared the skewers quickly and brought them to the fire. When she retreated this time, she stayed within listening range.

"Yellow Moon was a favorite wife to Swift Elk. He paid eight ponies to his men so that he could own her himself and not share her unless he wished. Once she was his, Swift Elk was popular in the band's gambling. The men would wager anything to be with her. She made him wealthy, for he lost often enough that the men thought their chances of winning her were high."

Sarah felt blood warm her cheeks as shame turned her stomach. She ventured a glance toward Mr. Taggert, catching the hardening of his gaze as Cloud Walker spoke at length about the bets Swift Elk had made. Mr. Taggert's gaze moved from man to man. He said not a word, didn't interrupt Cloud Walker's dissertation of her worth or the crafty way Swift Elk had used her. A chill whispered over her shoulders. If he let anger take him, he would lose the negotiation—and perhaps her freedom as well.

"What is the price you place on Yellow Moon?"

"Fifteen horses."

"I have only a rifle, a pistol, two horses, and a knife to my name. I am not willing to barter with them. You could follow us to Fort Laramie. There I can acquire a number of horses. Perhaps five."

There was a wave of hurried discussion. "It is a trick," Many Deer complained. "He would have the soldiers arrest us. We would be hanged."

"I haven't built my business by cheating your people."

Cloud Walker motioned the opposition to silence. "Shadow Wolf speaks truthfully, though he does not understand Yellow Moon's worth. You see the color of her hair? It is the color of white sand and yet she is still quite young. Swift Elk would have continued building his wealth for many years with her as his wife. It must be twelve horses. No less."

"She ran away from Swift Elk. If you take her back with you, it will be to kill her, not use her to grow Swift Elk's wealth. A dead woman has no value."

"She is too valuable to kill. But her actions will be punished."

"I have often traded with men from Swift Elk's band at my trading post on the Cheyenne River. I can give you a piece of paper that provides Swift Elk with an account. He can use the paper to trade for the goods he wants."

Many Deer made a disgusted noise. "It is a bad treaty."

"It is no treaty at all. It is a promissory note. Twelve horses similar to the ones I now own would cost me thirty dollars each. I would write the note for three hundred sixty dollars. You could receive payment from my trading post. Or you could take the three hundred sixty in goods from the store. Or in horse flesh. Or cattle. Or any combination that totaled three hundred sixty dollars. It is a generous offer. Most captives are ransomed for less. You are getting twice what the government would pay."

"I am getting nothing. A piece of paper that the rain could destroy."

"My word is not so easily destroyed. As you know, I don't have to make any payment at all. She is mine already. The payment I offer is in consideration of my affection for your people."

Cloud Walker motioned for the pipe to be refilled and circulated again. When it came to him, he drew a draft of smoke into his lungs and held that breath while he considered the deal. He released the breath slowly, letting a wisp of blue smoke into the air.

"I have thought on your offer, Shadow Wolf. I will accept it." He handed the pipe to Logan.

When the pipe had completed the circle, Logan took a sheet of paper and a pencil from his saddlebag and wrote out the promissory note. He handed it to Cloud Walker. "Take this to any of my trading posts. They will honor this contract."

Cloud Walker motioned for his men to take the cooked meat. They retreated to their horses and rode away, leaving behind the two ponies.

Sarah was frozen to the spot where she knelt. She heard the sound of Cloud Walker's band as it moved off into the shadowy range, an outcome so different from the night her home had been raided. Mr. Taggert was able to send them on their way with a promissory note. A piece of paper. Tears washed her cheeks. Mr. Taggert knelt in front of her. She lifted her gaze to him, wondering what kind of man it was that she now found herself traveling with across this savage land.

He didn't speak, didn't try to touch her. He studied her, waiting silently. "There is a little left of that antelope," Mr. Taggert commented. "Do you think you could get a few more pieces from it? We could cook them now for the morning. Then I will dispose of the carcass. We don't need wolves prowling around while we sleep. And I don't want to keep the fire going through the night."

She picked up his knife and cut a few more strips from the remains of the antelope. She skewered them, then put them on to cook. Setting back on her haunches, she caught sight of her hands, reddened with blood. Mr. Reimer, Mrs. Powell, and the driver were all dead. Life was so easily extinguished. Her world was in a crazy spin of loss and pain and deliverance.

"Look at me, Mrs. Hawkins," Mr. Taggert ordered. She forced herself to look at him. "Let's go wash up while that cooks. I'll give you privacy while I take the carcass off a ways. Will you follow me?"

She moved after him as docilely as a trained dog, her hands limp at her sides. He led her to the river's edge, then walked off to leave the carcass far away from their camp. She looked at the river, whose banks were swollen with the heavy spring flow, rippling and roaring. It looked deep in the dim light of the night. She'd seen a woman taken by a river once, another captive. Sarah didn't know if she'd been pushed into the rapids or if she'd chosen that death. It wouldn't be a painful way to go. Not really. Her lungs would burn a bit, but death would be fast.

She closed her eyes, feeling the pull of the water, its ebb and flow. She didn't want to die, didn't want to listen to the seduction of the river. But it called to her. The pain and the fear could end.

She didn't hear Mr. Taggert return, but when she opened her eyes, he was there. Watching her. He took her hands and pulled her down to a squat, dipping her hands into water so cold that her breath caught in her chest. He rubbed his hands over hers, up her wrists. He cupped a handful of water and smoothed it over her face. "It is done. It is over." He washed her face again.

She tried to focus on the river and its promise of peace, but his constant ministrations broke her focus. He drew her to her feet. Using the sleeve of his shirt, he mopped her face dry. She breathed in his scent, his essence. She breathed it again. Odd that his scent made her feel safe.

He took her hand and pulled her over to where she'd hidden her satchel. "See to your needs, then come up to the fire. And no more thinking about quick dives into cold water." Even in the shadow of the darkening sky, she could see his eyes burned with a chilling fervor. The intensity of his look cut through the haze of her mind.

"You're alive," he whispered harshly. "And I'm alive. And we will each of us live until we die. There is a reason for that, Mrs. Hawkins. We will not find it by cheating ourselves out of our remaining time."

Logan set out his bedroll, and opened Mrs. Hawkins's on top of it. When she returned from washing up, she came to a hard stop.

"No."

"'No' to what?" Logan asked.

"I won't do this with you. I won't be intimate with you."

"I didn't ask you to be. It's a cold night. Our blankets won't provide enough warmth if we sleep separately. I'll even keep my boots on."

She frowned at him, clearly not following his train of thought.

"I can't very well make love to you with my boots on. I might hurt you." He turned and had started to move off when he caught her comment, barely audible as it was.

"It wasn't love they made with me."

Rage stiffened his spine. "No, it wasn't."

He walked back toward her and kept his voice lowered so he wouldn't frighten her with the intensity of his reaction. "It was war. All of it. You, your husband. The Indians don't recognize noncombatants. It is how they make war, how they've made war for thousands of years. You're either an enemy or you're not. There is no gray area. You were a victim of war, Mrs. Hawkins. If you were strong enough to survive what the men who captured you did to you, then they let the women have at you. And if you were strong enough to withstand their treatment, you ceased being an enemy. You became worthy of marrying a warrior—which is exactly what happened."

Logan let his words sink in. He did not reach for her, did not speak, did nothing to break into her thoughts. The poisonous memories inside her had to come to the surface so that they could be expunged from her soul.

"My husband fought for us. They killed him as if he were no more significant than a gnat."

"He was a damned fool. He had no business being out here."

"He did what he did for the good of the Sioux, the people whose land was being stolen."

Logan shook his head. "I'm willing to bet he did what he did to line his pockets—at the cost of the Sioux. And you, Mrs. Hawkins, have paid for his foolishness with everything that you held dear."

He breathed the crisp night air and tried to calm the anger within him. He thought of her at the river earlier, the way she'd faded before him. "You have a choice now. You can choose to live, reclaim what is left of your life, fill it with the joy denied you thus far. Or you can surrender to your wounds. Let the past take you. Die of a broken heart. It's a decision only you can make."

Chapter 5

Sarah's eyes shot open. She held herself still, waiting for the fuzz of sleep to clear her head. She felt disoriented, trying to recall why she was sleeping outside, if she was still on the run with the warriors who'd taken her a year ago. Her coat rested over her, as did half of a man's coat. There'd been no coats that first trip. She ventured a look at the heat source next to her under the blanket. Mr. Taggert. He was awake, but lying still. Watching her. She pushed up on her elbows to search for Cloud Walker and his men.

"They didn't come back," her traveling companion said. His breath condensed in the cold morning air.

"Are we safe?"

"For now. Let's get moving. I think we're in Wyoming Territory now. With the horses, we should make Fort Laramie by midday tomorrow. Are you up for a hard ride? We've no saddles."

"Anything to get off this prairie."

"Then go wash up. I'll get our horses watered."

She took advantage of the privacy he offered. They ate a quick meal of the cold skewers from last night, then got the horses ready. Mr. Taggert spread their bedrolls across the backs of the horses as padding for the long ride ahead of them. One of the horses also had his saddlebag on it. He bent over, his hands cupped to boost her atop the pony. Her skirt was wide and covered most of her legs. He ignored the stretch of black stocking her skirt exposed.

He smiled up at her. "I got a bargain last night."

"How so?"

"I would have paid thirteen horses for you."

She frowned at him. "Mr. Taggert, I have no way of adequately thanking you for what you have done for me. No funds with which to reimburse you—"

He leapt up to the back of the second horse, her satchel in hand. Spreading the straps, he slipped them over his arms and settled it on his back. "There's no need to reimburse me, Mrs. Hawkins. You were in need of rescuing and I was in need of a wife."

Sarah tapped the sides of her mount, bringing him even with Mr. Taggert's. "I thought I made it clear that I do not intend to marry you."

He kneed his mount forward. "It seems only polite that you wait until I actually do propose before you refuse me."

Nearly an hour later, they crested a hill and came upon the ashen remains of the stagecoach. Sarah drew to a full stop and stared at the ghastly sight.

"Keep moving," Mr. Taggert ordered, but she was unable to comply. Two bodies lay near the coach, a man and woman. Naked and untouched by the fire, bloated in death. Several arrows were sticking out of them, their skulls bloodied. Mr. Taggert took hold of her reins and pulled her forward.

"We should at least bury them."

"I don't have a shovel. And I don't want to waste a day seeing to their final resting spot if it means we may have to find our own. This ain't a good spot to dawdle. When we get to Fort Laramie, we'll let them know what happened to the carriage."

Sarah couldn't tear her eyes from the still-smoking wreckage. As they came round the front of the carriage, they found the driver pinned to the coach with an arrow through his throat. His body was blackened, his slack jaw exposing a ghastly smile of white teeth.

Mr. Taggert kneed his horse to a trot, drawing hers along with him. Fear sliced through her hurt. Violence had become the fabric of her life, and every thread that unraveled terminated in blood, pain, and loss. She let him hold her reins, emptying her mind of everything but the rhythm of her mount, a fast rocking motion. Forward and back. Wind. Sun. These things were real. Only these things.

That night, as they lay side by side again between their opened bedrolls, Sarah held herself utterly still. She waited for Mr. Taggert to reach over to her, to use his strength against her. The blanket was not very wide. They couldn't lie on it next to each other and not touch. Every time he moved, she tensed. An hour passed. She stared up at the stars, waiting for him to do what men did to women. Waiting for him to disappoint her, too.

"I've been wondering something, Mrs. Hawkins," he said, breaking the silence.

Sarah gave up pretending to sleep. "What's that?"

"Where did you live before you got married?"

Before Swift Elk, before Eugene, before the terrible accident that took her parents' lives, before her father's fateful decision to emigrate from Pennsylvania to the Dakota Territory, she'd had a fairly normal, calm life. "Philadelphia."

"Do you miss it?"

Sarah considered whether she did. "I miss not living in fear more than I miss my childhood home. But a dream's an important thing, don't you think?"

"Yes. Was it your dream to come west?"

"My father's. He was a newspaper man. Over the years, he'd seen so many stories of the great adventures men had out west. He'd always longed to move here.

"We weren't a large family. There were only my parents and me. I had an older sister, but she died before I was born. My brother died in the war. Two years ago, when my father retired, he was ready for a change, an adventure. He bought a tract of land outside of Yankton."

She looked at Mr. Taggert. "My parents were so excited. They were going to realize a dream they'd held their entire lives. I was nineteen at the time. We rode the train out from Philadelphia to St. Louis, a city my father had always wanted to see. They spent some time gathering the provisions they'd need to begin their ranch. And then the accident took them."

"What accident?"

"They were trampled by a runaway freight team on a busy road. They died instantly."

Mr. Taggert sucked in a sharp breath of air. "Aw, honey. I'm sorry. Why didn't you go back home?"

"There was no home to go to. And I met Eugene then, at their funeral."

Mr. Taggert said nothing for a long minute. "Did you love him?"

Sarah sighed. The truth was, she didn't love him. Marrying him had simply been a practical decision. "Perhaps I could have. In time." Had things been different. Had *he* been different.

She looked over at Mr. Taggert. He was lying on his side with his head propped up on his hand. Her eyes had acclimated to the darkness of the moonlight. She could see there was no humor in his eyes. Nor lust. Only something that might be interpreted as fierceness.

"I'm not like any of the men you've known, honey. Not a damned one of them."

Life had broken faith with her, but this man had not. Not yet. "Good night, Mr. Taggert."

"Good night, Mrs. Hawkins."

Late in the afternoon of the next day, they descended into a wide, shallow valley. In the distance, several large, white buildings stood in regimental precision around a parade ground. Cattle and horses dotted the pastures surrounding the complex. Fort Laramie. At last. Sarah pulled a long draw of air into her lungs—her first easy breath in days. She straightened her gloves and pulled the cuffs of her sleeves down over her wrists. Mr. Taggert's alert gaze followed her movements. She forced a surface expression of calm.

They stopped outside the Officers Headquarters building. Mr. Taggert dismounted, then came around to help her down, his touch brief and entirely proper. "Would you like to come in with me? I'll just be a minute."

"Thank you." She shook her head. "I'll wait here."

When he disappeared inside the building, she took a look around. Heat shimmered in waves, distorting the dirt path around the grounds. No exercises were being conducted at the moment, perhaps due to the searing temperature. Nonetheless, soldiers moved around the buildings, busily seeing to their duties. A couple of women swept their porches. In shady side yards, children played a game of chase.

The office door banged shut. Sarah looked up to see Mr. Taggert following an officer who hurried over to her. "Mrs. Hawkins! Can it really be you? What a great pleasure to meet you and see that you are whole and hearty. Several of the men now assigned to us here were involved in your search. They feel their inability to recover you was the

greatest failure of their careers. They were close to
the devils who took you until that late spring storm
swallowed the trail."

"I thank you and your men for their labors on
my behalf, sir."

"Heavens, here I'm prattling on and I haven't
even introduced myself. I'm Colonel Miller. Logan
says he's escorting you to Cheyenne. Would you do
my wife and me the great honor of being our guest
while you're here at the fort?"

Sarah sent a quick look to Mr. Taggert. Would he
try to stop her from staying with the Millers? What
did it mean that he had claimed her? He said nothing, but gave her a small smile of encouragement.
"I'd like that. Thank you for your hospitality."

"Very good. Very good indeed. I'll just take you
over to the house then and introduce you to the
missus."

They walked down the dirt road that led to the
row of officers' homes. Before they could even approach the front steps, a woman stepped outside.
She smoothed her hands over invisible wrinkles in
her starched apron as she smiled a welcome to the
trio. "Logan Taggert! What brings you out our way?
Is it time for trading once again?" She took his
hands and leaned forward for a kiss. Logan gave
her cheek a quick buss.

"It is. White Bull is bringing some goods in for
me to look at. Then I'll be accompanying Mrs.
Hawkins to Cheyenne."

Mrs. Miller's eyes widened. "Mrs. Hawkins?" She

took hold of Sarah's hands and studied her features a little too critically for Sarah's comfort. "This is a miracle." Her eyes misted up. "Truly a miracle. We'd heard you'd been recovered at last. What a terrible tragedy. Colonel, I insist they stay with us."

"Not me, Mrs. Miller," Logan declined the offer. "I need to ride out and see if White Bull has gotten in yet. I'll bunk down with the men in the bachelors' quarters. But I would request that you take good care of Mrs. Hawkins." He set Sarah's satchel on the top step, then paused in front of her on his way back to the horses.

Sarah felt a little panicked that he wouldn't be near at hand. Strange. She hadn't felt anything like that since her parents' deaths two years earlier. "Will I see you tomorrow?"

He smiled at her. "You will. If you like, you can come to the trade with me. The women of White Bull's village produce beautiful pieces of beadwork clothing."

She didn't want him to leave, even as much as she feared he would stay. Anyone near her was in danger. She wondered if Eugene's enemies could find her here, and if they did, would they be foolish enough to try something? They hadn't found the papers at Fort Buford—maybe they'd given up. He stood close to her, close enough that if they whispered, the Millers would not be able to hear them. "Mr. Taggert, I don't know why you came with us, but you saved my life. I cannot find sufficient words to thank you for your selflessness."

"No thanks are needed." He stood silently before her, his pale eyes watching her.

"I cannot further delay you from reaching your intended destination." Finding his eyes too disturbing, she looked at his throat. "I shall have no trouble getting to Cheyenne on my own from here, I'm quite sure."

He leaned toward her. "Honey, you are my destination. Now, go on with Mrs. Miller. Get yourself to bed early. And sleep tonight. There are no stars to stare at inside a house, and nothing to worry about here anyway. You're safe." This last he whispered for her ears only.

He waved to Mrs. Miller, then picked up the reins to take their horses to the livery.

"I'll just walk with you a bit, my boy," Colonel Miller said. "You weren't by any chance on the stage from Fort Buford that we've been expecting?"

"We were. It was hit by Indians. Did you know Chandler's running a stage between Deadwood and Cheyenne? What's being done about that? He's causing trouble for every white man, woman, and child in the entire region—and any passenger who thinks he's safe on Chandler's stages."

"What happened? Were there other survivors?" A breeze pulled around the corner of the house, muffling the rest of their conversation.

"Oh, my dear! You were on that stage?"

Sarah nodded, seeing again the blackened carriage, the burned body of the driver. She closed her eyes, absorbed the feel of the breeze, forcing herself to block out yet another memory. If she were invisible, the wind would blow right through her. She imagined herself disappearing, in little pieces, until she was no more substantial than a spiderweb.

An arm settled about her waist, startling her. "Come inside, dear." Mrs. Miller smiled at her. "I have a new *Harper's Bazaar* just in from New York. Well, it's several months old, but it's new to me! Why don't we have a cup of tea and see what fashion statements we could make? I'll put some water on for a bath. You can soak off the trail dust while I wash your clothes."

They moved up the porch and stepped inside the cool foyer of the Millers' home. Sarah drew a breath and released it slowly, relieved to have walls around her once again. "I don't want to be a bother, Mrs. Miller."

"Nonsense! I am happy you're here. We have so few visitors." She smiled as she led the way back to the kitchen at the rear of the house. "Being an army wife, I know the hardships we face out here. If we don't help each other, who will?"

In the kitchen, a small stack of mail sat half opened on the table. She pushed the fashion journal toward Sarah, chattering about the exciting new designs while she bustled about, putting a kettle on to boil, drawing a screen around a tub, filling the tub with cold water, fetching a towel, soap, and a change of clothes for Sarah to borrow. When the preparations for the bath were finished, she made a tray of sandwiches and a pot of tea.

"Come to the sink, dear. We'll just let you freshen up a bit before eating our snack; then you can have a long soak in the water. I'll get your room ready—I'm sure you'd like to rest before supper."

Sarah moved to the wash basin that held a pool of tepid water. There was no way to hide the marks on her hands and lower arms, souvenirs of her stay with Swift Elk. She hardened herself to Mrs. Miller's inevitable reaction and began drawing her gloves off her hands. The older woman made no sound. Sarah unbuttoned her cuffs and turned her sleeves up, aching to dip her hands into the water and splash it across her face. She looked at Mrs. Miller, who kept her gaze on her face and did not appear to notice the burn marks dotting her wrists, the scars from tethers kept too tight, the lash marks that striped her hands.

Sarah picked up the bar of soap and rubbed at her hands and nails, then scrubbed her face. Mrs. Miller smiled and handed her a towel. "There, doesn't that feel better? There's nothing like a quick wash-up to restore a person's equilibrium after a long journey. I bet you're starving. Let's sit and have a bite."

Sarah followed her to the table.

"I've known Logan since he first came down from Defiance. He's grown into quite a fine young man, but don't you dare tell the colonel I said that. He's turned the head of many an army wife. Occasionally, he's graced us with his presence at a couple of our dances. While he was kind to all of us poor unfortunates stuck out here on the wretched frontier, he's never singled one of the women out. Never until you. It does my old heart good to see that he's found someone special."

Sarah yearned to tell the colonel's wife about her predicament, but she feared the way she would react. How did one tell a proper army wife that a trader had claimed her, had bought her from her Sioux husband? Doubtless she would think Mr. Taggert had taken liberties with her. She might even put her out of her house, leave her to find lodging elsewhere. In the end, she decided to say nothing.

"Mr. Taggert and I are just acquaintances. We only met a little over a week ago. I can't imagine that he could have formed such an attachment to me. I certainly hope he hasn't. I'm in no position to consider changing my circumstances. I would not be a fit wife for him."

"We'll see, my dear. We'll see. Now help yourself to a sandwich—or four. You need to store up energy for the journey to Cheyenne."

Sarah felt her stomach tighten at the thought of being back on the open prairie, traveling without cover. Any vehicle they used, even with an army guard, would be easy prey. She fingered a tiny sandwich that had been cut in quarters. "How long does it take to reach Cheyenne from here?"

"By horse, it takes about three days. By stage, it takes a little over a day. There are several stopping points between here and Cheyenne. They don't stop for overnights—they just pause long enough for a quick bite and a new team of horses every fifteen miles or so. It's tedious in the extreme, but quick. The next stage won't be coming through for another few days, though, so you'll have plenty of time to recuperate. You've had one ordeal after another, my dear. I'm glad you'll be here to let me fuss over you!"

Chapter 6

Logan whistled as he walked down the road toward the colonel's house the next morning, his arms full of the supplies he and Sarah would need for their trip down to Cheyenne. They wouldn't be leaving for several days, but he thought Sarah would be less fretful if she knew he'd acquired what they needed for the journey. He still had to pick up a couple of saddles, but he could do that at any time.

A unit of men was forming on the parade grounds, preparing for a detail. He adjusted his load and when he looked up, he noticed Sarah's Indian pony tied up outside the colonel's house. Sarah stood next to the colonel and his wife, wearing her bonnet, her coat draped over an arm.

Logan deposited his supplies in the grass near her. "What's going on?" he asked as Sarah and Mrs. Miller finished embracing.

"I'm going to Cheyenne, Mr. Taggert." She held her chin high, but the grip she still had on Mrs.

Miller's hand would probably leave a bruise. She looked tired. He wondered if she'd eaten last night, if she'd been able to sleep at all. He hadn't. He'd tossed and turned.

Logan looked at her, then at the column of men forming nearby. "No. I'll take you in a couple of days, as soon as I'm finished with the trade I came to do."

"The colonel has a unit of men riding out this morning. I'll be leaving with them."

He frowned. "What's the rush?"

"I have business to see to that cannot wait. I will find a way to repay you for the horses, Mr. Taggert."

"I don't care about the horses. I said I'd get you to Cheyenne, and that's what I aim to do."

"I'll be safe with the colonel's men."

"*I* can keep you safe."

A group of civilian men rode by. One shoved his hat farther back on his head and grinned at Logan. The hairs rose on Logan's neck as he flashed back to the first time he'd met that particular frontiersman three years earlier.

He'd been traveling between a couple of his trading posts in southern Colorado when he stopped in Poncha Springs for a steak and a whiskey, his mind on starting a friendly game of poker.

The steak was good and the whiskey smooth, but the game was a horse of a different color. One by one, the cowboys and vaqueros folded, leaving only Logan and the man sitting opposite him.

It was a hot night. No breeze stirred the stench in the dimly lit saloon. Even through the haze of smoke, Hugh Landry's hazel eyes were focused, unblinking. Skinner, they called him. His forehead was slick with sweat. His brown moustache was bushy and growing into a month's worth of beard. A cigar was clamped in the corner of his mouth, each exhalation adding to the gray fog in the room.

Three hundred dollars sat on the table between them. Logan knew Skinner only had twenty-five dollars left. He bet a hundred, intending to end the game. Skinner looked at Logan, his eyes narrowing as he weighed his next move. Logan rested his hand near his holster.

"You know I'm all in, but I can meet your bet."

"With what?"

Skinner reached for something beside his chair. Logan drew and cocked his gun, the clicks loud in the now quiet room. Skinner held perfectly still. Logan shook his head. "Not you," he said to Skinner. "You—" He nodded to the man on his right.

The man lifted Skinner's old parfleche. The beadwork was mostly gone, leaving skeletons of strings and knots behind. It was stained a dark color from wear and time. The man looked at Logan, then at Skinner. The room was absolutely silent as he reached his hand inside the pouch and withdrew a fistful of black hair and skin. He couldn't get it out of his hand fast enough. He turned the bag upside down and dumped the rest of its contents on the table. Five scalps. One with baby fine hair that might have been cat fur.

"I got twenty-five dollars cash," Landry said.

"And I can get a hundred and twenty-five for these. Will you take it?"

Logan uncocked his gun, but kept it near at hand on the table. "Where'd you get them?"

"Took 'em off a Cheyenne family. Easy as pie. Even had a pass at the squaw a time or two before I finished her."

Skinner. Jesus H. Christ. "Not interested in a bunch of hair. You got a horse?"

Skinner's eyes narrowed. "The horse ain't on the table."

Logan looked at the pile of money. "Then I guess you're out."

Skinner cussed. He took his twenty-five dollars back. "You can have the goddamned horse."

"And the cash. Your horse ain't much better than a mule, but I'll take him and the cash." Being horseless would, at the very least, slow the bastard down, keep him from attacking another Indian family for a while.

"Done. Let's see what you got."

Logan showed his hand, a straight flush. Skinner threw down his flush. The room erupted in noise. Someone clapped Logan on the back. A crowd gathered to see the scalps and hear Skinner's story as Logan took up his winnings. It was all Logan could do not to lose his dinner.

And now the bastard was here, fixing to make a journey with Sarah. Logan sent the colonel a dark look. "Tell me he isn't riding with them."

"He requested safe passage to Chugwater."

"He doesn't deserve safe passage. He's a god-damned scalp taker."

The colonel's face tightened. "I'll thank you to remember women are present, Logan. And Mr. Landry doesn't do that in this territory."

"You know as well as I do that he doesn't care if he takes an Indian, Mexican, or black-haired white man's scalp. And he ain't too particular where he does his scalpin'."

Mrs. Miller put an arm around Sarah. "You're scaring the poor child, Logan. Enough of that talk."

"She should be scared." He looked at Sarah. "You aren't leaving."

"I am."

"Is there a problem here?" Skinner's voice broke into the tension of the group. Before anyone could answer, Logan grabbed him by a fistful of shirt and dragged him away from Sarah. "Get back on your horse and keep your damned eyes to yourself." He shoved him toward his horse.

Skinner shrugged the wrinkles out of his shirt. "I was talking to the lady."

"And I answered for her." Logan stepped close to Skinner, almost nose to nose. "If I so much as hear you looked at Mrs. Hawkins on the way down to Cheyenne, I will hunt you down, cut out your bowels, and feed them to the wolves. Hell, I might just do that anyway for the sheer pleasure of it."

"You hearin' this, Colonel?" Skinner asked without taking his eyes from Logan. "You're a witness."

The colonel ground his teeth. "Lieutenant!"

The lieutenant dismounted and hurried over. "Yes, sir!"

"Escort Mr. Landry back to the formation, and then return for Mrs. Hawkins."

Logan kept Skinner in his sights until he'd rejoined the line of men. He drew a long breath, then slowly released it. He looked at Sarah's pony, which was saddled with a cavalry saddle, her bedroll tied to the back. "What are you going to eat on the long march to Cheyenne? Are the colonel's men carrying your provisions?"

"Mrs. Miller packed some items for me."

Logan cursed under his breath. "Mrs. Miller, would you please fill this canteen for her?" he asked as he handed over one of the new canteens from his pile of goods. He untied her bedroll, then opened it near the supplies he'd purchased. He set pouches of ground coffee, sugar, flour, oats, dried stew contents, and jerky at intervals on the blanket, then rolled the whole collection up. He tied that behind her saddle, then tied her coat and one of the slickers he'd just purchased over the lot.

Sarah twisted her hands. "Mr. Taggert, I can't accept these things. I cannot pay for them."

"I didn't ask you to." He leaned toward her, lowering his voice so that their conversation would not carry. "Why are you really doing this? Why now?"

"I have to."

"Where will you go in Cheyenne? How will I find you?"

She lowered her gaze. "There's a teaching position open."

"You're lying."

She looked up at him, her dark eyes liquid with tears. "Please, please, don't come after me."

Logan cupped her chin, forcing her eyes to meet his. "I will come after you, and I will find you," he growled before pressing a kiss to her forehead. He didn't care that everybody saw him do that. He didn't care that she stiffened at the contact. Damn it. She was his. Two weeks. He'd known her barely two weeks and already she'd turned him inside out. He pulled some coins from his pocket and pressed them into her hand.

"No. Mr. Taggert, you've done too much."

He turned from her. "Lieutenant, see that she arrives safely in Cheyenne. It may be that I can conclude my business here quickly. If so, I'll be able to catch up to you. If not, check her into the Inter-Ocean Hotel." He removed some money from his wallet and handed it to the soldier. Sarah had turned red at his proprietary air, from anger or embarrassment, he didn't know. Or care. "She's to wait for me there."

"Yes, sir."

Logan helped Sarah to mount. He held onto the pommel for a moment, glaring up at her. "Take your bonnet off."

"Why?"

"Because you're gonna wear this." He took his hat off. "It ain't pretty, but it'll keep your neck dry—spring rains are running late this year." He tied her bonnet to her gear. His hat was too big on her, but the straps would hold it in place. He reached up and drew the two cords tight under her chin.

"I'll see you in a week."

"Good-bye, Mr. Taggert."

"A week, Sarah."

He watched the unit depart, the column of dark blue uniforms softened by the cloud of dust stirred up by their horses. The colonel cleared his throat, drawing Logan's attention back to the middle-aged couple standing behind him. Colonel Miller clasped his hands together behind his back. Rocking forward on the balls of his feet, he lifted his eyebrows and gave Logan a piercing glare.

"I hope you're going to marry that poor woman, Logan dear, after that display," Mrs. Miller declared.

Logan frowned. "That display was for the benefit of the men. If they know I'll gut them—beggin' your pardon, ma'am—for mistreating her, they're likely to think twice before crossing that line." It was the only protection he could offer Sarah.

"My men are not dishonorable curs," the colonel sputtered, affronted.

"They aren't, sir. But Skinner and his crew are."

"I know you're awaiting the arrival of White Bull's people. Why don't you stay with us?" Mrs. Miller offered. "I promised my sister a pair of those beautiful moccasins you'll receive in the trade. I thought perhaps we could discuss a fair price. Bring your things inside and get settled. Who knows how long it will take White Bull to arrive, but I hope you'll be our guest. Come inside, Colonel. I'll make you both some coffee."

The colonel grumbled about the work awaiting

him at the office and took off. Mrs. Miller went inside.
The warm sun beat down on Logan's shoulders as
a cool breeze swept around him. He stood in the
scattered debris of his morning purchases. In the far
distance, he could still see the cloud of dust marking
the path the column of travelers took. Riding alone,
he could catch up to them before they reached
Cheyenne if he left within two days. He hoped White
Bull would arrive sooner rather than later.

Three days after Sarah left, Logan sat in the tepee
of White Bull, smoking a pipe. Logan had spent the
day visiting with White Bull's children, speaking
with the elders of the band, catching up with the
chief himself. Logan wished Sarah were with him,
wished she could see this side of the Sioux. White
Bull's wives had served Logan a delicious meal of
meatballs and flat bread. At last it was time for the
bartering. The women had arranged their beaded
products on a blanket outside the tepee, where the
soft evening light made the intricate works of art
even more striking. They offered a stunning array
of moccasins, pouches, shirts, dresses, belts, hair
pieces, necklaces, and earrings beaded in intricate
designs using the band's signature colors, white,
yellow, and orange.

Logan took his time examining each piece.
White Bull's people stood at a distance, stoically observing the trade, their excitement evident only in
their rigid posture. White Bull's head wife stood
across the blanket, staying nearby in case Logan

had questions about their products. Her eyes were sharp and danced over each piece he touched. He could feel the energy in the artwork, threaded into the suede with each tiny stitch. It was almost as if he could hear the stories the women had shared as they worked through the long winter months, feel their joy in the art they made and the benefit their trade with him would bring their band.

Once, long ago, he'd visited White Bull's tepee during just such a working night. The village had been quiet, the children all sleeping soundly. The men had gathered in one tepee, the women in another. And while there was much laughing and storytelling as the men shared a pipe, they sometimes would grow silent and listen to the stories the women shared. Their quiet voices carried in the cold, windless night, bringing to the men the myths that were the foundation of women's lives in the tribe.

It was the echoes of those stories embedded in the beaded pieces as much as the works themselves that Logan sought out. Over the years, he'd learned which bands produced the highest quality art, learned which infused their work with the energy that was addictive to him. Each band he traded with for beadwork made the same basic array of products, but each produced a different feel, a different arrangement of the miniature trade beads, used colors in different ways. The larger works were actually depictions of their warriors' exploits, of new sons born to the tribe, of funny exploits of village contraries, all told in geometric symbols—a code few white men knew.

Logan took his time examining each piece. When he sensed White Bull and his head wife were satisfied that he had given the work the appreciation it was due, he settled down to barter.

The pieces were highly popular at several of his trading posts, especially the ones on the edges of civilization visited by whites who didn't dare venture into the deep western reaches of Indian country. He paid generous prices for the goods, knowing it was the best way to ensure he'd continue to get quality work.

He'd liquidated his entire inheritance for the seed money to start up a series of trading posts. He helped the women artists help their people. It wasn't much. It wasn't enough even. But it was the difference he could make. And as the various bands of Sioux, Cheyenne, and Arapaho families settled on reservations, it became ever more critical that they be able to supplement their income. He met with them each spring to purchase the products they'd spent the winter creating. And he met with them each autumn to sell them the beads, threads, and needles they needed for the work.

Finally, when the trade was completed and the last pipe smoked, Logan packed up his new possessions and returned to the Millers' home. He let Mrs. Miller select the moccasins she liked for her sister and a few other things for herself; then he crated the remaining items and addressed them for delivery to his main trading post on the Missouri River.

There remained, now, nothing keeping him from catching up to Mrs. Hawkins. He'd never known anyone who'd affected his life as much as she had in as short a time. She was in trouble, he had no doubt of that. Life had dealt her a bad hand, several times in a row, and yet she still sat at the table and played the game.

That was courage.

And it was what drove him to find her. He ached to share his future with someone who could feel life as intensely as he could. She'd had no time to heal and mourn before this mad dash off to Cheyenne. He couldn't fix what was broken in her, but he could stand beside her, shelter her, protect her while she put the pieces of her soul back together. If he was lucky, she would step out of her past and see him.

He grinned, feeling foolish and possessive and happy. He'd kept a few pieces from his trade with White Bull as gifts for Sarah and couldn't wait to give them to her.

He took his leave from the Millers and started for Cheyenne. It was a new direction in his life and it felt good.

Sarah stepped through the arches at the entrance to the Inter-Ocean Hotel and out onto the busy sidewalk. The morning was bright and hot as she made her way toward the sheriff's—she was glad for the shade Mr. Taggert's hat provided. She tightened her grip on the papers she held as she sent a surreptitious look around the area, trying to see whether anything seemed odd, whether someone looked out of place, whether she was being watched.

Nothing caught her eye. Her stomach tightened as she approached the sheriff's office. What she was doing now was the conclusion of a yearlong nightmare. She looked forward to handing the stolen deeds over to the law and letting the sheriff unravel her husband's innocence or guilt. Then she would be done with it. Free to start a new life. Somewhere. Somehow.

It wasn't yet 9:00 a.m.—his office hadn't opened for the day. She walked over to a bulletin board of news alerts and wanted posters, absently reading the messages there to pass the time. Smack dab in the middle was a poster with her face and name on it, claiming she was wanted for forgery. It offered a thousand-dollar reward if she were returned to the authorities in Yankton, Dakota Territory.

Sarah's blood turned to ice. They'd gotten to the sheriff. There was no refuge to be had through him. In fact, whoever was after her knew she was here, in Cheyenne. She had to go, had to leave today. But where? The thought of leaving the safety of the town and riding off, unprotected, into the prairie filled her with terror.

She considered and quickly discarded the idea of hiding in her hotel room and waiting for Mr. Taggert. If her husband's enemies hadn't found her yet, it wouldn't take them long to ask the various hotel clerks if she were staying with them. Besides, it was too dangerous a situation for her to involve Mr. Taggert. She had to disappear.

Intending to hurry back to the hotel and make a plan—just get off the street before someone recognized her—she pivoted and slammed into the hard chest of a man. The three oilskin pouches she carried shot out of her hands. She gasped and swooped down to collect them even as he knelt beside her. She quickly retrieved two of them.

"Beg pardon, ma'am," he said, handing her the third. She lifted her gaze and caught sight of his sheriff's badge, then looked no further.

"Thank you," she said with a nod, hoping Mr. Taggert's hat obscured her face. She stepped around him and continued down the sidewalk, forcing herself to move in an unhurried stroll.

In her hotel room, she paced back and forth, trying to come up with a plan. She couldn't take a stage out of town because she had to bring her horse wherever she was going; she would need him at the other end of her trip and he couldn't keep up with the pace a stagecoach set with its constantly refreshed horse teams. Nor could she leave town by herself.

Then one name popped into her head: Jace Gage. She remembered what the captain had told her about the gunfighter who lived in Defiance. If she could learn how to use her gun, at least she'd have a fighting chance of defending herself if—or when—her pursuers actually caught up with her. Maybe, after she'd lain low in Defiance, her trail would be harder to follow. But how to get there?

She took another turn around the room. There had to be freight wagons that took supplies up to Defiance. It was just a matter of finding which wholesaler supplied the town. Maybe she could ride along with one of those teams on its next run. If it wasn't leaving immediately, then she could take lodging under a false name, stay hidden in her room.

She looked at her satchel. She couldn't run around town lugging her bag—it would bring even more attention to her. Nor could she risk letting the papers out of her sight. She needed pockets to store the papers and her money. With what she'd reserved from the Fort Buford wives' donation, what Mr. Taggert had given her, and the extra cash the lieutenant had not used to pay for her room, she had almost twenty dollars. It was enough to get her through her stay here in Cheyenne and the trip to Defiance, as well as to hire Mr. Gage for a few hours of instruction and to rent a room while she was up there.

With a plan firmly in mind, she took out her sewing kit and set to work modifying her undergarments.

Chapter 7

Logan took the room key the clerk handed him. "Thanks. And what room is Mrs. Hawkins staying in?"

"Mrs. Hawkins?" the clerk repeated, giving Logan a disdainful lift of his eyebrow. "Are you the gentleman who guaranteed her room?" The tone in his question made Logan's hackles rise.

"I am."

"Please wait at the end of the counter, sir. I will need to have you talk to the manager." He disappeared into a room behind the counter, emerging just moments later. "This way, sir."

Logan followed the clerk into the back office and sat in a chair the clerk indicated. After a brief introduction, the hotel manager presented Logan with a bill for damages.

"What is this? Why am I being charged for a new mattress, bed linens, lamps, and such?"

"The woman who stayed in that room, a Mrs. Hawkins, left it in tatters."

Logan frowned. "I'm not following—"

The manager, a thin, smallish man with spectacles on his nose, gave Logan a pained expression. "She sliced through the mattress, the sheets, the blanket. Lamps were knocked over, dressers were turned over, the washbowl was destroyed. We did not rent her the room in that shape, sir. And we cannot use it again until the debris has been cleared away."

Logan held the man in a cold stare. "What makes you think Mrs. Hawkins did this?"

"The room was checked out to her. Who else would have done it?"

"I sent her here because I thought she would be safe. I thought you had sufficient protocols in place to protect a woman traveling alone. She was attacked in your hotel and you're worried about replacing linens? Where is she? Did you kick her out?"

"I-I don't know. The maid service discovered the mess this morning. I don't know where she went."

Logan stood up and leaned his weight on two hands as he glowered down at the hotel manager. "Did you notify the sheriff?"

"No. We prefer to keep dealings such as these to ourselves. We don't need the City Council thinking we harbor hooligans at our establishment. The fewer reports of mayhem and trouble on these premises, the better."

"So, a woman, traveling alone, is attacked in your hotel and not only do you not offer her aid, but you don't contact the sheriff. What the hell kind of establishment are you running?"

"We don't know she was attacked, sir. There is no evidence to support that theory."

"Have you cleaned her room yet?"

"No."

"Take me there now."

"What about the bill?" The look Logan gave him was enough to make him change his mind. In fact, he couldn't get Logan out of his office fast enough. He rang for his clerk even as he stumbled through an apology. "Never mind, Mr. Taggert. It will be our pleasure to take care of this matter without troubling you further."

The room Sarah had stayed in was in a shambles. Furniture was flung about the space, drawers pulled free and tossed away from the dresser and nightstand. Lamps lay broken on their sides. A maid was trying to mop up the spilled oil before the damage could spread to the room below. Bed linens lay in heaps about the room. And beneath it all was what was left of Sarah's satchel, ripped apart, her meager possessions tossed everywhere.

"Get out," Logan ordered the maid and the porter.

He had to be in the room alone, had to put the pieces back together to figure out what had happened. The one thing that kept him from panicking was that there was no blood. Whoever had done this had either not found Sarah or had taken her alive. But if she'd been captured, she hadn't gone willingly. If she had been here when they'd come, she hadn't helped them in their search or there would have been no need to tear the room apart. And if she hadn't been here, then she was on the run.

He stared at the disarray in the room. What were

the vandals looking for? Had they found it? Bella had said Sarah's room had been ransacked at the fort. Someone was hunting her. She was out there, alone and in danger. Why the hell couldn't she have trusted him, told him what was going on? Christ, he'd saved her life—and her dignity—several times over the last few weeks. He'd proven himself to her, hadn't he?

Logan began gathering up her things. Some of her clothes were shredded, some weren't. He made a pile of the items that could be salvaged. Under-clothes. Stockings. A blouse. He held the pieces to his nose and breathed in her scent, sweet like fresh air and sunshine. Like flowers after a rain shower. That was Sarah. She couldn't smell like that and be a criminal, could she?

He thought of the merry dance his own mother had led his stepfather on, looking beautiful in the fancy clothes she ordered from a modiste on the biannual trips she insisted upon taking to Denver. Her hair was always artfully arranged, her nails polished and long. She presided like a grande dame over a family of men who had no interest in society, who only cared about cattle and range wars. She'd had many affairs, and even that had failed to make his stepfather take notice of her. Logan had watched his mother's machinations throughout the years of his childhood, vowing he would never fall for such tricks as an adult—neither hers nor those of his stepfather.

Yet here he was, crazy about a woman who, at best, had been so mistreated in life that she couldn't bring herself to trust him, and at worst, was neck deep in unlawful activities that had clearly turned against her.

He shoved a hand through his hair, taking a fresh look around the room. What was missing? Perhaps that, more than anything else, would tell him what he needed to know to make his next steps. He looked at the pile of her things. Her coat, her gun belt, and her bedroll—that was all that was not here.

He gathered the things that were not destroyed and stuffed them into a pillowcase, then left. Maybe the sheriff would know if something had happened in town yesterday. Logan walked into the sheriff's office. A man with a badge looked up.

"Can I help you, mister?"

"I'm looking for a woman who checked into the Inter-Ocean a few days ago. She went missing yesterday. The room she was staying in had been ransacked. I was wondering if there had been any trouble in town in the past few days? Any odd men come through?"

"Sir, this is Cheyenne. We have trouble every day. What's the name of the woman you're looking for?"

"Sarah Hawkins."

"The forger?" He walked outside and pointed to a wanted poster pinned to the bulletin board. "This the woman?"

Logan stared long and hard at the poster. That was Sarah, all right. "When did you get this?"

"About a week ago."

"Who brought it?"

The sheriff shrugged. "A courier. What's your interest in the matter? You a bounty hunter?"

"Mrs. Hawkins is my wife."

"Oh! Well, Mr. Hawkins—"

"Name's Logan Taggert. We were married in the Sioux tradition. She didn't feel it was binding, which is why we're not together. In case you happen to run across her, she's about five foot five, a hundred and ten pounds or so, with white-blond hair and brown eyes. If you find her, keep her here. She's mixed up in something and I don't know what, but it's got her on the run."

The sheriff uttered a curse under his breath. "I did see her. She was here. Wearing a brown home-spun skirt and a god-awful hat."

"That was her."

"I bumped into her. She was carrying some pouches, which I knocked loose. I helped her pick them up and she ran off."

"Was she alone?"

"Yep. Looked pretty scared, too."

"Why do you suppose a woman who was wanted by the law stopped by to see the sheriff?" Logan asked.

"Dunno. Maybe when you catch up to her, you could let me know. Where will I find you if I do hear anything more about her?"

"How far did you say Defiance is from Cheyenne?" Logan remembered hearing Sarah ask the captain at the fort. He'd thought no one went there except to make trouble or visit the lumber camps.

"Defiance. I'll be heading up to Defiance tonight. Send word to the sheriff there."

The sheriff nodded. "You one of the Circle Bar Taggerts?"

Logan didn't immediately answer. It had been a long time since he'd thought of himself as one of them. "Yes, I am." He'd go up to Defiance to find Sarah, but he'd be damned if he'd make a stop at the old homestead to visit his stepfamily. "Mind if I take that poster?"

The sheriff ripped it off the board and handed it to him. Logan folded it and put it in a pocket as he made his way over to the livery. He could take a fresh horse and leave now, but he'd taken a liking to the little mare, given the circumstances he'd acquired her under. He'd ridden hard to get here. His pony was too tired for the long ride ahead of them. So was he, for that matter. They both needed a brief rest before starting out that evening.

A hostler came over to take his horse. "Did you happen to see a woman come through here yesterday with a horse like this one?"

The hostler gave him a sharp look. "She came through, all right. So did a couple other men, looking for her."

"Who were they?"

"Mister, it's my job to look after horses, not poke my nose in anyone's business. I'll tell you what I told them. She said she was heading down to Denver to take a teaching job."

* * *

Sarah tied her pony to the hitching post by a two-story house with a sign out front that read MADDIE'S BOARDINGHOUSE. She knocked on the door. Footsteps sounded inside, then a slightly heavyset woman in her late fifties greeted her.

"Do you have a room available?" Sarah asked.

"I do." She stepped back and let Sarah enter. "I charge a dollar a day. You get three meals and a bath once a week."

"All right."

Maddie led her to a desk with a ledger on it. "How long will you be staying with us, Miss—?"

"Mrs. Hawkins," Sarah said before she could stop herself. Well, too late now. Hopefully by the time her husband's associates looked for her here, she would be long gone. "A week." Another seven dollars gone.

Sarah paid for the week in advance and signed the ledger. "Do you happen to know a man named Jace Gage?"

"I do. What's he to you?"

"I was hoping to take shooting lessons from him."

"You in trouble?"

"No. I'm just a widow who would like to know how to protect herself."

"So am I, but I don't feel the need to wear a gun." Maddie gave her an assessing look. "Jace owns the lumber mill outside of town. He's a family man now. If you're in some kind of trouble, maybe you should take it to the sheriff."

"I'll keep that in mind."

"Well then, put your horse up in the stable out

back. There's oats in the bin for it. I'll get a sandwich made for you. You look like you've missed a few meals. If you're going to be in training, you'll need to eat more regularly. Where's your luggage? I'll take it up to your room."

"I haven't brought any."

"Not in trouble, huh?" Maddie made a face as she handed over the key. "Second room on the right upstairs. Come to the kitchen when you're finished with your horse." The older woman went down the hallway, muttering about women and trouble coming back to Defiance.

Since she was the only guest at Maddie's that night, Sarah made use of her week's one allotted bath, then washed her clothes. She'd run from the Inter-Ocean without any of her clothes. Someone had been in her room when she'd come back from arranging a ride with a freight team, and it wasn't the maid service.

She should have waited for Mr. Taggert. She knew that now. She needed help. Lots of it. Losing him was the worst of everything that was happening to her. Nothing seemed to faze him. That man could talk a turtle out of his shell, face terrifying Sioux warriors and laugh, then cover her with a blanket and his coat and sleep only when he knew she did. She wished she'd met him before Eugene. Everything would have been so different.

After breakfast the next morning, Sarah followed Maddie's directions to the lumber mill. The day was dry and hot with only a halfhearted breeze to keep the heat from being suffocating. Mr. Taggert's hat blocked the sun from her face and helped with the glare. Though she probably looked ridiculous in it, it made her feel safe, as if it were a shield. He'd saved her life—more than once. A person rarely had occasion to meet a man as brave as he was. No matter what it took, she would find a way to repay the expenses he'd incurred on her behalf.

An hour outside town, she turned down a long drive leading toward the mill. There were several buildings on the compound, the closest of which was a private residence. The Gages' house had a fresh coat of whitewash. The garden was neatly tended. Off to one side was a large vegetable garden surrounded by a white picket fence. She started up the pathway to the house only to stop abruptly when she noticed a huge black dog standing at the top of the steps. He was on full alert. A row of exposed teeth made it appear as if he was smiling at her. But dogs didn't smile. And the angle he held his head showed he wasn't pleased to have a visitor.

God help her. The beast was huge and quiet. He would mangle her before she could even cry for help. She sent a look behind her, gauging the distance to her horse. The post beside the path's entrance held a bell. She stepped backward very, very slowly. Coming even with the bell, she pulled the cord and sounded the alarm as long and loudly as she could.

The front door burst open and a man came out. He wore simple clothes—a cotton shirt, a loose vest, and denim trousers. He was hatless. His hair was a sun-bleached brown. His face was open and friendly. He gave a curt order to the dog, which immediately settled down at his feet.

A woman came outside, standing slightly behind the man, holding a little girl. The woman was dressed like a man, except for the flowered apron that covered her from chest to shins. A young boy came out to stand in front of her. She put her hand on his shoulder, gently restraining him.

"Can I help you?" the man asked. His voice, a harsh whisper, took Sarah aback.

"I'm looking for Jace Gage."

"You found him."

Sarah swallowed reflexively. She should have listened to Maddie. Mr. Gage had a family. She was putting all of them in jeopardy. Now faced with the sight of his wife and children, she feared he would turn her away. He should turn her away.

"Mr. Gage, I need your help."

The woman put her daughter down and said something to her son that caused him to take his sister back inside. Crossing her arms, she came to stand next to her husband.

"What kind of help?" he asked.

"I need to learn how to shoot a Colt revolver."

"Why?"

"I'm a widow. My husband was killed in an Indian raid. I live alone now. I want to know how to defend myself."

The man and his wife exchanged a look. The

woman went back inside the house. "Come inside. We can discuss this over a cup of coffee."

She started forward but stopped when she saw the dog look at her with bared teeth again. "Wolfson, stop." The man ruffled the dog's fur. "He won't hurt you. He smiles when he gets excited. He doesn't bark much, unless there's something we really need to pay attention to. Mostly he just grins like a demon."

Sarah approached the house. The man stood back and let her enter first. There was a spacious parlor to her right, a large dining room to her left, stairs to the upper floor and a wide hallway straight in front of her. Mr. Gage led the way to the back of the house. They entered a kitchen that clearly was the heart of their home. Two overstuffed armchairs flanked a side table off in a corner of the room beside an open window. White, ruffled curtains wavered in the slight breeze. A rectangular plank table stood in the middle, surrounded by six ladder-back chairs. A massive, blue-enameled stove took up most of one wall, and a long counter ran the length of another, ending at the door. The sink was filled with morning dishes sitting in sudsy water beneath an iron-handled pump.

"This is my wife, Leah. I don't think I caught your name out front."

"Sarah Hawkins."

Mrs. Gage set a coffeepot to boil on the stove, then came over to shake Sarah's hand. Sarah met her eyes, instinctively sensing that Mrs. Gage's opinion of her would determine Mr. Gage's level of assistance.

"Mrs. Gage. How do you do?"

"Please, we don't stand on formality around here. I'm Leah and my husband is Jace. I hope you won't mind if we call you Sarah?"

"No, of course not."

"Have a seat. Tell us what trouble you're in," Jace said, indicating a chair at the table.

"I bought a gun at Fort Buford. I don't know how to use it very well."

"Why did you come to me? Plenty of men know how to use a gun."

"A friend of mine at the fort said you lived here. You were the closest gun expert I knew of. I was hoping you could give me a few pointers. I could pay you ten dollars."

The Gages exchanged a glance. Leah set coffee mugs on the table. Their two children lingered by the back door, curious about the stranger. "Joseph, Elisa, come meet Mrs. Hawkins." Both children did as they were told. Their eyes sparkled with mischief and curiosity. Sarah liked them immediately, and once again she worried about the trouble she might be exposing them to.

"Wow, look at that gun belt she's wearing, Dad." Joseph looked at her. "Do you know how to shoot that gun, ma'am?"

"No."

"My dad does. He can shoot a plate into eight pieces. He can blow the center out of a coin tossed into the air. He can—"

"Son, that's enough. Take your sister outside to play," Jace quietly ordered.

Sarah saw the tension in Leah's face, and couldn't blame her one bit. She hated guns, too. She stood up to take her leave. "Forgive me. I was presumptuous. I should never have come here. Thank you for the coffee. I'm sure you're right. Someone else can teach me how to use the gun. Maddie said I should ask the sheriff."

"You haven't finished your coffee," Leah said.

"Sit down," Jace ordered, his harsh voice brooking no argument. "A woman traveling alone who wants to learn to shoot is a woman in trouble. Why don't you tell us what is going on?"

Sarah couldn't look at either of the Gages. She sat frozen for an instant, then drew her gloves off. Setting her hands flat on the table, she waited for their comments. Neither said a word.

"I was taken captive in a Sioux raid. I lived for a year among Swift Elk's people. The Indians aren't settled. Not at all. It is dangerous living out here. I want to be able to protect myself." She still didn't look at either of the Gages, but she felt the glance they exchanged.

"All right." Jace broke the silence. "We'll start this morning. But I won't allow you to pay me."

Sarah's gaze flew to Jace. His cold blue eyes watched her. She looked at Leah, who offered her a tentative smile. "Jace is the best in the world. He'll have you handling that piece in no time."

A breath broke from Sarah's lungs. Her relief was palpable. "Thank you. Both of you."

A short while later, Jace had checked in with his foreman, and Leah had made arrangements with their housekeeper to watch the children, so both Gages were free to work with her. All three headed out front on their way to an empty pasture off to the side of the house. They'd just gotten to the edge of the yard when a rider came thundering down the drive—on a horse very like the one Sarah had ridden.

She froze in place. It couldn't be. Surely it wasn't Mr. Taggert riding up the drive! It was! He wore a new hat, tan like the one he'd given her. Several days' growth of beard darkened his jaw. He dismounted and dropped the reins in front of his pony, then walked toward them. His gaze touched each of them, but settled on her. He looked furious.

She'd never been so happy to see anyone in her life. How had he found her here?

"Logan Taggert! As I live and breathe!" Leah exclaimed as she launched herself into his arms. Sarah frowned, wondering how they knew each other.

He caught her up in a tight hug.

Jace folded his arms. He didn't look very pleased to have another man holding his wife.

Leah pulled free and drew Mr. Taggert over to them. "Jace! Logan's here!"

Jace gave him a grudging smile and stuck out his hand. "So, you're the man who sends my wife all those letters. Good to finally meet you."

"All those letters," Leah scoffed. "He writes once or twice a year. If we're lucky."

"Great to meet you, Jace," Logan greeted him. "I gotta say though, I'm disappointed."

"How's that?"

"Thought you'd be able to teach Leah to be more female by now."

Jace laughed. "You might have grown up with my wife, but you don't know her like you thought you did."

"And this is Mrs. Sarah Hawkins." Leah pulled her forward.

The humor left Mr. Taggert's face. An icy wind seemed to sweep around the small gathering. He looked her over in a quick glance, his eyes, his face hardening. "Yes, I know."

"You know each other? How?"

"She's my wife."

That announcement was met with shocked silence. Sarah quickly filled in the silence with, "We're not married, Mr. Taggert."

"Then why did I give twelve horses to Cloud Walker for you?"

"You can't buy a wife, Logan," Leah admonished.

"Sarah, is Logan why you came here?" Jace asked.

"No," she answered him, but she only had eyes for Logan.

"Why didn't you wait for me at the Inter-Ocean?" He leaned toward her, the tightness of his face the only clue to his emotions.

"I couldn't."

"Why?" Logan fought the pull of her gaze. Her eyes pleaded with him so convincingly. He'd seen his mother trot out that very look a thousand times to any man within reach, including his stepbrother. To a man, they fell for it every time, right up until she lay in her deathbed, shot by a scorned lover. He didn't want Sarah to be like that. He wanted her to be the woman his heart told him she was.

"I'm in a bad situation. I didn't want to draw you into it."

"And yet you've pulled my friends into it."

Sarah swallowed hard. Just that quickly, the refuge she'd sought here, though she knew it was temporary, no longer existed. She looked at Leah and Jace. "He's right. I shouldn't have come here. I thank you for being willing to help."

Leah frowned and moved to block her retreat. "Logan, quit being a bully." She wrapped a hand around Sarah's waist and led her toward the front steps. "Let's go back inside and discuss this like calm, rational adults. Something's wrong. Jace and I can help."

Leah set a pitcher of cold water on the table. Jace filled glasses for each of them while Leah got more coffee brewing on the stove. Sarah sat at the table and looked at the forbidding faces of both men. Her problem was too big for her to handle alone. She didn't want to involve them, but perhaps they would have some idea of what she should do or someone who could help her.

Using the table for cover, she lifted her skirt and withdrew the oilskin pouches from the pockets she'd sewn on her petticoat. She handed them to Mr. Taggert. "I'm not sure where to begin."

Mr. Taggert leaned back in his chair and folded

his arms. "How about you start before the trouble began?"

"That would be in St. Louis, I guess. I told you about the accident that took my parents' lives," she said to Mr. Taggert. "They were hit and killed by a runaway freight team in a terrible accident," she said, bringing Jace and Leah up to date with the information Mr. Taggert already knew. "I met Eugene at their funeral. He was a friend of my parents. My father was a newspaper editor in Philadelphia. Eugene was a reporter. My father had edited many of Eugene's news pieces, I learned. It was strange to run into him in St. Louis. He told me so many stories of their work together that I almost felt as if my parents were still alive. When he found out that I was left alone, he offered to escort me back to Philadelphia."

"Did you go back?" Jace asked, an edge in his voice.

She shook her head. "I couldn't. There was nothing to go back to. My parents had sold everything to realize their dream of moving west. They had purchased a small spread outside Yankton. Moving there was something they'd worked toward for years. I wanted to see their dream fulfilled. I told Eugene that was where I was headed. He was thrilled. He was heading off to the Dakotas to investigate a story about the corruption rampant in the Indian agencies. We talked endlessly for a week. He was a shoulder to cry on. He helped me get through the first shock of losing my parents. When the week ended, I didn't want to lose him. He felt the same way. We married before the justice of the peace. He left the next day for Yankton."

"He left you the next day?" Leah asked.

"There were people waiting for him. He had appointments to keep. Yankton was still fairly rustic. He wanted to locate the land and get a cabin built before I came out. We divided the money my parents left me, half for me to live on until he returned, half for him to set up our homestead."

Jace shook his head.

"Let me guess. You never heard from him again," Logan said.

"I did get letters from him. In the beginning. They became more infrequent. I decided late the next spring, after a year of being apart, to follow him to Yankton. My funds were running low. I had no choice."

Logan leaned forward and propped his arms on the table. "What happened when you caught up with him?"

She was silent a moment, lost in her memories. "He was not happy to see me. He said it was too dangerous for me to live there. He wanted me to go back to Philadelphia. He had discovered one of the assistants to the Indian agent was forging fake land deeds and selling them. He'd infiltrated the group responsible, using a different identity. He said some people knew him as Gene Mapleton, that if someone addressed him as such when I was around, I was to show no reaction, and in fact I should claim to be a cousin of his."

"Did you ever see your ranch?"

"Yes. He had built a cabin there. We stayed there nearly a month before things began to fall apart." She sighed. "He showed me those deeds." She nodded to the papers on the table. "He said Pete Bederman, the assistant agent, had faked them. He wanted me to draft more like them. When I refused, we fought." She paused. It hadn't just been an argument. He'd bloodied her nose and mouth, said Pete would do that and worse to both of them if Eugene didn't produce more fake deeds for him to use. That was when she'd realized what a terrible mistake she'd made marrying him.

"He was gone frequently during that month, for days at a time. And when he left the next morning, I'd decided I had to leave as well. I hid these papers in a trunk. I didn't know what was going on, but I knew it was illegal and I didn't want him to use those deeds. I had a neighbor store them. When I came home that evening, we fought again. He was upset that I hadn't been home copying deeds. And then Swift Elk and his men raided our home. My husband died that night."

"Someone knew these papers were still out there," Logan said, looking at the different deeds.

"Bederman?" Jace asked.

"When I came back to the fort," Sarah said, "I sent word to my old neighbor to have my trunk sent to me at the fort. She'd stored the chest in the loft in her barn. She said her home had been hit by thieves who had ransacked their meager belongings, that she was glad she had stored it in the barn—they hadn't found it. It was all that remained of their household. I thought nothing of that, until my room at the fort was also ransacked. And then my hotel room at the Inter-Ocean. I believe they were looking for these documents."

The documents were passed around the table. "Gene Mapleton—your husband's alias—is listed on one of these deeds," Jace commented.

Sarah nodded. "He said he had to buy one so that Pete Bederman and his associates would believe his false identity. That false identity was one of the reasons Eugene didn't want me to be with him. The settlement we lived in was close enough to the fort that some people knew him by another name."

Mr. Taggert and Jace exchanged a look. "I know Bederman," Mr. Taggert said. "Some strange dealings have been laid at his feet. I wouldn't put it past him to be running these bad deals. He's angling for an Indian agent assignment in the Dakota Territory. He's made no secret of the fact that he thinks those lands should be opened to white settlement."

Sarah looked at Leah. "So you see, Mr. Taggert was right to condemn me for bringing trouble to Defiance. If he found me, Mr. Bederman could, too."

"What were you doing at the sheriff's office in Cheyenne?" Logan asked.

Sarah sent him a sharp look, wondering how he knew about that. "I was going to give him these deeds and ask for his help." She looked at the three people gathered around the table. "But there was a wanted poster listing my name on it. I'm wanted for forgery. I did not draft these or any deeds."

Logan made a face. He pulled a stiff piece of folded paper out of his pocket and handed it to Jace. "It seems you are indeed a fugitive."

"I've never forged anything in my life. I've never lived outside the law." She looked at Mr. Taggert. "I didn't do this."

Logan studied her, letting his face reveal nothing of his thoughts. He neither accepted her innocence nor her guilt. If her story was to be believed, she'd been easy pickings for Hawkins. "How about the sheriff here? Is he trustworthy?"

Jace nodded. "Took us a couple of years to find one worth having, but Cal Declan is a good man. You want to bring him into this?"

"I think we'd better. And then I'm going to get Mrs. Hawkins out of town."

"Good idea," Leah said. "She'll be safer if no one knows where she is. It would be hard to hide her here, with so many people around. Maybe the sheriff can locate Bederman, see what he has to say about this." She looked at Logan. "Your family misses you. You should stop by and see them. We share any news we hear of you from your rare communications with us. We all worry about you."

Logan frowned. He sent the obligatory Christmas letters to his friends and family. Most years. His feelings for his father and brother weren't settled, even now. He wasn't too anxious to see them. He'd traveled this close to home many of the last spring seasons to trade with his Sioux friends and had never felt the desire to go up to the ranch and see his stepdad.

"I have some trading to do with a group of Sioux." He looked at Sarah, who sat stiffly in her seat. "And then, I guess I will take Mrs. Hawkins to the Circle Bar. She can wait there while I track down Bederman."

Two hours later, the four of them sat in front of a frowning Sheriff Declan. He stared at the papers spread out on the table before him, fingering the wanted poster. "I agree something doesn't smell right. You said your husband died in the raid?"

Sarah nodded. "His body was found in the burned remains of our cabin. He was buried on our property."

Sheriff Declan's gaze moved to Logan. The two men regarded each other silently for a long moment. "I know your family, Mr. Taggert. They're upstandin' folk, but I don't know you. I can't release Mrs. Hawkins into your custody—you're no kin of hers. I have no choice but to place her in protective custody until we get this figured out."

"Cal! No! She can stay with us," Leah offered.

"No," Sarah calmly rejected her offer. "It is too dangerous. Mr. Bederman will find me. He's hunting me. He went to a place as remote as Fort Buford, tracked me to Cheyenne; he'll come to Defiance, too. I will put you and your family in grave danger if I stay at your house."

Logan looked at Sarah. He didn't want her out of his sight. When he'd first seen her this morning, he'd felt a maelstrom of emotions. Relief, rage, confusion—all of it was only now beginning to settle down into fear. Some part of Sarah's mind still believed her husband was innocent. Logan didn't hold so revered an opinion of the bastard. Eugene Hawkins had been a dangerous man playing a deadly game. He'd stalked her at her parents' funeral, made himself indispensable to her, then taken her money and her land and left. What kind of a man did something like that to a grieving woman?

He wanted Sarah under his protection. He'd found her. He'd rescued her. He was keeping her. "We can step over to the church and say the words in front of the preacher. Right now."

He was ready to have a wife. She needed protection. It was as good a reason as any to get married. He wasn't in love with her, so he wasn't in danger of falling for her machinations the way his stepfather had for his mother's shenanigans. And they were putting her troubles before the law. If she was guilty, then the truth would come out. And if she was innocent, she deserved to have someone stand up for her.

"I can't marry you, Mr. Taggert."

"Sheriff, do you have a room where Mrs. Hawkins and I could have a private conversation?"

Cal nodded toward the back of the jailhouse. "There's a small kitchen back there. Leave the door open."

Logan stood up and waited for Sarah to precede him into the room. He held the door open for her, then closed it behind him, disinclined to let the others overhear their private discussion. Crossing his arms, he spread his feet and faced her. "I suppose we both have questions and issues about getting married. You first. What are your objections to our getting married?"

Sarah turned a fiery shade of red. "I will never again be intimate with a man." She stared at the floor while making that announcement. "I will not share a marriage bed with you."

"That's it?"

She flashed a look at him, then returned her gaze to the floorboards. "That's it."

"Did the men who ravaged you leave you with a disease?"

She shook her head, her color deepening. "No. The doctor at Fort Buford examined me. There is a chance that I cannot bear children, which isn't an issue because I will never become pregnant."

Logan studied the woman who stood so rigidly before him. Life had dealt her a rotten hand of cards. Her choices had been made for her at every turn. And here he was forcing her into yet another direction she might not want to go. He knew he would be a good husband to her, but there was no way she could know that. And her experiences with men so far had been anything but healthy.

He remembered the panic he'd felt seeing her ransacked room, knowing she was alone and hunted. After a few hours' rest, he'd started for Cheyenne, nearly killing his pony to get here as fast as he could. Maddie had been his first stop in town. She always knew what was happening, knew all the gossip. If Sarah had come to Defiance, Maddie would know it. And she had.

He looked at Sarah, trying to figure out what it

was that kept tugging at him. His old hat hung by its thong off the back of her neck, a beat-up, trail-worn wreck of a hat. It was no fashion statement. Why was she still wearing it?

"Mrs. Hawkins, you're still wearing my hat."

"Yes." She looked at him. "Do you want it back?"

"No. I bought another. But why are you still wearing it?"

Her gloved hands gripped each other tightly. "It keeps the rain off my neck." She whispered the words he'd said to her when he'd put it on her.

"Is that the only reason?"

She looked up at him and then away again, folding her hands around her waist. "You are the kindest, bravest man I've ever met. Wearing it reminds me of you."

Logan felt gut-punched. Heat filled him like a dozen shots of whiskey. "I think there's room for negotiation here. I *want* to get married. You *need* to get married. The outcome is already established. At stake are what each of us gains and each of us surrenders. You don't want intimacy, and I do. How about this? We will share a bed, but I will not claim my marital rights. I will not touch you in an intimate manner. I will do nothing that you don't want me to do. You determine our intimacy, or lack of it." He stepped closer to her. Crowding her. "I do claim the right to court you, to woo you away from your fears. I have the right to rid you of your enemies. I have the right to protect and provide for you. I have the right to hold and comfort you."

She looked up at him with tears in her eyes. "But why would you want to?"

His stomach clenched. He forced himself not to reach for her. "Because I'm lonely. Because I think we will grow to care for each other. Because it's about goddamned time someone did."

Impossibly, she straightened her back further. She held her head up and looked him in the eye. "Then, Mr. Taggert, I have the right to help you in your work, to go where you go, to be a part of your life."

"Agreed. Ultimately. But not until I have dealt with your husband's enemies. After that, we will not be separated." He wanted to lift her chin. He wanted to press his mouth to hers, to feel her surrender, but he would not break his vow. "Mrs. Hawkins, will you marry me?" He held his breath, wondering if he would force her to accept him if she said no.

She studied his eyes, weighed her choices. "Yes, I will, Mr. Taggert." She swiped the moisture from her cheeks and sent him that look of determination that he was becoming so familiar with.

He grinned down at her. Unable to stop himself, he touched the tips of his fingers to her cheek. "Thank you."

The door swung open and Sheriff Declan stood there. "Well? What's it gonna be?"

"Mrs. Hawkins has agreed to become my wife."

"Great. We'll get Reverend Adamson to perform the service in the morning."

"No. We'll do it now," Logan countered.

Leah and Jace came to the kitchen door. "He needs time to prepare," she pointed out.

"We're not waiting."

Leah let out a gleeful shout as she ran into the room. She hugged him, then Sarah. "Come—we'll go to your room and pick out a dress while the men get everything arranged."

"I have only this dress." Sarah looked down at it and tried to straighten the worn homespun material.

Leah looked at Logan, as fierce as a mama bear over a cub. "Sally and Jim have two ready-made dresses in their general store. They're machine made, but surely one of them will be serviceable for the wedding."

"Then go get them." Logan handed Sarah his wallet. "Get what you want, whatever you need." Sarah was reluctant to take his money. He bent close to her ear as he folded her hand over his leather billfold. "It falls under my right to provide for you. Go with Leah. I'll be ready when you are."

"What will you wear?" Sarah asked him.

"Don't worry about him. I'll loan him something suitable," Jace assured her. "He'll be as pretty as he can be when you see him at the church."

Leah pulled Sarah from the room, but stopped a moment in front of Jace. Grabbing his arms, she kissed him quickly and said, "Logan's getting married! Can you believe it? Oh, I wish Audrey were here!" She was gone before Jace could react, dragging Sarah behind her.

The men stared after the women in stunned silence. Logan would have liked to have Audrey— another childhood friend of his and Leah's—there for the ceremony. But she lived four hours from town. There was no way she could make it before morning. And if they waited for her and her family, they would need to alert Logan's father and brother, who lived a day's ride north of town. It would be days before their nuptials could be concluded, and that was days too long. He wanted Sarah under his protection now.

"Well, then. Why don't we go get Reverend Adamson ready, Logan? Sheriff—mind alerting Maddie? She'd never forgive us if she weren't invited."

Chapter 8

Several hours later, the dark shadow of the church entrance yawned before Sarah. She stepped up the stairs, trying not to feel overwhelmed. This was not at all how she'd thought the day would end when she'd awoken this morning. She clutched a bouquet of sweet lilac flowers. Maddie had loaned her a veil of fragile lace, aged to ivory. The outfit she wore was a pink linen skirt and matching jacket with a white, high-necked blouse.

Maddie, Sally—the storekeeper's wife—and Leah had helped her bathe and do her hair. She was terribly self-conscious of her scars, but no one had said anything after the first shock of seeing them wore off. In the bustle of having her nails done, her hair dried and braided and quick tucks made in her new outfit, she'd closed her mind to the recent horrors. That time was over. She was here now. Safe. Embraced by these people who knew and loved Logan. Everyone they had met loved him, even Cloud Walker and his band.

She was very fortunate indeed to have come to this point in her life. It was hard to believe that little more than two years ago she'd married another man, a man who'd never loved her, a man who, if she were honest with herself, never meant to return to St. Louis for her. Logan, a stranger still, had shown her a higher regard than Eugene ever had.

Leah came to the door and peered out at her. "Ready?" she asked.

Sarah nodded, anything but ready. She stepped inside the church. It wasn't dark at all, but lit brilliantly from sunlight pouring through the tall, stained glass windows on the west side of the building. Two tidy rows of pews lined either side of the aisle, leading her eyes to the front where Logan stood, solemnly watching her. He was freshly shaved. His hair was still damp. He wore a dark suit that showed his tanned face and blond hair off to quite an advantage. Seeing him, the church and its occupants faded from her vision.

"I want to marry you," he'd said at the sheriff's office. He wanted this. She had nothing to offer him. No dowry. No joy. Not even the promise of future children. Only the certainty that her past was quickly catching up to her.

Yet still, he'd said he wanted her.

"Mrs. Hawkins, won't you please hand your flowers to Leah to hold?" Reverend Adamson asked. She did as he requested, hiding her ungloved hands in the folds of her skirt as she faced Mr. Taggert. "Now, if you would set your hands on Mr. Taggert's?"

She drew a breath, locking her eyes with Mr. Tag-

gert's gray gaze, willing him not to look down, willing
him not to withdraw from her now. He smiled at her.

"Do you, Sarah Worthington Hawkins, take Logan
Samuel Taggert to be your lawfully wedded husband . . ." She looked at the reverend, her mind a
whirl. Was this real? What if this was another bad
decision? It was hard to breathe.

"Mrs. Hawkins. Look at me." She moved her
gaze to Mr. Taggert's. His gray eyes held a warmth
in them, as if he was about to smile. Faint lines radiated out from his eyes, paler in the short furrows
where he squinted from the sun. "Breathe, honey.
I never break a bargain. You have my word about
how our lives will unfold. Tell the reverend if you
take me as your husband."

"I do."

More words. Jace reached over and handed him
something. He took her left hand and held her
third finger out so that he could slip his ring on her
finger. A ring. A bright, wide, gold band. She stared
down at it. Her first wedding ring had been a small,
thin band. The Indians had taken it and had given
it to one of their wives. She was already a terrible
wife—she hadn't thought of a ring for Logan. He
pressed something cold against her right hand. His
ring. He'd thought of his ring. He held his left
hand steady for her, his long, blunt, ring finger ex-
tended. At the reverend's prompting, she slipped
his ring on his finger. He grinned at her.

"I now pronounce you man and wife. Mr. Taggert,
you may kiss your bride."

Logan looked at her. "May I kiss my bride?" he

asked her. She nodded almost imperceptibly, her mouth pressed shut. She prayed she wouldn't vomit as she tried unsuccessfully to block out memories of other men, other faces moving above her, laughing, touching her with their mouths, with their hands.

He turned her away from the small crowd and bent toward her without actually kissing her. He cupped her cheek with a hand. "You did just fine. Now you're mine, and I will take care of you."

She met his gaze and released a long, shaky breath. Then they were suddenly engulfed by all of Mr. Taggert's friends. Like dust in a wind burst, they moved as a group down the aisle and out into the sunlight. Sarah filled her lungs with the warm afternoon air. There was much laughter and chatter. She was feeling apart from it all, until Mr. Taggert reached down and took her hand in his. She looked up at him, but he was talking to Jace and Jim, the storekeeper. It was an unconscious gesture. She tightened her hand around his, glad for his strength.

They crossed the street and entered Maddie's kitchen. The smells of coffee, roasting meat, and all the fixings filled the room. Maddie had sneaked down to her kitchen while Sarah was being prepared for the wedding to make an extensive feast for them. Leah walked over to the cupboard and began setting out dishes. Sally poured coffee and brought cream and sugar to the table. In short order, the roast was carved and the table filled with bowls of mashed potatoes, green beans, fresh bread, and sweet butter.

Jim popped corks on a couple bottles of champagne he'd brought down from the store. "I'm sorry your family couldn't be here," he said to Logan as he filled glasses.

"There wasn't time," Logan answered. "Maybe, when things settle down, we'll have another reception. Until then, I'm going to keep Sarah out of town so that she won't be a magnet for trouble while Cal does some research and sees what he can discover."

Cal met Logan's look. "And when I do get to the bottom of things, I'll handle it within the boundaries of the law."

Logan grinned. "That would be the ideal resolution."

"That will be the *only* resolution." The two men shared a look.

"Now, now, boys. We can't fight during a wedding celebration!" Sally broke the tension. "Here's to the newly wedded couple. May your lives together be filled with love, laughter, and the blessings of many, many children!"

Logan lifted his glass and sipped the cold champagne, watching as Sarah did the same—quietly and without looking at anyone. He wondered if he would be able to chase away the shadows in her eyes, the horrors in her mind that were always so close to the surface.

They ate a leisurely dinner, catching up on each

other's lives and the changes that had come to Defiance after Logan left. Between his college years and the time since, he'd been gone almost twelve years. Maddie and the Kesslers had aged, but were the same in so many ways. Jace and Cal were new additions to the community, but they fit in as easily as if they'd been lifelong residents.

The warmth of the gathering made Logan edgy, and he didn't like to think why. It was well past sunset when he stood up and offered the group a polite smile. "I think it's time my wife and I retire. We need to hit the trail early tomorrow."

Sarah felt her limbs turn wooden. Mr. Taggert helped draw her seat back so that she could stand. He exchanged polite words with those gathered. She kept her eyes pinned on the table, the floor, her feet—anywhere but the people in the room who thought they knew what was about to happen. She moved silently beside Mr. Taggert, causing him no problems, no reason to challenge her. Would he remember his promise? Was he different behind a door than he was in public as Eugene had been? Would it matter? Who would fault him for seeking the rights due him in their marriage bed?

They went up the stairs and paused in front of her room. She didn't know what she was allowed to do. She unlocked the door, but didn't open it.

"My room is just next to yours. I'll come over in a half hour. Will that give you time to settle? I need to write a couple of letters. My family and friends should hear about us from me."

She did look at him then. "How will your family react to our being married?"

He met her look. "It doesn't matter. You will be safe at their ranch. And I won't leave you with them long." He opened her door for her.

"It is a bad bargain you made, Logan Taggert."

"It is the best bargain I ever made, Sarah Taggert. I told you I would have gone as high as thirteen horses."

When he entered Sarah's room a short while later, the lamp had been turned low. She was in bed with the blankets pulled up to her chin. He moved silently across the room, his feet bare. He'd washed and shaved, then donned a fresh pair of denims and a loose cotton shirt. He usually slept in just his drawers, but he felt it would be awhile before his wife would be comfortable enough with him that he could resume that habit.

He turned the light out and lay down next to her, on top of the covers. His wife. He liked the sound of that.

"Good night, Mr. Taggert."

He turned on his side and looked at her lying stiffly next to him. "Mrs. Taggert, do you think, now that we're married, we might use each other's given names?"

She looked at him, turning only her head to do so. "I guess that would be all right."

"Are you tired?"

She straightened and shut her eyes. "I feel like throwing up."

Logan laughed, appreciating her honesty. She didn't pretend to be comfortable just to appease his vanity. It was a good start. "Would a foot rub help?"

"No! No, it would not."

Logan settled on his back, next to his very stiff wife. "When we leave here, we'll head north for about a week. We're meeting with a man named Chayton. He's Sioux. His mother was a white captive. He is unbelievable with horses. I wonder sometimes if he hasn't found a way of speaking to them without words. I trade each year with his wife, whose beadwork is the highest quality I've ever seen."

"Does he have white wives?"

"No. He has only one wife. Laughs-Like-Water. They have two kids, a boy who's about six and a little girl who's four or so."

"You sound fond of them."

"Chayton is like a brother to me." More a brother than Logan's own stepbrother was. "When I left home, he was the first person I met. We almost killed each other, but we ended up hunting together instead. He had gone to search out a herd of wild horses. Laughs-Like-Water's father had set a high bride price on her—five horses. Chayton had asked her father to not accept any suitor for her until he returned at the end of the summer. I stayed with him that entire summer and helped him catch his horses. Her other beaux offered the requested horses and many gifts. One, whose father had many horses and was the wealthiest man in the village, even offered ten horses. But Laughs-Like-Water made her father keep his promise to Chayton." Logan paused, remembering Chayton's ride into the village, followed by twenty horses.

"What happened?" Sarah prompted him to continue.

"Summer ended. We were a long way from his people. An early snow hampered our return. He was sick with worry that her father would have waited only until the end of the summer moon."

"Did she wait for him?"

"We didn't know yet. He rode into his village at dusk, leading his herd. I rode drag, but no one paid attention to me. Chayton brought great wealth to his people, and he'd done it by his own hand. He didn't trade on the strength of his father. That night, he stood with fifteen horses outside Laughs-Like-Water's tepee. He gave a command, and the horses rose on their hind legs as Chayton cried her name. He gave another command and they went down on one leg. It was magnificent. Long seconds passed. I watched him wait. It seemed a lifetime. At last her father emerged. He looked impassively at the gift Chayton offered. Three times the bride price he'd asked."

"Logan! What happened?"

He smiled at her. His wife was a romantic. "Laughs-Like-Water's father called for her mother to come out and take the horses to the corral. He accepted the bid. Chayton and Laughs-Like-Water have been together ever since. He has become a legend among his people. All the warriors bring him their horses to train. What he does with them is nothing short of magic."

"You make the Sioux sound so different from the people I knew."

"There are good and bad among all peoples, Sarah. I think you've just gotten to see mostly the bad."

When Sarah woke the next morning, the sun was high, flooding her room with light. Disoriented, she looked around the unfamiliar room, listened to the sounds of the house. People were talking in the kitchen. The tantalizing aromas of coffee and breakfast floated in the air. She remembered every minute of the whirlwind yesterday had been.

Logan! She jumped out of bed. They were supposed to have left early this morning. The morning was well along. Had he gone without her?

She rushed to wash and dress. Hands shaking, she gathered her things and put them in a pile, having no satchel to pack them in. She stepped into the hall. He'd said his room was next to hers. She tried the one to the right. It was empty. Same with the one on the other side. He was gone. All of his fancy words, his promises. He'd still left her. She wrapped her arms about herself as the hallway seemed to spin.

"You're up!"

Her head shot up as the familiar deep voice slipped into her mind. He was coming up the stairs bearing a cup of coffee. "I thought you'd left."

"Of course not. It occurred to me there was no reason to rush off at the crack of dawn. You've had quite a few hard days. I wanted you to rest." He handed her a cup of coffee. Her hands shook as she took it.

She looked up at him, his image wavering in her eyes. "I thought you were gone."

He pulled her into an easy hug. "Aw, sweetheart. I'm sorry I frightened you." He rubbed her back. "Come down to breakfast. Maddie's been cooking for hours. I hope you're hungry." She leaned into his chest, drawing a long breath and slowly releasing it. He seemed to be waiting for her composure to return. He could read her far too easily. She hated letting him see how dependent she was on him.

She sipped her coffee, using the motion to shield herself from him. She wondered, as she followed him to the kitchen, if he would be different once he was away from town and these people he knew so well. Would he keep his promises to her when there was no one around to know if he didn't?

Chapter 9

A massive covered wagon drew up in front of Maddie's boardinghouse a short while later that morning. Their ponies were tied to the tailgate. Sarah sent Logan a questioning glance. "Are we traveling in that? Is it safe?"

He grinned. "It's safe. We'll be out for a couple of weeks. I thought you'd rather ride in a wagon than on a horse for that amount of time. Besides, I need to take a fair amount of supplies to Chayton and hope to be picking up a good collection of artwork from his wife. We could either bring two pack mules with us, or take the wagon." He shrugged. "It just seemed easier."

Sarah's gaze traveled across the hard planes of Logan's face. His eyes were alive with excitement.

"Come—I'll show you. It's a chuck wagon." He took her hand and drew her around to the end. The backside of the wagon was a custom-fitted cupboard, with cabinets, panels, and compartments. "There's a table that folds down for food preparation. The drawers are hidden behind the table's board. Its leg folds up and over to the side. We're stocked with coffee, flour, sugar, beans, oats, grits, cornmeal, salt, pepper, baking powder—any dry goods you might want. The cabinets hold utensils, pots, and pans."

He took her around to the front bench, past a large water barrel tied to the side of the wagon, along with various ropes and lanterns. The driver's bench sat high atop another cabinet. Logan helped Sarah up to the bench. He followed her up and stepped over the front seat into the interior of the wagon. There were two benches on either side with a table between them. They ended at another cabinet, on top of which lay a mattress, complete with sheets, quilt, and pillows.

"Logan, this is a house. On wheels. Where did you get it?"

He grinned. "The livery owner bought it awhile back from a logging crew. He's repaired all the bad wood and broken hinges and made a new tarp for it. Took him awhile to get it cleaned up for us this morning—which was another reason I decided to leave later than planned. The linens are new—picked them up from Jim's store. Maddie gave us the pillows and quilts."

"It's too much. You wouldn't have done this if not for me. I don't want to slow you down."

"I'm not in a hurry, Sarah. Not anymore. I'm dragging you across the territory. I want you to be comfortable."

Sarah looked away, shocked by the depth of his thoughtfulness. Her father had been a kind and gentle man. He'd done everything in his power to make her mother's life what she wanted it to be. Her own marriage to Eugene had not been anything like the magic her parents shared.

Logan climbed back onto the seat next to her. "I brought your things down and packed them under that bench. We're all loaded up. Ready to start?"

She drew his old hat up and cinched the thong beneath her throat. "Ready."

Maddie stood in her drive and waved to them. "You take care of Sarah. And don't be a stranger, Logan. We've missed you."

He nodded to her with a quick tug at his hat, then slapped the reins. Sarah looked at Logan. Her husband. So many times over the last couple of years, her life had taken a turn she'd never seen coming. Her family's move west. Her parents' deaths. Her first marriage. Her capture by the Sioux. And now her marriage to Logan. It was like living in a river full of rapids and falls, the current moving so fast that anything resisting the raging waters would be destroyed.

Logan's hands were light on the reins. He looked relaxed, a man very much at home in this wild territory. She felt his courage, doubted he'd ever encountered something or someone he couldn't handle. His hat shielded the upper half of his face, but sunlight touched his chin, the hard outline of his jaw. She couldn't believe he'd found her, that they were married. Her gaze lingered on his face, drinking in the sight of him.

She forced herself to look at the land slowly

passing by, but saw nothing of its green lushness. Her mind was too filled with gray eyes, eyes that seemed to read souls. She knew she had no secrets from him, not when he could look at her and know her wounds.

She folded her legs up on the bench and wrapped her arms around her knees. "Why have you stayed away from your home and family so long?"

A muscle worked in the corner of his jaw. He shrugged. "No good reason. Habit, I guess. Being gone was easier than returning."

"Why?"

He sent her another quick look. His face was a careful mask. He sighed. "I spent four years back East getting my degree. I planned to take a job there, but my stepfather wanted me to come home. He had plans to have me marry his neighbor's daughter."

Sarah was speared by an unfamiliar blast of jealousy. "Did you get married?"

He shook his head. "My stepbrother fell in love with her."

"Is that why you left?" Sarah held her breath, waiting for the devastating news that he still felt the loss of his first love. Or worse, that he'd only married Sarah so that he wouldn't have to return home alone. She blinked away her tears, quickly, before he could notice them. What was, what might have been, was in the past. She and Logan, for better or worse, were married. She would do her best to help heal that old wound. She would make him proud.

"Maybe it was. But it isn't why I stayed away. I'm happy for my stepbrother and Rachel. They were meant for each other. She mended the things that were broken in Sager's spirit. There could have been no other for either of them."

"Why, then, did you stay away?"

"My stepbrother and stepdad are a bit overpowering. I didn't want to live in their shadow. My brother will inherit the ranch we grew up on. And in marrying Rachel, he gets all of her father's land, too. There was no place for me. So I left to find where I belonged."

"What happened to your parents? Your stepdad raised you?"

"My father died when I was very young. I don't remember him at all. My stepdad met my mother when I was only a few years old. They married and he brought us out here, to his ranch. He is really the only father I remember."

"Was he a good father?"

Logan considered her question. He sent her a quick look. "My stepdad lost his first wife to a Sioux raid. She was pregnant when they took her. Sid, my stepdad, searched for her for years. When he finally learned she'd died, he also discovered that she had borne him a son. I think Sid cared for my mother and me, but he was gone a lot searching for his real son. I was left alone with my mother, who was angry about having to live in so remote a spot. She was a bit unbalanced. Her rage grew over time. We all lived in fear of upsetting her."

"I'm sorry, Logan." She reached across the bench to touch his arm. "Is she better now?"

He shook his head. "She passed away eight years ago."

"Oh, Logan!"

He shrugged. "It's done. My brother came home when he was a teenager, and left again almost immediately. Again my father searched for him. And then, when I graduated college, my father and his neighbor hatched a plan to have me marry Rachel. Sager had come back about then. I thought we could try to be a family, but it wasn't possible." He gave her a wan smile. "And that, Mrs. Taggert, is the whole sordid story of my life."

Sarah moved her hand down to clasp his hand, glove to glove. "That is *not* the sum of your life, Logan. You are part of this wild country. You're friends with everyone. You can speak Sioux and probably a dozen other Indian languages. You understand tribal customs. You ride across this land without fear, as if you welcome the challenges that might come your way. You don't let men bully you—or any strange women you happen to run into. You are an extraordinary man. I am glad you are my husband."

Logan studied her beautiful brown eyes, struck by the fierceness of her defense. He pulled his hand free and wrapped it about her shoulders, drawing her closer to his side. "Thank you," he whispered. She had reached out to him just now. And she had let him hold her last night. It was a start.

After hearing the story of her first husband, Logan knew theirs had been no real marriage at all. Eugene Hawkins, or whoever the hell he really was, had used her to fund his trip west. He'd never intended for his resourceful bride to follow him to the wilds of the Dakota Territory.

Logan had asked Sheriff Declan to look into her husband. He had a sneaking suspicion that Eugene had been mired in the corruption he'd uncovered before his death—he was not the bumbling innocent his wife believed him to be. Not for the first time, he regretted the bastard was already dead. He'd have liked to kill him personally. Slowly. Painfully. Drawing from him blood for every injury he'd done Sarah—through intent or ignorance.

The evening wind had calmed to a slight breeze, stirring cool air around the dusky sky as Logan secured their camp at the end of the day. The fire was banked. The horses were tied to a corral line. He turned around and saw his wife standing there in her boots and nightgown, a blanket over her shoulders. Her thick, white-blond braid was pulled forward over one shoulder. She stopped all motion when he looked at her. He wondered if she was even breathing, because he wasn't.

He moved toward her, his stride stiff, his every sense locked on her. The evening's pastel orange and pink colors bathed her face and hair, a wash of color that made her skin glow. He looked at her mouth, imagined it against his, imagined her opening for him, giving herself to him even as he gave himself to her.

"Do you need help getting into the bed? You'll have to climb up there." He pointed to the chair beside the table.

"I don't need help."

He held still as she moved past him to the wagon. Her blanket brushed his arm. He caught the faint scent of her, fresh and sweet-smelling. He forced himself to go to the river's edge. He took his time with his evening routine, wanting to give her plenty of time to get settled before he joined her.

When he returned to the wagon, he untied the rear section of the canvas, folding it back so that the bed was exposed to the open air. The June evening was long. They could lie together and watch the darkening sky.

Inside the wagon, he changed into a fresh set of clothes that he reserved for wearing to bed. He hadn't worn a nightshirt since his childhood and didn't intend to start now, but he couldn't join Sarah wearing only his drawers. Besides, the night was cold. He took up his pistol, rifle, and knife, setting them at the foot of the thick mattress while he climbed up. He took the outer half, preferring to keep Sarah somewhat sheltered by the interior of the wagon. She moved stiffly to the far side of her half while he arranged his weapons in easy reach.

He sat on his edge of the bed, facing the open end of the wagon, his legs folded. "Sarah, come and sit next to me. We'll watch the sunset."

He looked so boyish sitting on the edge of the mattress, facing the night. Carefree. She looked beyond him, to the prairie and the sky that met it at the horizon. To the east, where night was gathering, the sky had turned gray. To the west, the sky was a vibrant orange, the clouds shades of pink, vermilion, and apricot.

She couldn't resist his request. She crawled over to one side of him and sat cross-legged as she drew her blanket over her nightgown. Birds were sounding their nesting calls. The grasshoppers were growing quiet, their noisy clatter replaced by chirping crickets serenading one another. It seemed the world was settling down, but she knew that was an illusion. It was just a change in shifts, from day hunters to night hunters. The open, endless prairie was vast and lethal.

Logan watched the changing colors, listened to the changing sounds, felt the cool night breeze with rapt attention. She looked again at the land surrounding them, trying to see it from his eyes. She knew what was out there—coyotes, wolves, and snakes. Humans more dangerous than any animal. She shivered.

"Cold?" Logan asked as he adjusted her blanket. Frosty air chilled her foot. She moved to cover herself again, quickly, before he saw the scars on the bottom of her feet. Too late. He grabbed her wrist and stopped her.

"What is this?" he asked, staring at her foot.

She tried to move so that her feet were together, folded away from him, but he took hold of her ankle. "Let me see your feet."

"No. Please. Please don't look at them."

"Show me your feet." His voice brooked no argument. She moved so that the soles of her feet faced him. She watched the prairie, wishing the sun was setting faster, wishing for the cover of darkness.

He lifted her feet and put them in his lap. She

held perfectly still as he brushed his hand over the puckered, seared skin. "Christ. What did they do to you?" He touched her other foot. She couldn't feel much of his stroke. He gripped a foot in each hand, her terrible scarred feet. His eyes watered. "What did they goddamn do to you?" he asked again, his voice a harsh rasp.

She swallowed, fixed her gaze on her knees. "I tried to run several times that first month they took me. I ran anytime I could, though every time they found me and beat me. I had heard some of the women talking about a unit of soldiers that was searching nearby for me. The warriors feared I would escape and bring the soldiers back upon them. They had the women burn the bottoms of my feet so that I couldn't run."

He swallowed hard. "Do they still hurt?"

"No. I can't feel much of anything there." He was pressing her feet against his chest, so tightly that his knuckles were white. She could feel the heat of his body warming her cold soles, feel the drum of his heart. Then, in one swift movement, he caught her up, moving her to his lap. He drew her blanket over her, wrapping her tightly in the fabric, covering her feet, binding her against any resistance. His arms were like steel bands around her. She waited for the panic to overtake her, the wash of nausea, but it never came. Instead, she felt shielded, protected from everything outside the sphere of his control. She relaxed a bit in his hold.

His chin rested on her head. "I'm sorry. I'm so goddamned sorry." He drew a ragged breath that she felt from his throat down to his lungs. "I don't know how you survived."

Logan struggled to squash the rage building within him. Her husband had been a selfish bastard and a greenhorn, too ill-equipped to deal with the realities of life in the territories. He'd done nothing to protect her. He had, in fact, exposed her thoughtlessly to the war brutalizing the plains.

The thing that terrified him was that he knew the scars on her feet and hands were not the worst of the ones she bore. He had to find a way to control his unbounded rage, else she would not feel safe to show him the rest of her wounds.

"Sarah, honey, I cannot undo what was done. None of it. But I can promise you that your life with me will not be one of pain. I will put your happiness before my own. I will share my world with you. I will make amends with my family so that you have a family. I live for the day that I see joy in your eyes." He pulled away and looked directly into her face. "I live for that day."

Sarah stared up at him, rendered speechless by the vehemence in the rigid planes of his face, the tears on his cheeks. A sob broke from her. She wrapped her arms around his chest. He understood. He was possibly the only person in the world who could have understood, she thought. Her ear rested against his heart, which beat like a drum—in a solid, deep rhythm. She let it flow into her, a balm for her ragged spirit. "Logan, don't let go of me."

His arms tightened. "Never."

"I'll try to be the wife you need me to be."

"You already are. Honey, you already are."

Sarah woke the next morning to the warm cocoon of the feather mattress, pillows, and heavy quilts. Only her face was exposed to the cold morning air. She could see her breath in the morning light that filtered through the wagon. She squirmed deeper into the covers. Logan was gone, but the space where he had been was still warm. She rolled into his side of the bed lazily.

She heard a crackle of fire, caught the scent of wood smoke and coffee. She breathed it again, a moan of enjoyment involuntarily breaking from her. She lifted her head. Logan had opened the tailgate table and was preparing breakfast. Cubed potatoes were sizzling in a pan over the fire just off to the side of him.

She leaned up on her elbows and looked down at him. He grinned up at her. "I didn't mean to wake you. I was trying to be silent so that you could sleep as long as possible."

Sarah couldn't speak, could barely breathe. She had long since lost faith in anyone's ability to be kind to someone else, but Logan had an endless well of kindness and patience. He stood before her in his denims, his cotton shirt open but tucked in. His canvas jacket hung loosely on him. He wore no hat. His blond hair was cut raggedly as if he'd trimmed what he could with his straight razor. His beard darkened his hard jaw.

He stole her breath. And her heart. He'd wanted this marriage. He wanted the intimacy granted a husband and wife. It was the only gift she had to give him. And though he was so deserving of that and more, she didn't think she could open herself to physical intimacy. Even for Logan, the man who stood like an archangel between her and the world, cooking her breakfast.

He read in her face the words she couldn't speak. He came closer to her and reached up to take her hand. "Give us time, Sarah. It's all I ask."

Tears filled her eyes. She gripped his hand tightly, finally offering him a nod.

Chapter 10

Nearly a week later, Sarah could feel Logan's increasing tension as they made their noon stop. He'd kept them to the low valley by the river, using the land and trees for cover. She took the horses to the river, two by two, watering them and letting them feed on the rich grasses along the bank while Logan moved to higher ground, searching their back trail.

His expression was shuttered when he returned. He moved about, performing the routine midday chores of refilling their water buckets, giving each horse a measure of oats, helping her make lunch. They had rested barely a half hour when he hooked the team up and secured their ponies behind the wagon.

"What is it, Logan?"

"We're being followed." He studied her. "There's an old ridge of granite boulders about two miles from here. It will give us better cover than we have here."

"Are they Indians?"

He shook his head. "White men." He helped her up to the front bench. "If we don't make it to the rocks before the shooting starts, I want you to get in the back and stay low."

He shouted to the team, encouraging speed with a snap of the reins. The wagon lurched forward. Sarah held on to her seat, terrified their headlong pace over the rough terrain would bounce her from the bench. A few minutes later, a long, low range of boulders came into sight. Logan charged straight for the natural bulwark, pulling up only when they were inside the ring of boulders. He set the brake and leapt off the bench.

"Take the ponies through the boulders," he ordered as he unhitched the wagon team. He reached under the bench and pulled out his rifle and a box of cartridges. He handed Sarah her gun belt. "Shoot anyone who comes through there unless I tell you it's clear."

She led the ponies down a narrow path into a small clearing. Knee-high grass filled the space within another ring of granite boulders that were taller than a two-story house. An ancient scrub pine stood off to one side, growing thick and wide. Sarah released the horses, letting them wander and feed. Logan was right behind her with the wagon team.

He paused beside her. Cupping the back of her head, he drew her close and pressed a fast kiss to her forehead. His eyes met hers. "If anything happens to me, you are to go to my father at the Circle Bar. I have written to him about our marriage. He knows of you."

Sarah nodded. "I will."

His hand tightened on her neck. "Swear it to me."

"I swear it."

Logan released her. He cocked his rifle as he slipped through the narrow path. The ground thundered with the approach of several riders, men she hadn't even seen trailing them.

"That's far enough." She heard Logan warn the riders who had been after them.

"You there, you traveling with a woman?"

"What's it to you?"

"She's wanted by the law."

"What for?"

"Claim jumpin'."

"You the law?"

"No, friend, we're the wronged. She took our property and we want it back."

"You mean those bogus land deeds? Deeds to land that the Sioux own?"

"They won't own it for long. Give us the girl and the papers—we'll let you live."

Logan laughed. "Don't have them. We gave them to the sheriff in Defiance. Why don't you go see if he'd be willing to oblige you? Course, he may not have them either. Think he was sending them by special courier down to Sheriff Bennett in Cheyenne."

"Well then, I reckon we got ourselves a standoff. There's three of us and one of you. Who do you think's gonna win?"

"I gotta tell you, my money's on me," Logan answered confidently.

"I say we just shoot him and get the girl," one of the men said to the other riders.

Sarah peeked around the boulder. Three men sat on their horses several yards in front of Logan.

"Yeah. We need her for leverage. I don't want to tell the boss we lost her again. And I for one don't want no sheriff in on this."

"Relax. Bennett thinks she's a forger. I talked to him when I pinned up the wanted poster."

Their voices carried as if they stood in the ring of stones, their debate amplified despite the distance. Without warning, gunfire erupted, ricocheting off the rocks with sharp, whining barks. She stumbled back into the shelter of the clearing. The horses ran in circles, trying to find their way back out. She took her hat off and flapped it gently to keep them from charging down the opening.

A movement at the top of the rocks caught her attention. A man knelt up there, preparing to leap down to a lower boulder, pistol in hand. He straightened to make the jump. Suddenly his arms flew out to his sides, his gun dropped, clattering over the boulders. He tumbled forward, an arrow between his shoulder blades. Sarah slapped her hand over her mouth to keep herself from screaming.

A Sioux warrior shouted. He leapt from boulder to boulder, dropping down into the ring of rocks. Reflexively, her hand went to her gun. She drew it, her hands shaking. Her legs grew weak. She watched the ridge of boulders, looking for the other braves she knew would be there. She pressed the hammer back. She was shaking so terribly that she doubted she would hit her target.

The shooting had stopped out front. Her heartbeat was pounding in her ears. The warrior was tall, almost as tall as Logan. He wore his hair parted on the side, his ponytails bound in red cloth. He had a strong nose, high cheekbones, and a square jaw. He pushed his way through the horses. He bent and sliced the scalp from the man he'd killed. Straightening, he looked right at her, the patch of hair and skin dripping blood in one hand, his bloodied knife in the other. His face wasn't painted—he hadn't expected to be doing battle today.

She gasped a deep breath, feeling the wash of fear flooding her body, hot and cold. Time folded back on itself. This was just like what had happened outside her small cabin a year ago. The warrior who'd appeared then had been the first to push her to the ground, the first of seven. Then he'd smashed Eugene's head in with his tomahawk and sliced off his scalp.

The warrior before her now moved forward. She shook her head, tears streaming down her face. She lifted her gun and pointed it at him. Even holding it with two hands, she couldn't keep it steady. He stopped where he was, assessing her. Without taking his eyes off her, he wiped his knife on his leggings, then sheathed it. He pushed the scalp into a pouch. Hands free, he started toward her again.

Waves of nausea fed the fear within her. *Never again.* He held up a hand to her. A bloody hand. If she shot him and missed, he would brutalize her before killing her. She turned the gun on herself and pulled the trigger.

She heard the click even as two angry male voices shouted, "No!" and "Sarah!" She was jerked around, into the hard wall of a man's chest. *Logan.* She knew his scent before her mind could even register that it was his arms holding her like steel bands. He took the gun from her hand and tucked it into his waistband.

He pulled back, his hands tight on her arms, his face a mask of terror. He was shouting at her, his white teeth flashing. His hands patted her arms, her shoulders, her neck, her head. Over and around, searching for a wound. He took her upper arms again and pushed her back, looking over her blouse and skirt. He drew her forward, folded her into his arms. His breathing was ragged. She could feel him shaking. His hand cupped the back of her head, pressing her face into the strength of his shoulder.

Slowly, sounds began to return to her. The warrior said something as he stopped beside them. She felt the pressure of his hand on Logan's shoulder, then he was gone. Logan stroked her back, his iron grasp slowly easing. She felt the deep breath he drew. He kissed her forehead.

"That is Chayton." His words rumbled through his chest, against her ear. "He is like à brother to me. He will not harm you. Nor will he let harm come to you." He drew back, cupping her face with his hands. "He will protect me and mine as I do him and his. It is his band that we go to visit."

Logan kept his arms wrapped around her, drawing a ragged breath. A chill swept through him. He'd almost lost her. By the grace of God, she'd fired the empty chamber he'd told her to keep the hammer against. She was cold. He rubbed his hands up and down her arms.

He didn't want to leave her side, but needed to clean up out front—especially knowing that Chayton had probably taken their scalps as well. "Wait here for me. I need to take care of a few things."

Logan led the wagon horses through the pass. Chayton was there, waiting solemnly. He held three bloody scalps. The bodies, including that of the man Chayton had killed in the inner pasture, were nowhere to be seen.

"I regret frightening your woman. I am thankful she didn't shoot me. I did not expect her to try to shoot herself."

Logan lifted his hat and ran a hand through his hair. "She was held as a captive of Swift Elk's band. They did not treat her well. She is still recovering from her wounds."

"She was the one known as Yellow Moon."

"Yes."

"We heard Swift Elk was enraged that she left him."

"I have paid him her bride price."

Chayton nodded. "That is good. He is a fearless warrior, but his hatred of your people has twisted his mind. I am surprised she survived. But I am glad she did." He grinned at Logan. "Laughs-Like-Water feared you would never find the mate you sought. She has sensed the loneliness in you for a long while. Is Yellow Moon the wife of your heart?"

Logan studied Chayton. "Yes."

"That will make my wife happy."

"Chayton, on my way out, I crossed paths with a man who is dangerous for your people. A bounty hunter who takes Indian scalps for money. His name is Hugh Landry, but they call him 'Skinner.'"

Chayton's face hardened. "If I see him, he will die."

"He and his men have buffalo guns." Logan looked at his friend. "Maybe it is time to move your people to the agency." Chayton's life was bittersweet—his family gave him great joy, but the future his people faced meant an end to the way they had existed for years beyond remembering. His chief had decided to keep the band out of the agencies, fearing the horror stories about starvation and abuse and even massacres perpetrated against those who had surrendered.

"Laughs-Like-Water is pregnant. Would you have me take my family to the agency where they will starve us? They will take my gun and horses so that I cannot hunt. They will tell me and my wife to grow plants in the soil, but they will not give us seeds or tools. They will want us to grow plants where there is no water. They will feed us rancid meat. We will not be able to hunt to take skins for our tepees. And even if they allowed us to keep our guns and to hunt, they have killed all the buffalo. What would we hunt? The earth weeps with the destruction your people have wrought, and you would have me put my family in their hands?"

"I would have you survive, my friend. There are white people from here to the morning sun. Soon, there will be white people from here to the evening sun. We cannot be stopped."

"Your people are a disease infecting our lands."

"Come to the Circle Bar with me. Bring your family. There will be work for you. You will be safe. You could train horses."

"I will not leave my people. And I will not cut our visit short out of fear of your scalp-taker. Laughs-Like-Water has waited all year for this trading trip. She and the other women have worked hard and have earned this time. I will give her the joy she wishes—before we are locked away and cannot travel to meet you."

"If you are locked away, I will come to you."

Chayton turned away, his face an expression of hardened nonchalance. He waved to the chuck wagon. "What is this monstrosity?"

"I've brought many supplies to you, more than I could carry on a single horse. Give me a hand with these horses. I want to move away from this spot. Sarah and I will camp by the river near here for the night and will meet up with you tomorrow morning." When the horses were once again hitched to the wagon, and they had pulled the wagon out of the small pasture, Chayton left to return to his family.

Logan moved back into the inner pasture. Sarah sat with her knees folded and her arms around her legs. She rocked herself and stared across the enclosure to the opposite rock wall.

He knelt facing her and leaned back on his haunches. "Sarah, talk to me." She didn't acknowledge his presence. "I can't believe how close I came to losing you today." He slipped his hand under one of hers and brought it over to his chest. She stopped rocking, but still did not look at him.

"Honey, if it had not been Chayton in here today, if an enemy had taken you, I would have found you."

She turned slowly to meet his gaze. "The soldiers came looking for me. They spent months looking for me. They didn't find me."

He nodded. "I bet they even came to Swift Elk's village, didn't they?"

"He had the women hide me outside the camp. I was not allowed to speak or move. They kept me beneath a buffalo hide they were preparing for a tepee cover. I thought I would suffocate. I fought until I couldn't breathe. They beat me, and still I fought. And then one of them kicked me. I don't remember much after that. When I regained consciousness, the soldiers were gone."

"There is nowhere that you could be hidden from me. If we got separated, I would find you. You must never, never attempt to take your life again. I need you to believe in me, even if you can't yet believe in yourself."

She studied his eyes as she evaluated his words. "I want to believe in you," she whispered.

He smiled at her. "I believe in you. I believe that you will heal, that you *can* heal. I believe that we will have an extraordinary life together—one I don't want to miss a minute of." She reached for him, her gaze both unconvinced and yearning. He went to his knees, drawing her up with him, against him. He held her tightly enough to calm the trembling within her. Having her in his arms was heaven. He didn't move and barely breathed for fear she would remember where she was. When at last she began to pull away, he eased his hold, moving a hand down her arm to thread his fingers with her smaller ones.

"Let's make a few more miles today. Tomorrow morning we will meet up with Chayton and his family."

The fire crackled a few feet from their wagon. The air moved in a slight breeze that carried the scent of new sage and snow from the distant mountains. Sarah lay beneath the heavy quilts, drawn tightly against Logan's side. His denims were rough against the bare skin of her calves.

Neither of them was the least bit sleepy. He had held her like this for a week, never seeking more from their intimate time together. She leaned up on her elbow, looking at the firelight reflected from the canvas cover, playing across the shadows and hard planes of his face. She reached a hand to touch the rise of his cheekbone, tracing it down to the lines bracketing his mouth. She looked at his eyes, saw the pale edges of his irises that were centered with deep black circles. His stare was unblinking.

"I want to be your wife."

They lay so close, neither needed to speak in more than a whisper. "You are my wife."

"In every way."

He sucked in a sharp breath. "You aren't ready for us to join our bodies. We have our whole lives together. I will not rush this part of our relationship. I like holding you. I like watching you. I like that you feel comfortable lying next to me. It is all I need for now."

Her thumb brushed back and forth across his cheek. She lay half across his chest. She could feel his heartbeat drumming against her chest. "I don't think it's all that I need."

"Then take the lead. Kiss me. I won't kiss you back unless you ask me. Hold me. I won't hold you unless you ask me."

She studied him. Heat swirled within her, warming her in ways she hadn't experienced since those first days Eugene had courted her, before she knew what it was to be a man's wife, to be Eugene's wife. So far, nothing about being Logan's wife had resembled her time with Eugene. She wondered if this would be different, if his kisses would be anything as wondrous as she imagined.

She drew herself up, across his body, bringing her face even with his. He made no move to restrain her, to take over their embrace. The dark intensity in his eyes was unmistakable. He watched her every move. She drew her thumb across his mouth, learning the contours of his lips. Logan was quick to smile, quick to meet a challenge, so very sure of himself. Slowly, slowly, she lowered her mouth to his, a chaste touch that was anything but innocent. She moved her lips to the left over his closed mouth, to the right. She could feel his breath against her upper lip. His nostrils were flared, his control hard-won.

She lifted up to look at him, momentarily losing

herself in his eyes. They were like ice over a black, fathomless lake. She bent to his mouth again, reveling in the control he granted her. She took his upper lip between both of hers, feeling the texture of him. She moved in the opposite direction with his bottom lip. She liked the feel of him. She liked his scent, a musk that was his alone. She could do this. She could surrender to him. It wouldn't be terrible, wouldn't be like the other times.

A flash of what would happen exploded in her mind. Grunting. Pushing. Ripping. Laughing at her pain. It hurt. It hurt. She couldn't do this.

At once she withdrew, pulling away from him so fast that she would have fallen from the bed had he not grabbed her, steadied her. "Whoa!" He eased her back onto the bed. "What happened?"

"I can't do this."

"You can't lie still and go to sleep?"

"I can't be your wife. I want to, but I can't. I can't do it."

They were lying on their sides, facing each other, she at the very edge of the mattress. He kept a hand at the curve of her waist. It was constricting. It was reassuring.

"You are my wife. There isn't anything you have to do or not do to be more of a wife to me." She looked at his chest. She was out of the covers, exposed to the cold air of the night. His hand moved from her side, up to her face to push the hair from her cheek. "There's a big difference between being taken and giving yourself. I will not take you. When you are ready, you will give yourself to me. We will both know when that is. For me, right now, I want nothing more than to hold you in my arms and know that you are safe, that your heart beats so close to mine. I'll sleep on top of the covers if you like, so that you'll feel safe."

She shook her head. "It's cold."

He smiled and tugged at the covers. "Then get under here."

Chapter 11

"Wait until you see what Laughs-Like-Water has brought for the trade. She's been working on her items all winter. She's quite a skilled artist," Logan said with a grin the next morning, as if all that mattered was the warm sunshine and the brilliant blue sky. As if he had no concerns at all about the Sioux camp they were riding into.

"Laughs-Like-Water was the one who taught me to listen to the pieces of art, to hear the stories woven into them."

Chayton called out, ending further discussion. Not a breath later, two children ran toward them, squealing with joy.

Logan set the brake and pulled the children up to the bench, settling them between him and Sarah. "This is Little Hawk and that's White Bird," he said, introducing Chayton's children. They peppered Logan with so many questions that Sarah could not make sense of much of what they said. When Logan pulled a package of hard candy out of his vest pocket

and gave it to them, they settled down immediately.
They looked up at her and smiled, their teeth white,
their faces tanned already from the early summer
sun. The little girl watched Sarah with big eyes the
color of molasses. She reached out hesitantly and
touched Sarah's long braid of blond hair.

No sooner had they drawn up beside the camp
than several women hurried forward to tend the
horses. They must have handled wagon teams before,
for they made short work of unhitching the horses.
Logan climbed down and helped Sarah to the
ground. People gathered around them in a circle,
patting Logan's shoulder, greeting him like a son. A
dog barked excitedly.

This wasn't a warrior band. The difference was
immediately evident. There was an elderly couple,
Chayton's children, and a few teenage boys and
girls. There was no hostility, no distrust, just joy at
the return of an important friend. It looked as if
Chayton had brought only his immediate family to
the trade.

"The boys are apprentices to Chayton and the
girls to Laughs-Like-Water. It is an important thing
to be apprenticed to such highly regarded people
as Chayton and his wife," Logan leaned down and
explained in English. "The older couple are Chayton's parents."

Chayton came through the small crowd of people
to stand in front of them. He put a hand on Logan's
shoulder, welcoming him to their camp. "Come and
greet my wife," he invited as he led the way to his
tepee. Logan took Sarah's hand as the crowd parted,

giving them room to follow Chayton. They paused outside the entrance to his tepee where he called to his wife.

Quickly, as if she had been awaiting his summons, a woman emerged from the low opening. Her hair was parted in the middle and woven into two tight braids. Beaded tethers bound the braids at the top and bottom. She wore a buckskin dress with a wide sash beaded in lines and geometric shapes of green, white, and orange. The sides of the skirt were opened, revealing a pair of fringed leggings that terminated in beaded moccasins. She was beautiful. Sarah caught herself staring and tried to cover her lapse of manners.

Chayton smiled at Laughs-Like-Water. "I have big news! Shadow Wolf has married! This is his wife, Yellow Moon."

Laughs-Like-Water approached Sarah. She took hold of Sarah's hands and gazed into her face. Her eyes were a warm brown. Emotion danced freely across her face, like sunlight skittering through the branches of a tree. Her hands were strong, her grasp firm. Sarah studied Chayton's wife as she was herself studied.

"I am glad for you, Shadow Wolf, but her eyes tell stories that make my heart ache," Laughs-Like-Water said without looking away from Sarah. "If there is anyone who can fill you with laughter, Yellow Moon, it is Shadow Wolf."

Impossibly, Sarah felt certain that Chayton's wife saw into her soul. She did not answer the woman.

Laughs-Like-Water gave her hands a squeeze and then released them. "Let us help with the horses."

Sarah led their two horses to a patch of grass where another horse grazed untethered. She was surprised that he was not secured.

"He will not run. He listens to Chayton's magic."

Sarah wasn't sure what that meant, but Logan had said he was an extraordinary trainer. She set to work removing saddles, wiping the horses down. She took them to the river to drink. When they were finished, she tied them to the corral line that was already in place.

"Shadow Wolf said he came to trade with you," Sarah said as she waited for Laughs-Like-Water to finish with the horse she was tending. It felt odd to call Logan by his Sioux name, but it fit him. He was fierce and protective. Observant and patient. Like a wolf watching from the shadows.

Laughs-Like-Water straightened and smiled. "We have met with Shadow Wolf for many years. In the days following the fall hunt, we meet to trade for the beads he brings. Then all winter, I sew them into clothes, leggings, pouches, and such. In the spring, we meet again, to trade for the products I've made. Chayton is very proud of my work. And the money Shadow Wolf pays for it helps our people through the winter when hunting is poor and we need to trade for supplies."

Sarah studied Laughs-Like-Water. She had not known anyone like her during her stay with the Sioux. None of the women she'd lived with chatted so openly—not even among themselves.

When the horses were settled, Laughs-Like-Water grabbed Sarah's hand and hurried with her back to camp. Caught up in the other woman's excitement, Sarah laughed. "Do we begin the trade now?"

"No." Chayton's wife slowed to a walk. "First we make a feast. It is not good to rush these things. If I hurry to put my wares in front of your husband, he will think less of them. He will think I value them so little that I wish the transaction concluded rapidly before he can give much thought to what he is purchasing."

A large fire pit was already roasting a deer haunch. Chayton's children were tasked with keeping the meat rotating. Fortunately, their duty didn't impact their game of chase. Every few minutes, they rotated the skewers, then hurried off again to play.

Sarah helped Chayton's wife and the other women make flat bread. Then she brought some supplies from their wagon to make a few extra treats. Using one of the flat breads as a crust, she made an apple torte from Logan's store of dried apple slices, cinnamon, and sugar. She ground coffee and set a large pot of it to boil over the fire. When it was ready, she poured a cup for Logan and sweetened it with a bit of sugar. Chayton's father and his apprentices sitting near him watched her serve Chayton next. Coffee was such a common thing to her, but to Chayton and his people, it was a treat. Fortunately, she had enough tin cups for each of them to have one of his own.

When she looked up, Logan was watching her, seeing how she interacted with the people he was so fond of. She smiled at him. His eyes widened; his hand froze with his cup midway to his mouth. Sarah returned to Laughs-Like-Water. She didn't know what had come over her, but she was excited to be here. She knew what a savvy negotiator Logan was, and she hoped he would be generous in his transaction with Chayton's wife.

When the meal was nearly ready to be served, Laughs-Like-Water set a blanket on the ground. Her young apprentices brought out several large bundles. Logan faced them, but he never let his gaze wander in their direction. He was acting as uninterested as Chayton's wife in the transaction that would follow their meal.

Sarah knelt across the blanket from Laughs-Like-Water as she unrolled her bundle and set out an amazing variety of items, all of which had been beautifully beaded. There were moccasins, ceremonial leggings and shirts, dresses, earrings, bracelets and necklaces, breechclouts, tobacco pouches, medicine bags.

"This is impressive, Laughs-Like-Water. Did you do all of this?"

Chayton's wife smiled at her. "I did the first year. But Shadow Wolf said he would trade for as much as we could produce. So now, all the women of the village help me with these over the winter. Each contributes as she may. Some prepare the skins, others watch the children, others cook for us. My apprentices, whose eyes are young and hands are steady, show great talent. We spend the summers thinking up the patterns we will make, and the winters making them. Do you like them?"

"Yes. You are very talented."

Chayton's wife picked up a pair of beaded earrings stitched across a circle of suede backing. "I give these to you."

Sarah reached for the earrings. She knew how much work went into the pair and was shocked at the generous gesture. "They are stunning. I am speechless." She looked at Laughs-Like-Water. "I have no gift to give you in return."

Laughs-Like-Water smiled. "I did not give you a gift expecting one in exchange. I gave you a gift because it gives me joy to do so."

The women and children arranged the items for Logan to review. Laughs-Like-Water sent the children to the river to fill the water pots. Sarah looked at Logan, uncertain whether she was permitted to join him. He smiled an invitation. When she approached him, he moved over on the blanket to make room for her.

"Those are beautiful earrings."

Sarah fingered the beaded discs she was already wearing. "Laughs-Like-Water gave them to me. She's quite an artist."

"Every year, she enlists the help of more women. It's become quite an undertaking. My customers are very pleased at the quality they produce."

Laughs-Like-Water served Logan several slices of venison on a flat bread. She gave her husband a similar portion, then called the children over to share the one she took for herself. For a moment, time slipped away, taking Sarah back to her days among Swift Elk's people. Then, she had eaten what little they'd spared, sometimes going for days without.

"This is for both of us, Sarah."

She looked at the roasted morsel he held out to her. Her stomach growled. She glanced up at him, too late remembering to shutter her expression, hating that he could see how hungry she was. "Thank you."

He ate slowly, feeding her bigger pieces than he took for himself. When she became aware of his actions, she tried to refuse what he offered. "It would be an insult not to finish what has been prepared for us," he whispered, leaning close. She acquiesced, eating every piece he gave her.

When the others had also finished, the time for trading had come. As before with Cloud Walker, Chayton started a pipe. He offered its first smoke to the four directions, the Earth and the sky, then passed it around to the men.

Sarah felt unaccountably nervous for Chayton's wife. She didn't know what Logan would use to trade for the pieces of art Laughs-Like-Water offered. Logan knelt before the blanket where the items were spread. Several times, he would pick up a piece and examine it closely. He discussed the various colors and pattern choices represented in the different pieces.

Sarah looked at Chayton, who stood off to one side, arms crossed. His expression was impossible to read. She knew the more stoic a Sioux was, the greater import a subject held. Even the children stood silently—and still—next to him.

"This is a fine collection of work, Laughs-Like-Water."

"It is a larger bundle than ever before."

Logan lifted a man's shirt, studying the colors banding the chest and the patterns embedded within it. He picked up a pair of women's moccasins, carefully looking over the designs that covered the top of each foot and circled around the ankle. He touched piece after piece, sometimes studying them, sometimes looking away pensively as his thumb moved over the beadwork pattern.

"What is the price you ask for this collection?"

Laughs-Like-Water shot a glance at Chayton. He met her look, but did not give away a single clue as to how she should answer. Sarah's stomach tightened.

"I ask four hundred dollars for the bundle."

Logan's brows lifted. He whistled under his breath. "That is considerably higher than our last trade."

"I had help from many more women. I have many more families to share the proceeds with. And apprentices of my own now, too."

"I will give you two hundred and fifty for the lot in coins, and another twenty-five dollars worth of supplies." They quibbled a bit more. Sarah brought over coffee. They sat down and sipped the dark liquid, taking a break in their negotiations. In the end, Laughs-Like-Water got the price she wanted.

Logan counted out the money and handed it to her, which she promptly gave to Chayton. The goods were packed up and handed to Logan, who turned over the supplies he had brought with him for this transaction. Laughs-Like-Water stoked the fire, adding more wood.

Logan took chocolate bars out of the wagon and handed them to Laughs-Like-Water to distribute among her family. The children, who were growing sleepy, instantly revived. Chayton's son climbed into Logan's lap. White Bird came over and sat in Sarah's lap. She looked up at Sarah with her huge eyes, as brown as the dark chocolate bar she ate. Sarah smiled as she smoothed the girl's silky black hair from her face. White Bird held the bar up for Sarah to bite. Sarah took a little nibble, then snuggled White Bird more comfortably in her arms.

She set her chin on the top of White Bird's head as the chocolate melted in her mouth. This was something that would never be hers. She would never have a child of her own to sit trustingly in her lap. Moisture filled her eyes, distorting the campfire. She blinked it away and caught Logan watching her. His expression was rigid, as hard as she'd ever seen it.

After Laughs-Like-Water settled the children in their blankets a short while later, Chayton told his wife about the scalp hunter. The joy leeched from her face. "We must warn the village. Should we leave at once?"

Logan shook his head. "Skinner was heading south. Tell your people to go north."

"They've come south for the hunting," Chayton

said. "We are allowed to hunt these lands. It was agreed upon."

Logan made no comment. It didn't need saying how few treaties were fully honored or at least how few were considered as anything more than temporary agreements. With gold having been discovered in the Black Hills, none of this land would be open to the Sioux for long, even as far west as where they were now.

The women retired shortly after that. Logan wandered over to the horses. He took a group of them down to the river to drink. Chayton joined him with another group.

"I have a bad feeling about Skinner, Shadow Wolf."

Logan frowned at the moonlight that glittered on the river. "These are bad days."

"They are good days to be white," Chayton scoffed. "Bad days to be one of our people." They returned the horses to the corral and brought down another set, both men working in silence as they considered the future.

When he joined Sarah in bed, his mind was still churning. He felt what Chayton felt. Something was coming.

Sarah had originally gone to Defiance to learn to handle her pistol. It was time he worked with her. Hopefully, she would never have to use her gun. But if the need arose and she was untrained, that would be his fault.

A sound slipped into his consciousness. Faint, but unmistakable. Their wagon was parked near

Chayton's tepee. He and Laughs-Like-Water were talking in quiet murmurs, punctuated here and there with groans and sighs. Logan looked over to Sarah, wondering if she heard the two lovers. Her eyes were open. She was staring fixedly at the canvas overhead.

He reached his hand over to hers under the cover. She was clasping the bottom blanket in a fist. *Christ.* Her breathing was so faint, he thought she might be holding her breath.

"Let's take a walk. We'll look at the stars." He slipped off the bed to retrieve her boots and to step into his. He fetched her coat, then helped her out the back way, over the table. She pulled her coat on. He took her hand and led her a short distance away, where the only sounds they heard were crickets and the occasional hoot of an owl.

Several granite boulders were strewn about, remnants of the same ancient line of mountains where they had defended themselves yesterday. Logan leaned back against one and drew Sarah against his body. He reached down and slipped his hand over hers, folding his fingers around all but her index finger. He wrapped his arm around her waist and set his cheek against hers. She was stiff as a board, poised for flight. Or a fight.

"It's important to know the constellations. Navigating out here on the prairie at night is as difficult as at sea. Look up." He pointed with her finger to the sky, his hand over hers. "See the stars that start there and make this pattern, like a cup? That is the Big Dipper. Its tail points to the south. The peak of the cup points north. Once you know that, you cannot be lost. My father's ranch is about a week southwest from where we are now."

Sarah turned in his arms to look at him. "Why are you telling me this?"

"Because reading the stars is a skill you should have so that you aren't dependent on me or anyone. If you have to travel at night, you'll know where you're going." He turned her back to focus on the sky and pointed her finger again. "Look to the south. There. That's Centaurus, a warrior creature half man, half beast. And up here is Hercules, his student, the one who caused the mortal wound that led Zeus to make a constellation out of Centaurus. And there, to the west, is Gemini." He moved his hand to her chin, lifting to position her gaze where it needed to be. Her skin was like velvet against his cheek, beneath his palm. He couldn't help stroking her there, up and back.

She turned to look at him. "How is it you know so much about the stars?"

She didn't pull away from him. Her face was so near his that her breath touched his lips. "I learned in college. Thought I might become a surveyor, but I realized the knowledge had other, more practical applications." He gave her a slight smile. "My mother wanted me to pursue a political career, but I had no such lofty ambitions." He wondered what her skin would taste like.

"I think what you are doing is much more important. The politicians don't know what's happening out here. You've made friends among the Plains people.

You have influence here. Was she disappointed that you went in a different direction?"

Logan shrugged, feeling the need to be brutally honest. As his wife, there were things about him that she needed to know. "She was shot during an illicit assignation with a lover. You see, you aren't the only one with secrets."

She turned in his arms and wrapped her hands around his neck. "I'm sorry, Logan. I didn't mean to pry. I know so little about you."

She was leaning against his body. He hoped her coat shielded her from the growing evidence of the effect she was having on him. "My stepfather runs a large cattle operation north of Defiance. My step-brother has a spread right next to him."

"Are they safe up there?"

"They have been so far. My brother, Sager, was raised by the Shoshone. He, his father-in-law, and my father are pretty savvy when it comes to making the alliances they need to be successful. That includes trading with the local Indian populations. They're safe."

"I'm looking forward to meeting them. I hope they accept me."

Logan shrugged. "If they don't, we won't ever need to see them again. You can help me with my trades. Maybe one day we'll build a museum of the people of the plains so that children for generations to come will know them as we do."

"You love them, don't you?"

"I love many things about them. They honor each other and respect their differences. They're courageous and resourceful. They live in harmony. They find joy in little things. They seek counsel from the spirit world. Their laws are structured by the rules of nature. It's a different way of living, a way that can't coexist with our ways. It is important to know them so that they will not be forgotten."

"And yet they killed my husband and raped and tortured me. How does that fit with the people you know?"

"Their way of life is worth fighting for. They must fight the only way they are able, using any means they can. But even in fighting they destroy themselves, for we cannot allow our people to be harmed. And we far outnumber them. It is a battle that was lost before it was started." He brushed his knuckles against her cheek. "I am sad for them. And sad for us. And very, very grateful that I found you. I will keep you safe, Sarah."

She wrapped her arms around his waist and laid her head against his chest. He tightened his arms around her. Unable to stop himself, he kissed the top of her head.

Chapter 12

Sarah watched Chayton's family disassemble their camp. In very little time, their great tepees were packed onto travois, along with their elderly family members who were too frail to walk the long distance to the next camp. Chayton was taking his family back to their village. He had decided to talk their people into going north, away from the dangers of scalp hunters like Skinner.

Chayton brought his family by for a last farewell. They confirmed their plans to meet again in September, when Logan would bring Laughs-Like-Water the beads and supplies she would need for her work over the winter. The small band of Sioux moved slowly away, the noise of dogs and children gradually fading.

Sarah folded her arms, watching them. "I am sad to see them go."

Logan wrapped his arms around her waist and drew her back against him. "That is how I feel whenever I part company with Chayton and his family.

These are dangerous times for his people. For many people." He rubbed his chin over the top of her head. She folded her arms over his. She was becoming comfortable touching him, being touched by him. It warmed something deep inside himself that had been cold and empty a very long time.

"Thank you for bringing me with you to meet Chayton's family. They're good people."

"Every society has its good and bad people. Your introduction to the Sioux did little to show you the truth of their ways—at least ways as they are when they aren't at war." He rubbed her arms. "I think we should hit the trail, too. You ready? We'll be at the Circle Bar in a week or so."

Sarah turned in his arms to look up at his face, wondering at the words he didn't say, wondering how he would react if his family disapproved of her.

After their noon stop that day, when they had eaten their lunch and the horses had been fed and watered, Sarah started to pack up the wagon.

"Leave it," Logan told her. "It's time I showed you some things about your gun. Bring the revolver and your cleaning kit."

Sarah hurried to do as he asked, excited to finally have the lessons she sought. They mounted the ponies and rode a fair distance from the wagon and the corralled wagon team. After securing their mounts in a stand of cottonwoods, they walked a good ways off so that any debris from their practice would not come near the two animals. The ponies were battle trained—he wasn't worried about their being startled by the sound of gunfire.

The gun belt Sarah wore would have fit a large man, but it was wrapped twice around her waist, covering most of her middle section. "Remind me to order a gun belt that actually fits you."

She smiled at him as she held her hands out to her sides. "What do I do first?"

"Unload your gun."

"Why? How can I learn to shoot if it isn't loaded?"

"This ain't a game, honey. You have to first know and respect your weapon before you go making it deadly. Take the bullets out."

She opened the loading gate and spilled the cartridges into her hand. Logan reached over and took them from her.

"Now what?"

"Now show me how you handle your piece."

She set the Colt back in its holster and drew it out fast. He didn't make any comment. She did it again. And again. Logan crossed his arms and waited for her enthusiasm to wane. When her movements began to slow down, he smiled.

"A pistol doesn't have the accuracy a rifle does, nor the impact a shotgun has. Speed is not your friend when handling a Colt. Now try one more time, slowly. You aren't an expert gunfighter and you never will be." She sent him an injured look. "Not because you're a woman. Because you haven't the heart for it. Your pistol is for self-defense. If you rush your shot, you could lose your opportunity to hit your target. So let's see you take your piece out slowly, with intent."

She did as he asked. "Don't look at me, honey. A bullet tends to go where you're looking, and I won't ever be your target. Pick one of those trees over there, the same one every time." She repeated the exercise a few times. He could see the focus in her gaze. Their practice had stopped being a game. Good.

"Now, take your piece out and cock it."

This she struggled with. The hammer was much firmer than she'd expected—harder to do when she wasn't panicked. It took two hands for her to accomplish the task. "I'm sorry. This isn't as easy as it looks."

"No need to apologize. This ain't about being pretty. It's about getting the job done. The more comfortable you are with it, the better shot you'll be. And let me tell you, there is something poetic about an enemy staring down the barrel of a Peacemaker. You just take the time you need and enjoy the power, 'cause you're about to kill your enemy. And dead is dead, whether it takes two hands or one."

She nodded at him, absorbing his words.

"Now uncock it and do it again." She did. "And again."

She repeated the exercise until it began to feel familiar. He could see the tension ease out of her stance as she became comfortable with what she was doing.

"You hear the clicks it makes when you cock it?" She nodded. "Four clicks. You got to remember to listen for them. Each one means something. Quarter cocked. Half cocked. You load at half cocked. Three-quarters cocked. Fully cocked. You can fire on the fourth click. Now, lift it up and sight down the barrel. See that dead branch in the tree just to the right of the boulder? It's about twenty yards away. Think you could hit it?"

She nodded.

"Well, darlin', I guess you're ready to actually shoot something." He handed her a cartridge and watched while she opened the loading gate and loaded it. She holstered her gun and waited tensely for him to give the order to shoot.

"Honey, do this." He flapped his hands. "And this." He rotated his head. "You gotta relax. I know you respect that weapon so there's no need to fear it. See if you can hit that dead branch. Remember what I taught you. There's no need to be fast. Fire when you're ready."

Sarah took a deep breath and calmly removed the Colt. She drew the hammer back. Click. Click. Click. Click. She sighted down the barrel with one eye closed. And pulled the trigger. The recoil slammed against her hand, making her fall backward.

Logan squatted next to her, wincing. "Well, I guess I didn't account for that. Now that you know it's coming, you'll be better prepared. Let's do it again." He gave her a hand up.

"Did I hit it?"

"No, ma'am, you did not." He handed her another round. "Holster your piece and start from the beginning."

They repeated this several more times, until she

finally did hit the branch. She holstered her gun and started jumping up and down, clapping her hands. To Logan's everlasting bemusement, she launched herself at him and started kissing his face. He was a goner before her arms had fully closed around him. He caught the back of her head, holding her immobile while his mouth came down on hers. He slanted his mouth against hers, using his jaw to urge hers to open. Her arms tightened around his neck, lifting her body up closer to him. She wasn't fighting him, thank God, because right at that moment, if he didn't taste her mouth he thought he might just die.

He swept his tongue between her lips, between her teeth, searching for her tongue. When he felt it rise against his, stroking, sliding, demanding, fire shot through his groin. He had to fight his every instinct to push her to the ground. He gentled his hold on her, giving her the freedom to pull back.

She did not. His tongue made another sweep of her mouth. If he didn't stop now, he wouldn't be able to. He slowly eased his mouth from hers, but he didn't release her body. She was a little bit of a thing, bony hips and shoulders and big, round breasts. He bent his head and kissed her neck, willing his body to calm down, an impossible feat.

"Well, I guess that's enough for a first lesson." He set her back on her feet. He hadn't even been aware he'd lifted her up.

"Thank you, Logan. Can we try again tomorrow?"

A drumming started in his head. She had to know they'd end up kissing again. "Oh, yeah. We'll practice every day."

* * *

Logan watched Sarah hang up the last of their laundry two days later, scattering clothing over branches and boulders. She wore a loose muslin blouse with the arms folded up to her elbows. Her hair was pulled back in a thick braid, but the silky strands seemed discontented to stay confined. They played with the wind, slipping forward to stroke her face under the brim of his old hat.

He felt like the air was sucked out of him, watching his beautiful, broken, ragtag wife. She'd begun to smile again. Frequently. Anytime she made some small achievement. A bit of camp food well prepared. Her improving skills with her pistol. Hell, even the wind made her smile now. But still there was a shadow in her eyes when she looked at him. He couldn't let her continue to live in fear.

She trusted him enough to let him touch her, hold her hand, hold her in his arms as she fell asleep. But he wanted more. Much, much more. He wanted her heart. Her soul. He wanted her to know that she was perfect, strong. Resilient.

He looked away, at a loss as to how he could reach her. If they continued on the path they were on, they would have a friendly but incomplete marriage. He'd grown up watching his parents circle each other, neither quite knowing how to deal with the other, both miserable and alone.

He saw to the horses, mulling over the situation while he groomed and fed them. Gradually, an idea took form. She wouldn't like it. Not one bit. But he could see it done without breaking his promise to her.

When he came back to camp, she was putting away the last of their supper dishes. She poured him a cup of coffee. He watched her, bracing himself for her reaction. The sun was beginning its descent, washing the rugged land around them in warm orange hues.

Setting his coffee down, he retrieved a bar of soap and a couple of towels. "Time for our baths."

She nodded, burying her face in her steaming tin cup. "Go ahead. I'll take mine when you're finished."

"No. We'll bathe together."

He had her full attention with that. Her eyes went wide. Fear tightened her expression. "You said we wouldn't be intimate."

"I said I wouldn't claim my marital rights. This isn't intercourse. It's just a bath. Water. Soap. Two clean bodies. Nothing scary."

"I don't want to bathe with you."

He touched her cheek, the tense line of her jaw. "I have shown you that I will not break my word. You know that from my friends, from people like Cloud Walker who'd never met me before but knew of my reputation. When we negotiated our marriage, I claimed the right to hold and assist you. This falls in that bucket."

He set the towel and soap down, then started to undress. He pulled his vest off, dropped the straps of his suspenders, and pulled his shirt from his waistband. "Take your clothes off, honey."

She stood immobile. Her skin, which before had had a rosy hint from the washing and the hot June evening, was now ghostly white. "Please, Logan. Please, not yet." Her voice was a whisper, broken and raw.

"Now, darlin'. I can't help you heal if I don't know the extent of your injuries."

Her face went blank. She set her gaze absently on the ground at his feet and began to unfasten her skirt. He stepped around her, taking one of the chairs so that he could remove his boots and socks. When he looked up, her shirt and skirt were piled at her feet. She stood with her back to him, wearing only her camisole and drawers. She'd removed her petticoats earlier to wash them with the rest of the laundry. She made no move to take off her underclothes.

He leaned back in his chair. "Everything, Sarah. I would see your skin, your scars. I want to know what you're hiding from me. I want there to be no secrets between us. Only this. Only the truth. Only trust."

Still with her back to him, she loosened the string at her waist and pushed her drawers from her hips. Red lines marred her alabaster skin. Angry puckered marks showed where she'd been poked with burning embers. Rage rose like a beast within him. This woman, so brave, so resolute, had been taken from her home and thrust into a band of angry warriors hell-bent on the destruction of all white men, women, and children. How she had survived was a mystery he would never unravel.

She pulled her camisole up over her head. The marks were heavier across her shoulders and arms. Tears made his vision waver. "Turn around," he ordered quietly, half afraid to see worse scars on her front.

She moved in a tight circle, turning to face him. Her face was still downcast. She clutched her camisole in front of her, between her breasts. Her legs were long and slim. Pale curls covered her sex. Her stomach was concave, her hip bones clearly visible. He had been feeding her three full meals a day and several snacks between times, but she had a ways to go to return to a healthy weight. Her stomach stretched up to a narrow rib cage, and breasts that were stunningly perfect, round and full despite her slim weight. Her nipples were upthrust, tight with tension. Her hands clasped the little bit of cotton fabric in a white-knuckled hold between her breasts.

"Move your hands. Let me see all of you."

Sarah took a breath. She felt herself withdraw, pull inward. It didn't matter what he thought of her. There was nothing she could do about it. He was her husband. He could do anything he wished. Anything at all, as she well knew. She kept her eyes averted and lowered her camisole. Logan sucked in a breath. She wanted, perversely, to start singing, to hum loudly, to drown out his voice, his thoughts. Her mortification.

"Good God, honey," he rasped, leaning forward. "Is this what you've been hiding from me?"

A tear slipped down her cheek. She braved a

glance at his face. He stared at her chest, a look of awe on his face.

"Come here. I want to see it closer." He smiled at her. "I thought you had a scar more terrible than all the others. I was terrified of what you would show me."

"I am scarred. It's a great blue scar they carved into my chest. I cannot wash it away. It hurt. I begged them not to do it. I begged and begged." She gasped and stopped herself, realizing how much she was revealing.

"Come here, sweetheart. Let me look at it. It's a tattoo, not a scar."

She moved woodenly forward. What did it matter what he did to her? It would be no worse than what Swift Elk's braves had done, time and again. She stood between his legs, waiting for him to start grabbing at her, hurting her. The trout she'd eaten at supper threatened to come up.

Logan put one hand on her waist. His hand was large and warm. It seemed to cover half her side. He traced the outline of the blue image with his other hand, his touch as light as butterfly wings.

He shook his head, then looked up, looked into her eyes. "I travel all over these plains, buying items from different tribal artisans. Some of it I sell. Much of it I keep. But some of it I save in a special warehouse. Pottery and blankets by Navajo artists, beadwork by several Sioux and Cheyenne families. All of it tells a story. Each piece bears the echoes of a people, their stories, their dreams, their sorrows. I search high and low for these treasures."

He held her with both hands at her hips as he stared up into her eyes. He shook his head. "I heard the story of your spirit when our eyes met. I knew, in an instant, that you were special, but I never expected you to be a work of art. Exquisite beyond any I've ever seen."

Sarah blinked the tears from her eyes. "I am not a work of art. I am scarred and ugly. They did this against my will. Swift Elk said it was his mark so that all the men he let use me would know I belonged to him."

"Swift Elk is a damned idiot, a cruel goddamned bastard who makes war on women. But the women who did this did not brand you." He traced the images again, his touch whispering over her skin like the faintest of breaths. "The women who drew this felt your pain. They drew the story of you." His hand flattened against the blue tattoo. "They marked this over your heart so that your heartbeat would broadcast the truth of you out to the world. It was a protection of sorts."

Sarah wiped at the moisture on her cheeks. He smiled up at her. "The name they gave you was Yellow Moon. The moon is incredibly important to a tribe. It lights the village, illuminates predators and enemies who might try to attack it in the shadows of the night. The moon is the circle in the center of these two funnels." He drew a finger over the shapes as he explained them. "This upper half shows the darkness of the night. The clouds push down threateningly. This lower one shows the village lit by your glowing light. They show that you were the light of the village. It is quite an honor they did you."

He held her waist again. His face was close enough to her body that she felt his warm breath on her skin. Her breasts thrust embarrassingly forward, but he didn't seem to even notice that she stood nude before him.

The silence stretched between them as they looked into each other's eyes. Slowly he stood up, so close that she had to arch her neck to look up at him. "Laughs-Like-Water gave me a salve for your scars. She made it from mock orange that she gathers when they go to the mountains. She said it has soothing properties that will help any soreness your wounds cause. After we bathe, I will put it on your skin. You will let me do this because you have already given me permission to see to your care."

Sarah slowly leaned into him. He was a force of nature, irresistible, unavoidable, determined. She wrapped her arms around his waist as she laid her head against his chest. His skin was warm. She liked his smell. When his arms slowly closed about her, something inside her shifted. He accepted who she was, what she had been, what was left of her. He looked at her, clothed or nude, as if she lit his world, as if she were his Yellow Moon.

Logan tried not to breathe too deeply, tried not to do anything that would make her fear being in his arms. He ran his hands up her back. Her bare skin was soft like velvet. His arms tightened around her, drawing her closer, closer against his body until her breasts were pressed against his chest. His body hungered for hers. He could feel himself swelling, hardening. His hand moved up her spine, beneath her braid, cupping the back of her head as he held her against himself.

"I've waited for this, Sarah, waited every day of my life to hold you in my arms. I can't believe I found you. If I'd been a half hour later, I would have missed running into you." He nuzzled her hair. "I would have found you, though. I know it. I would have heard your call. You heard mine. You went to my town, my people." He drew back so that he could see her beautiful face. He rubbed his thumbs on either side of her jaw. "We were meant to be, Sarah."

Sarah did not argue. His belief in their souls being meant for each other was a way of thinking she didn't understand. She wished she had heard his call before Eugene came into her life, before her world had turned black. Logan knew her dark secrets. All of them. Even the ones she hadn't yet told him. There was no need to say anything else. She wasn't the first white woman who'd come back to society with shocking accounts of her treatment while a captive. Perhaps it was time to start over, begin her adult life now, with Logan. Let the past go like the ghost that it was.

"We should take that bath, before the evening grows cold," she prompted.

He handed her the bar of soap, a small washing cloth, and the towel. He unfastened his pants, loosened the string of his drawers, and pushed them both down his hips. His erection sprang free, jutting straight forward.

He was huge. A chill spiked through her as she stared at his member. "Ignore it, sweetheart. I desire your body. I cannot hide that fact. But we have an agreement, and I will not break it." He took her hand and led her toward the water.

She set the towels on a rock by the bank, then stepped into the cold river. They knelt a few feet in so that the water came to their waists. Her hands were on her legs, her eyes downcast. He could feel her withdrawal. He took the soap from her and lathered up the cloth, then set it back on a nearby boulder. Lifting one of her hands, he began to wash her. He started with the tips of her nails, focusing on each finger, swirling the cloth around her palm, the back of her hand. He wrapped the cloth around her wrist and pushed it up her arm.

Despite the chilly temperature of the water, Sarah felt a strange heat flood her body. She looked up at Logan, bracing herself for the look of lust and possession that would be all over his face. He would see her slight reaction to his touch, her pleasure. He would break his promise.

She did not see what she expected. He was calm, entirely focused on the strokes his hands made over her skin. He was a man filled with self-possession, not one lost to his passion.

She could not draw her eyes away from the hard profile of his face. His brows were a tawnier shade than his sun-bleached blond hair. A day's growth of beard darkened his jaw. There was a hollow between his cheekbones and his jaw that made him look edgy. Predatory. His bottom lip was more rounded and full than his upper lip. He must have felt the weight of her gaze, for he looked up at her. His lashes were a dark brown, softening his piercing gray eyes. Sitting this close to him, she could see the thin rim of dark blue that outlined his irises.

Watching her, he moved the cloth over her collarbone, one of his hands still holding hers. Involuntarily, her fingers tightened against his. She wanted to feel his hands on her body, but she had to satisfy herself with the touch of the cloth as he moved it over her neck, around her chest, between her breasts, over her ribs, beneath her breasts. Her breathing grew shallow as she anticipated the cloth rubbing over the hard peaks of her nipples.

He paused, adding more lather to the cloth. He reached forward and took hold of one of her breasts, pressing it into more of a peak as he moved the cloth over and around the soft flesh. He lavished the same attention on her other breast. She couldn't help arching into his hand, wanting more. More pressure, more heat. The feel of his hand against her skin.

He wrapped an arm about her waist and lifted her from the water so that he could wash her stomach, her hips, her thighs. Her body felt on fire. The touch of the cold water did little to soothe her.

"Straighten your legs out for me," he directed, setting her on her bottom on the smooth river rocks. He lifted a leg and drew the cloth around one lean thigh, over her knee, behind her knee. Resting her foot on his leg, he used both hands to draw the cloth over her calf, her shin, around her ankle. He washed her foot, moving tenderly over the scars on her sole.

He reached for the soap, lathering the cloth so that he could repeat his ministrations on her other leg. Sarah shut her eyes, giving herself over to the sensations set aflame by his touch. "Kneel again," he said. She complied. He reached a hand around her waist again, lifting her. Her knee was between his legs. She felt his erection brush her leg, but before she could push away, he swept the soapy cloth between her legs, against her feminine core. A sensation she'd never felt before flared at his touch. She bucked against his hand, arching, seeking more. And then his hand was gone. He brushed the cloth against her buttocks, between them, over the small of her back, up the center of her spine, over her shoulder blades to the back of her neck.

Her body was wet and slick against his. His skin was warm. She moved her hands over his shoulders, feeling the muscles that bunched and cabled as he held her, washed her. Her face was pressed to his throat. She rubbed her face against the hard column of his neck, feeling his body tighten as she did so.

"Turn around and lie down so that I can do your hair," he ordered, his voice a rough whisper. She pulled away from his body and lay down, exposing the front of her body to the air and the lapping touches of the river current. Her head was between his knees, kept aloft by his hands. He brushed the soap bar against the top of her head, starting a lather that he drew down throughout the rest of her hair. His strong fingers massaged her scalp, wringing a little moan of pleasure from her.

She felt his hands moving once again over her body, rinsing the soap from her skin, stroking her with cool detachment. When the lather was gone, he drew her to her feet and led her to the river's edge, where they'd left the towels. He took one and draped it over her head, squeezing the moisture from her hair. He wrapped the towel around her body, then folded the corner in at the top to hold the cloth in place.

"Go back to the wagon and get into bed. Don't dress. I want to put the salve on you." She didn't immediately move, couldn't seem to lift her leaden feet. His erection pointed fiercely at her. She realized she wanted what he wanted, wanted to be intimate with him. Wanted him to wipe out the memories of all the others. She spun on her heel and hurried to the wagon, shocked by that realization.

Logan trudged back into the river to see to his own bath. He'd thought the cold water would ease his raging desire, but touching her body, feeling her reaction to him, seeing her passion, had only deepened his need for her. He ducked his head beneath the water and then soaped up his hair, his back to the wagon. He knelt in the water, felt the current flow over him, curling around his erection.

He drew the soap bar down his chest to his cock. He was in pain, aching for release. He couldn't go to her like this. Never in his life had he broken a promise. He would not break his promise to her. He palmed his shaft, imagining her body against his, her slim arms around his shoulders, her legs spread over his. His hand slipped down his shaft, squeezing, releasing, clamping as her body would do when he took her. He began to slip his fist up and down, faster and faster. He was so close. His thumb circled the crown of his penis, over and over, then fire shot from his balls as his semen burst from him, shooting into the river.

He slumped back on his haunches, dragging deep, calming breaths into his lungs. When the cold water had cooled the fire within him, he finished his bath and returned to the wagon. He pulled on a fresh pair of drawers and collected the jar of salve. The skin tied over the mouth of the jar was saturated with the oil inside and spread the sweet scent of mock orange flowers. He tucked the base of the jar near the embers at the edge of the fire, letting it warm while he shaved and did his teeth.

Sarah lay between the cool cotton sheets. She'd washed them just that morning. They smelled of sunshine and fresh air and moved against her bare skin in unfamiliar ways. She was used to wearing a nightgown to bed, except for the dark months when she wasn't allowed to wear anything at night in Swift Elk's camp. It had been better when he had taken her as a wife, simply because he shared her less frequently with the other warriors. Some nights she'd been able to sleep through without any demands being made upon her person.

The memories flooded her mind, chilled her body, reminding her why she couldn't be intimate with Logan. She couldn't do it. It would hurt.

The wagon shifted as Logan entered. The sun

had dropped below the horizon, but it was still light enough beneath the canvas covering to make out the pale glow of Logan's gray eyes. Sarah swallowed hard and looked away. She gripped the edges of the sheet in a white-knuckled hold. She could do this. Logan wouldn't hurt her. It wouldn't be like before. Just get it over with, she told herself. Tension threaded through her stomach until she feared she would be ill.

She looked at Logan again. He was naked except for his drawers. The terrible bulge between his legs was less pronounced. He held a small clay jar. A sweet, floral scent drifted up to her. It was a pleasant smell that she filled her lungs with.

"I hope you like this salve. Laughs-Like-Water makes several batches a year. The people of her village rely on it to ease their wounds and sore joints." He climbed up to sit on the edge of the bed. "I have warmed it at the fire. Will you trust me to touch you again?"

Sarah studied his icy gray eyes. He had shaved—his face looked a bit less stark. She did trust him. It was her memories she didn't trust. It was as if an invisible wall stood between him and her, as unscalable as a fortress. She nodded.

"Then take the sheet off you."

She hesitated only briefly before drawing the sheet away. She lay back, blanking out her mind, concentrating only on the sweet scent of the oil Logan was pouring into his palm. He sat at the end of the bed and lifted one of her feet. He massaged the oil into the bottom of her foot. She was embar-

rassed to have him touch her scars, but his hands
kneaded and massaged until her tension seemed to
fall away. She looked up at him, meeting his eyes.
He finished with her first foot and started on the
other one.

A breeze blew through the wagon, making a
muted sigh as it caught on the edges of the opening,
stirring the sweet scent of the salve around them.
"Close your eyes. Sleep if you will. You are safe with
me, Sarah Taggert."

She did close her eyes, but only because his look
sent a heat swirling through her that she was not
willing to accept, a heat that told her surrendering
to Logan would be a wonderful experience, that
whispered he was the missing answer to a question
she'd long held.

His hand rubbed the heated oil into her calves,
knees, and thighs, kneading her muscles, melting
her bones. His hands brushed the tops of her
thighs, almost touching her hips. It was all Sarah
could do not to push into his hands. Her reaction
made no sense to her. She hadn't wanted any man's
hands on her like this, not even Eugene's.

Logan tipped the oil jar and poured out a thin
stream of the warm liquid on her belly, drawing a
line from hip to hip. He set his hand on her lower
abdomen, spreading the oil into her skin, moisten-
ing his fingers with it. His face was a mask of con-
centration, but a slight flush gave away the fact that
he wasn't as unaffected as he pretended to be
about what he was doing. He moved a hand up to
her ribs even as his other hand moved the oil into

her feminine curls. He massaged the oils between her legs, letting his hands slip into the folds at her entrance.

She tightened her legs, bringing her knees up defensively. His hands stilled as his eyes sought hers. Slowly, he shook his head, watching her until she'd straightened her legs out once again. He moved his hand from between her thighs, easing the oil up to her ribs, careful to work the healing salve into the old scars of burns, cuts, and lash marks.

He tipped the jar and poured thin streams slowly around one nipple, then the other. A low vibration began somewhere deep inside Sarah, like the beating of distant drums, visceral and rhythmic. His big hands palmed her breasts, pressing, massaging. It was entirely too stimulating. When his thumbs and fingers trapped her nipples, rolling the peaks back and forth, she almost cried out. What was he doing to her? It was torture. It was wonderful. She couldn't take any more. She wanted it to never stop.

Her hands came up to capture his, holding him to her. He smiled, a dark and lazy curving of his mouth, a mouth she suddenly wanted to taste.

It was the oil. It was giving her a madness. A fever. She ached all over. Wanted—something. Not his body. Not to surrender. Never that.

He took her arms and drew them up over her head, capturing her wrists in one hand as he continued his ministrations with his other hand. She stared into his eyes, wondering if he knew what was happening to her. He was leaning on one elbow, his chest so near hers, his heat singed her.

He flattened his hand, rubbing it so just the hard peak of her nipple brushed his palm, back and forth, around and again. Her breath was coming in short gasps. He smoothed his hand over the blue drawing on her chest. He reached over and spilled a bit more oil onto her chest. He rubbed it into her skin, up both sides of her throat, his fingers massaging the base of her neck.

He turned her face to him as he massaged the oil into her jaw, her cheeks, her forehead. "You are beautiful, Sarah." His voice was a raw whisper. Her gaze dropped to his mouth, which hovered so near her own. He grinned. She sensed he knew about the madness stealing through her, closing in around her fear, urging her to reach for him.

"Time to roll over."

Sarah closed her eyes, severing the strange connection she felt between her and Logan. She rolled over, lying still while he repeated the whole process from her feet up. He took great care to ease the oils over her back and shoulders, where old marks discolored her skin. By the time he'd made his way back down to her hands, she doubted she could have formed a coherent sentence.

She heard him set the jar of oil aside. The bed shifted as he stretched out beside her. She pushed herself up. "I should dress."

"No." He looked at her, his thoughts impossible to read. "I want to hold you like this tonight, skin to skin."

She scooted in close to him, resting one of her knees between his. She could feel the press of his erection against her belly, but she gave no sign she was aware of his arousal. He pulled a pillow up under her head. She wrapped an arm around his chest, leaning in to him, hearing his heart beat against her ear.

"How do you feel?"

Sarah heard the rumble of his voice through his chest. "Warm and tingly on the outside. And very, very afraid on the inside."

"Afraid?" He moved so that he could look at her. "Of what?"

"Of losing you. Of needing you. I want to know if this is real, if it will last." *When you'll become like all the other men I've known.*

He smiled a lazy, very male grin. "You'll have to stick around and see. Maybe you can tell me the answer in fifty years or so. Go to sleep now, sweetheart."

It was a long time before sleep claimed her. She kept thinking he would realize he held a naked woman in his arms and assert his marital rights. If that happened, she schooled herself, she would forgive him. He was a kind and gentle man. He was fearless, full of light and love and joy. If he needed her, she would not turn him away. She would not.

Despite her vow of acceptance, she held herself very still, fearing as much as hoping he would bridge the divide she'd set up between them. But he did not. He simply held her, slowly stroking her back. His breathing was even, almost inaudible. She wondered if even in his sleep he still sought to comfort her.

Eventually, her mind surrendered to her fatigue. Sleep twisted her senses. The arms that held her became someone else's. Swift Elk had bartered her yet again in a game of chance. And lost. One of his warriors was pulling her away, forcing her out of the village, over to a slight dip in the prairie, giving them privacy only when they lay on the ground. She didn't fight him, didn't resist. Swift Elk would punish her by letting all of his men have a turn with her. One was better than seven.

He pressed her to the ground, freeing himself from his breechclout, pushing up her dress. She fought the terrible panic, the rising nausea, the need to run. She fought it and lost. She clawed at the muscled arms binding her, raked her nails down his hard chest. She screamed. She screamed and screamed and screamed.

And woke herself up.

She was in a bed, in a wagon. Her attacker was near her, also sitting up, his hands stretched toward her as if he would grab her. She was naked, as he seemed to be. Where was she? The nightmare wouldn't leave her mind. It flashed back and forth until she didn't know which reality was true.

"Easy," the man said. She knew that voice. "Easy." Logan. He didn't touch her. He didn't need to. He was poised to pounce on her. She would never get away. She gulped a deep breath of air.

Logan watched as Sarah blinked at him, watched the last vestiges of the nightmare retreat back into her soul. She was balanced precariously on the edge of the mattress, near the back opening of the wagon. "You're okay, honey. No one's gonna hurt you. No one's gonna make you do something you don't want. We got our agreements, remember?"

He slipped off the bed, into the core of the wagon to find a pair of pants he could pull over his drawers. Holding her bare body, skin to skin, had been hours of torment. His body burned for hers. The pants would at least help cover his raging need. He should never have made her sleep naked. He'd finally given in to the sleep he needed, leaning in to her warmth, resting partly on his stomach, partly on her, one leg between hers. It was heaven. Until she started screaming.

He lifted the chest beneath the bench seat at the table and withdrew a nightgown for her, then fetched another blanket. She sat where he'd left her, the sheet drawn to her chin. She stared at him with wide-open eyes, her gaze dark in the shadowy space of the wagon. "I've brought a nightgown for you. Will you put it on?"

She tucked the sheet beneath her arms and reached for the nightgown. She pulled it over her head, buttoned the sleeves and the front opening, then rose to her knees and drew it down the length of her. Logan fetched a tin cup of water and handed it to her. She held it a moment, staring vacantly at it. Her hand was shaking. She tried to fight off the wave of sorrow that threatened to consume her. She held a hand to her mouth as the sobs came.

"Whoa there." Logan climbed back up to the bed. He set the water aside and pulled her huddled body into his arms. "You just go ahead and cry it out, my sweet wife. Cry as much and as long as you need to. I've got a hold of you, and I'm not letting go." He pretended a bravery he did not feel. Her sobs sliced at his soul even as her tears burned the cuts she'd opened on his chest.

He wished he could undo what had been done to her. An empty wish. How many women who had been taken captives didn't survive their return to white society, their spirits so broken, they couldn't fight off common illnesses. All he could do was show Sarah another path, one filled with love, and stand impotently by while she decided to live or die.

He closed his eyes. This was his fault. He'd pushed too far this evening. Her sobs began to subside, but tension throbbed through her body, tying her to her fear. He lifted her face, smiled down at her as a crazy idea took root in his mind. He swept his thumbs across her wet cheeks.

He eased free of her and slipped off the bed. He grabbed a shirt and pulled it over his head. She frowned at him, looking as disgruntled as a wet kitten. He grinned, then turned from her to keep himself from taking her back into his arms. He fetched his moccasins from the bench trunk where his things and the beadwork he'd purchased from Laughs-Like-Water were stored. He dug through until he found a pair of moccasins that would fit Sarah. "Come outside. Don't change."

A few minutes later, she came around to the back of the wagon. Her stride was hesitant. She looked at him, a worry frown wrinkling her brow.

He smiled. "Sit down," he said, directing her to

one of the two chairs they used when the table was folded down. She did as he ordered. He knelt before her. Lifting her nightgown, he untied her boots and drew on the exquisitely beaded moccasins he'd bought with her in mind.

"Logan, what are you doing?"

"We're going for a run."

"You want to run. Now? At night? Give me back my boots. I'll ruin these."

"These are yours." He looked up at her, his hands on her knees. "Everything I have is yours." He opened her cuffs, folding the fabric back at each wrist. "Open your collar a bit. You'll not like the restriction at your throat."

He stood up, held a hand out to her. "Ready?"

"This doesn't make sense."

"Humor me. Run."

"Where?"

"It doesn't matter. Just run. Go. Feel the night air take away your fears. Run."

He was crazy. That had to be the explanation. She started walking north, deeper into the prairie, letting the bright moon light her way. He walked behind her. Close. Like other times. Other terrible times she'd been taken in the grass. Used. He was behind her.

"Run."

She wanted to run. She wanted to run and run and never stop. She picked up her pace. She couldn't outrun him. Men were built for speed, and he was so close behind her.

"Run, Sarah," he ordered.

And then she did. She lifted her hem and ran. She quit looking at the terrain streaming by her, quit fearing a misstep. Her legs moved fast. The cool night air pulled at her hair, brushed past her neck, stole her breath. Her legs stretched beneath her. She lifted her nightgown high up her thighs. Each step brought her farther from something, closer to something. Freedom. She settled into a steady, swift pace, feeling the muscles of her legs working. She forgot that Logan ran behind her. She lost herself to the run until she ceased to even be aware she ran. It seemed she floated effortlessly through the night, with no tethers, no destination, no worries. Just going. Somewhere. Anywhere.

Logan came even with her. She looked at him and laughed. She stretched her arms wide, lifted her face to the night sky. She never wanted to stop. She lost track of time. She wondered if Logan had been right, if she could surrender her nightmare to the sky and the wind and the night, let her spirit be healed.

She pictured the wind not just slipping over her but through her, filtering out the pieces of her soul that harbored memories of the evil done to her, lifting it away like dust caught on white lace. It was working. She could feel herself growing lighter, easier. She felt fearless, endless. Whole.

Gradually, she became aware of her body growing fatigued. She was hot and thirsty. She slowed to a walk, then doubled over and held her knees. "I can't run anymore."

She straightened and looked at Logan, who had

kept pace with her the entire time. She smiled, panting. "That was amazing. It helped. I feel better inside."

Logan watched her, and there was no humor in his face. "You laughed."

Sarah's stomach tightened. Had she broken a rule? Had she done something wrong?

"It was the most beautiful sound I've ever heard." He looked over her head at the night sky and drew a deep breath. "I thought I would have to wait years before I heard that." He said no more, but started back to the wagon.

She fell into step beside him and reached for his hand. He looked at her. She smiled. "I want to run every day."

"Then we'll run every day. I'll do anything to hear you laugh again." He lifted her hand and kissed her knuckles.

"Will the nightmares end, Logan?"

He drew a long breath and released it slowly. "I don't know. We can't make them end. We can only reach for each other when they come."

"I love you, Logan Taggert."

He stopped, forcing her to stop, too. He drew her close, holding her only by their joined hands. "You love me?"

"I do."

"I cannot live without you, Sarah."

"Nor I you."

He nodded. "Then we will find a way to live." He wrapped an arm about her waist and continued walking. "We'll have a good life, honey. I will give you joy."

"You already have."

The sky was growing light when they reached the wagon. The horses were restless, needing water and feed. "Why don't you go back to sleep?" Logan suggested. "I will see to the horses. We are not in a hurry to get where we are going."

She shook her head. "I will make us breakfast while you see to the horses. Better keep them away from me." She grinned at him. "I'm hungry enough to eat one of them!"

Logan turned away, locking the sight of her teasing smile away in his heart. He heard again her shocking outburst of laughter when they'd run, the purest of sounds. He longed to hear that sound again, to feel the joy she cast on him and the entire world with her arms opened wide.

He began to whistle. Maybe, just maybe, they would survive her injuries.

The long, cooling hours of dusk were giving away to night. Sarah had washed and put away their supper dishes. Logan had seen to the horses. He was preparing for his evening ritual of bathing, brushing his teeth, and shaving. She had already washed her face, brushed her teeth, and was in her nightgown, ready for bed when she went to sit on the fold-down table and watch him shave.

He'd hung a mirror off the side of the wagon and had laid out his grooming items on the table.

He took his suspender straps off his shoulders and dropped them at his sides, then pulled his shirt free. Realizing she was watching him, he grinned at her. "What are you doing?"

She shrugged. "Watching you."

"Why?"

"I like looking at you. I don't think I've known a man as beautiful as you."

He moistened his toothbrush and dipped it into a tin of tooth powder. "Men aren't beautiful. Girls are," he argued, speaking around a mouthful of toothbrush.

She smiled. Folding her legs in front of her, she wrapped her arms about her shins and watched him. "Everywhere we've been, the women found you very pretty indeed."

He spit the concoction in his mouth out and rinsed. "I wouldn't know. I was too busy keeping men away from you."

He drew his shirt over his head. Four angry scrapes were slashed across his chest. More lesions marked his upper arms. "Logan! Good heavens! Look at you. I did that, didn't I? I thought I was dreaming, but it was real."

He set his jaw as she jumped off the table and turned him to see the scratches. She'd fought the warriors who first captured her, fought them mercilessly, slashing at them with her nails, her teeth, her feet. There had been too many. They'd simply held her down for each to take his turn. The man she'd scratched so terribly had wanted to just kill her, bash her head in with the flat side of his tomahawk.

She sent a terrified glance to Logan, waiting for his punishment. She'd backed herself against the side of the wagon. She could easily have slipped from his hold—he was not restraining her. He held her chin, his face bent near hers. He was saying something to her, his words low and soothing.

". . . I will always protect you. You will never be harmed in my care. Hear me, Sarah. I will always protect you. You will never be harmed in my care."

She blinked. He was repeating himself, repeating his vow, murmuring it so that it slipped into her soul, calming the fear, doing battle with her memories. He was Logan. He would not harm her. She had hurt him, but he would never hurt her.

"I'm sorry."

His eyes were unblinking, his gaze fierce. "You were afraid. You did not know what you did."

"I didn't want to hurt you."

He smiled, achingly patient, endlessly calm. "You haven't hurt me. These are just scratches."

"I will get the salve Laughs-Like-Water gave us."

He nodded. "I'll wash first, then you can put it on."

In the wagon, Sarah sank down onto one of the benches, her arms wrapped about her waist as she took a moment to compose herself. She'd lashed out blindly last night, intending to harm, lost in a memory, a thing no more real than an ephemeral thought. What had been was done. It was a situation that no longer existed, one that would never exist again. It had the ability to harm her only through her own mind. She had to be strong. She had to fight her own demons.

When she rejoined Logan, he was halfway through a shave. White foam covered one side of his face. He scraped lines of it off with his straight razor, holding the skin at his neck taut, moving his jaw to give the blade access to his beard. Finished with the shave, he splashed water on his face, then mopped off the extra dots of white with a towel. He cleaned his blade and shaving brush, emptied the water, then put his shaving kit away.

He turned to her. She waited, barely breathing, forcing herself to appear calm. "So, wife, heal me." He set his hands on his hips and grinned down at her. She poured the oil into her palm, savoring the sweet scent that filtered into the air. She rubbed her palms together, warming the oil as she faced him. He had a light feathering of blond hair on his chest—a chest covered in sculpted muscles that tapered from broad shoulders to a narrow waist. She pressed her palms to his skin, over the red slashes. She drew her hands down the marks, moving lightly, careful not to press very hard against his skin.

"More." Logan bent his head to her, his mouth very near her ear. "Use more lotion."

She poured a bit more into her palm, then lifted her hands against his chest. "I am so sorry, Logan." She looked up at him.

He watched her with a hard, steady regard. His pupils were dilated, darkening his pale eyes. "I forgive you," he whispered.

She filled her palm with more oil and started to work on one of his arms. His arms were thickly muscled, so different from her own. He didn't flinch as she eased the lotion into his skin. It felt strange to be touching a man. She poured another measure of oil and worked on his other arm. The heat of his skin warmed the lotion, deepening the sweet fragrance in the air between them. She took her time with his other arm, in no hurry to move away from him.

When she could no longer pretend to be treating his scratches, she moved her hands over to his stomach. Spreading her fingers, she pushed her hands up through his chest hair, feeling the bulges and hollows of his chest until her palms stopped over his heart. Her gaze moved up, over his collarbone, his neck, his jaw. His bottom lip was fascinating, rounder than his upper lip.

"I want to kiss you, Logan."

"Then kiss me."

"I'm afraid I will be ill."

He grinned. "Maybe you will, maybe you won't. Give it a try. See what happens. I won't kiss you back unless you ask me to."

She looked into his eyes, then reached up to wrap her arms around his neck. Lifting herself onto tiptoes, she pulled his head down to hers and did what she'd been longing to do—touch her mouth to his. He did not hold her, did not press against her. He kept his mouth closed, moving ever so slightly in response to the pressure she exerted.

She ran her lips along the soft skin of his newly shaved cheek, then pulled back just enough to focus on his eyes. "I think it would be all right for you to kiss me back."

A smile lit his eyes. "Tell me what you want."

"Hold me."

His hands immediately came up to grip her shoulder blades, his arms banding around her, hard, protecting. He bent toward her, waiting for her to take the lead. She kissed him once, twice.

He growled in frustration. "Honey, let me show you how to kiss your man." He turned his head, setting his mouth across hers. He captured her lips in his, pressing and releasing his way around the entire circumference of her mouth. He opened his mouth. She did as he did, felt his tongue enter her mouth. She reached forward to touch her tongue to his, softness to softness, incredibly intimate. She pressed against him, holding him to her ever more tightly. His hands at her shoulders lifted her as his mouth worked against hers.

She'd never been kissed like this before. It filled her with incredible warmth, heating her from the inside out. She broke the kiss and started it over again; this time she did to him what he'd done to her. He opened himself to her, took what she gave. She sent her tongue into his mouth, searching for his. He met her thrust, passed her tongue, entered her mouth. In and out. Over her tongue, under it. Sliding back and forth.

She was melting inside. She could feel his body's response—his erection pressed against her belly. This was Logan. Her Logan. He would not harm her, would not laugh at her or shame her. What was between them was between only the two of them. She would not be ravaged in front of others.

He broke the kiss. "I think, wife of mine, that if

you don't want nightmares again tonight, we'd best stop with kisses."

She lowered her heels, running her hands down his arms. She flattened her palms against his ribs as she pressed her forehead to his chest and worked on calming her breathing. "Will we run tonight?" she asked after a minute.

"If you like. We can talk all night if you want. We can sleep in each other's arms. We can make love. We can do anything you wish. For the rest of our lives."

She kissed each of the scratches on his chest. "You're a brave man to sleep with me again."

"Honey"—he lifted her chin so that he could see her face—"your demons aren't ready to give up their hold on you. We aren't out of the woods just yet." He brushed the white-blond hair from her face. "But I see the path out even if you don't. I won't leave you in the woods. Just don't let go of my hand."

She took his hand, leading him up into the wagon. "Let's sleep. Then run again in the night."

"Logan," a sweet voice whispered into his dream. "Wake up. It's time to run." He opened his eyes to find Sarah leaning over him, one hand on his chest. He couldn't see much of her expression in the dark. She was wide awake, but still warm from sleep. He smiled as he ran a hand up her arm. Cupping the back of her nape, he drew her to him.

"Now?" he asked, his mouth against hers.

"Now."

"Did you have a bad dream?"

"No. I just want to run."

"Hand me my moccasins. Get yours on."

They climbed out of the wagon, wearing only their underclothes. The cool night air slipped around them. There was a faint hint of light in the eastern sky. It had to be nearly 4 a.m., Logan thought.

"Which way?" he asked Sarah.

She turned her back to the east and walked backward, grinning at Logan. "Toward the sunrise. We'll be the first to see it this morning." She spun on her heel and took off, settling into a comfortable pace. It was easier to run in just her drawers and camisole. She could feel the wind slip over her skin. Neither of them spoke; they just ran in silence, at one with the land and the air and the world around them.

The pale glow at the far horizon deepened, brightened. Logan looked over at Sarah, amazed at her endurance. When light began to penetrate the dark, he could make out the pink color of her cheeks. She'd tied her hair back, but several silky strands pulled free and blew back from her face.

She slowed down, then stopped. He did the same. They were both breathing heavily, steaming into the air around them. The day would be blazing hot, but the nights were still cold, the chill lingering into the morning.

She set her hands on her hips and faced the slowly brightening horizon. Pastel colors washed over the land, tinting her white cotton undergarments in lavenders and pinks. She was something to see. He couldn't stop staring at her. All the fear was gone from her face as she watched so expectantly for a dawn that was still hours away.

What would he give to have her look at him that way? "We should head back."

She looked at him and nodded, but neither of them turned back to the wagon. Instead, she took a step toward him. His body tightened. Heat pooled in his groin at the intent look on her face. His mind told him to turn away, start walking. Desire held him rooted to the spot. She pressed her palms against his ribs. He sucked in a breath. Their run had brought a sheen of sweat to his skin, which the air was now cooling. Her hands were hot against his skin.

He tried to stay still, tried to know her only by scent and not by touch, not by his mouth, not by his skin. He drew her sweet scent into his lungs, locking it inside him until his lungs screamed for more. She stepped closer. He shut his eyes, hiding from the ache that rose from his heart. She leaned forward. He felt her heat. Her lips pressed against his skin. A whisper only. Like butterfly wings. Barely there.

Slowly, slowly, he lifted his hands, afraid to cage her in his grip, afraid she would step away, afraid of how much he needed her. God, his heart was tearing apart. He dragged the tips of his fingers up her back, over the thin cotton of her camisole. He bent his head over the top of hers, encircling her body with his. Had any man ever loved a woman as he loved Sarah?

Her hands moved in a slow stroke up his chest. His dick thickened, growing hard against her belly. There was no way to hide his hunger for her, as close as they stood, wearing as little as they did.

He wished they could stand there forever, tired from their run, waiting for the dawn, safe and happy.

She lifted her face to him. He looked away from the shadows in her eyes. He smoothed the hair from her face. Her skin was impossibly soft, like velvet beneath his fingers. He was vaguely aware of her hands stroking down the length of his sides, over his hips. She moved between their bodies, cupping his heaviness.

He sucked in a breath, his eyes shooting to her face. He'd said she could touch him anywhere, anytime, but this was too soon. She wasn't ready to be intimate. But he couldn't pull back because she was reaching out to him. He couldn't go forward and he couldn't go back, he was stuck on a frozen lake, waiting for the ice to crack beneath them, drowning both of them in the terrible hidden currents of her memories. It was too soon. He was afraid. So goddamned afraid of losing her.

He drew her hands away from his hardening cock and lifted both of them to his mouth, baring her palms so that he could kiss the center of her hands—one, then the other.

"Please. Logan. Let us be together. Now. While I am not afraid. The longer we wait, the more I fear our joining. Let us just get it over with."

"I want to make love to you, Sarah. I don't just

want intercourse. I don't want a simple joining. I want you to feel what I feel for you. I am in no hurry."

"Please. You need me. Let me give you ease. Let me do what I can to help you."

He shook his head, aching to accept what she offered. "I am not so selfish that I would take you while you still fear me." He bent forward, burying his face in her neck, hungry to feel her skin against his face, to smell her scent, to taste the salt on her skin.

"Logan, help me to get through this. Make me your wife."

His arms tightened around her. One hand slipped under her long braid, cupping the back of her head. He kissed his way up the column of her neck to the corner of her jaw. He nuzzled her cheek, finding a path to her lips. He kissed the corner of her mouth.

There were too many shadows standing between them. Perhaps she was right in wanting their first coupling behind them, so that she would know there was nothing to fear and much to enjoy. It was a good plan. Logical. Humbling in the trust she placed in him. But his desire for her was utterly combustible, like a spark catching in a grain silo. His hand shook with the restraint of his will. This first time had to be for her pleasure alone. He would have to be more careful with her than if it was her very first time.

He bent his forehead to hers as his hands moved to her shoulders. He could feel her breath on his mouth, fast and shallow, pumping her fear and excitement over his soul. He drew a deep breath, then released it slowly. Again. Again. He willed her breathing to match his own slower rhythm as his hands slowly eased down her arms to catch her hands.

Pulling them out to their sides, he drew back to look at her, his beautiful wife. She stood before him, washed in the early morning light, ethereal. He wondered if he let go of her hands, would she disappear?

He leaned back as he started walking in a slow circle, pulling her around with him, wanting to spin away the threads of fear that clung to her. He stepped faster, grinning when she sent him a questioning glance. Faster. Her braid swung free. She laughed, like music spilling into the night. He could live on that sound. Around and around they went.

"Stop! I can't take anymore!" she begged. He drew her close, falling to the ground with her on top. The world continued to spin around them. She laughed and buried her face in his throat, gripping a fistful of his hair. He put his nose in her hair and drew a deep breath. He kissed her temple, the corner of her eye, her cheekbone, the soft skin beside her ear.

He drew her up his body, dragging her against his erection. He felt the wave of tension that rippled through her. He moved his legs between hers so that she straddled him. The weight of her body on his cock excited him, sending hot blood to his groin. He ached to join their bodies. He moved his cock against the cradle of her hips.

She stiffened as she lay against him. Bracing an arm on his chest, she pushed herself up. He lifted his knees, giving her a backrest to lean against. Her eyes were enormous pools of dark worry. He sat up. Cupping her chin, he kissed her closed mouth as his hand came up to cover her breast. She drew a shocked breath. He felt the pull of air against his mouth. His cock tightened, rocked against her sensitive core.

He kissed her chin, the space between her chin and lip, then took her mouth again, twisting his head when she opened to him, hungry to taste her. His tongue found hers, warm and wet. He groaned into her mouth, unable to stop the sound as his body quickened around hers. He broke the kiss, then matched his lips to hers once again. He moved his head in the other direction and took her mouth from a new angle.

Her nipple pebbled against his palm. He cupped both breasts, letting his fingers play with the hardened peaks. Her fingers on his shoulders gripped and released him as she arched against his hands.

His jaw opened, leading hers to do the same. Their lips barely touching, their tongues danced and played, rising, pushing, sliding against each other.

He broke the kiss to press his mouth against the corner of her jaw, the soft skin beneath her chin, the side of her throat. His hands shook as he lifted them to the buttons of her camisole. When he released the last one, he looked at her as he parted the fabric, baring her breasts.

His gaze dropped to the twin mounds, shockingly luscious on her slim frame. He sucked in a sharp breath. Her hands tightened on his shoulders, the pressure from her thumbs stiffening, warning of her tension.

Taking hold of her waist, he lifted her body toward his mouth. He nuzzled the side of one breast, his beard scraping against her sensitive skin as he pushed against the heavy mound. Her nipple peaked even tighter, aching for his touch. He ignored its thrust toward his face, turning his attentions instead to her other breast, kissing the soft flesh, lifting its weight against his face.

A groan slipped past his mouth as he sucked the softness of her breast. She knelt before him now, bearing her own weight, freeing his hands to take hold of her breasts. She watched everything he did, her hands now pulling him closer. He lifted her breasts, careful not to touch her nipples, knowing she ached for him to do that very thing. His thumb and forefinger tightened around the base of her nipple, pointing it toward his face. Her nostrils flared, her face tightened with anticipation. She gasped as his tongue flicked out to stroke her nipple.

Her thumbs were no longer pushing against him. She was pulling him closer. Logan covered her nipple with his hot mouth. Her hips bucked against him, pressing against his cock. He swirled his tongue over her taut peak, then sucked hard, gripping her other nipple between his thumb and forefinger, doubling her pleasure.

He switched his attentions to her other breast, freeing his hand to move down her belly, lower to her mound, where the fabric of her drawers kept his hand from her soft skin. He ground the heel of his palm against her clitoris, gently, the pressure there and gone, there and gone. She pushed against his hand. His fingers found the opening in her drawers. He slipped a finger beneath the fabric, stroking over the folds of her sex, between them. She was wet, ready for him. He moved two fingers through her slick folds, letting his thumb massage the hardening nub, knowing from her body's involuntary movements he was giving her extreme pleasure.

His fingers slipped into her opening. Her eyes grabbed at his, fear chilling the heat that had flooded them seconds earlier. The shadows swirled like living entities between them, a fog of memories that were as real to her as she was to him. He knew she was leaving him, pulling back into her memories.

"Sarah, look at me." She blinked, focused on his face. "Say my name."

Her eyes on his, she reached between their bodies, her fingers finding the hard length of him.

"Say my name. Do it now," he ordered.

Tears pooled in her eyes.

He caught her face in his hands as she loosened the tie of his drawers and freed him. "Say my goddamned name, Sarah. I am your husband. I am the *only* one who will know your body, the only one who has ever known your body. Others have taken what you *give* to me. They never knew you as I will. I will keep you safe. I will honor you with my life, my love. I will never, never harm you."

"Logan." The sound broke from her mouth as she speared herself on his penis.

God, she was tight, slick, a sheath made just for him. His hips bucked up against her in an involuntary movement. All expression slipped from her face. It was as if she just got up and left, leaving her body still joined to his. She pushed up and down, faster and faster, the movements learned, practiced, impersonal. *Mechanical.*

A chill washed over him. She was no longer aware of him, of their union. She was doing what she'd learned to do, moving her body in a way that drew an answering response in his. She was fucking the demons in her head, not making love to him.

His body cooled. The breeze blew against the tears on his cheeks. He didn't know what to do. He didn't want her to be absent from their coupling. Ever. She was fragile. He couldn't criticize her. This was how she'd survived. Leaving herself, separating her mind from her body.

He took hold of her hips, keeping her absolutely still until she opened her eyes and looked at him. He wasn't entirely certain she saw him.

"Who am I?" he asked the shell of his wife. She tried to move her hips. His cock throbbed, buried to his balls in her hot sheath. He would not let her move. "Who am I, Sarah?"

"Logan." Her voice was barely a whisper.

Still holding her immobile, he pumped into her. "Again. Say it again." He lifted her just slightly, enough that he could push into and out of her.

"Logan."

He lurched into her. "I am your husband. The man who loves you above all else. Say it. Know it."

Her chin trembled. "You are my husband. You love me."

He would not let her move, even as his cock filled her, bumping against her womb, gently, tenderly, his eyes locked on hers. "I love your body. I love your soul. I love your mind. I love everything that you are. You are mine, Sarah Taggert, mine and no other's. I will not share you. I will honor you with my life, my body, my love. Do you hear my words? Do you understand what I am saying?"

She blinked, freeing the tears to wash down her cheeks and splash onto his chest. She nodded.

He wept as his body took hers. "Who am I?"

"Logan."

"Who are you?"

"Sarah. I am Sarah Worthington Hawkins Yellow Moon Taggert."

He smiled. He nodded. "You are everything to me. Everything. Say it."

A sob broke free. "I am everything to you."

"Everything," he growled.

"I am everything to you."

"Look at me."

"I am."

"Don't take your eyes away from me. I am making love to you. I worship your body. I pay homage with mine." He thumbed her sensitive nub as he pushed the hard length of him into and out of her, his release so close to breaking free. But he would not take his pleasure before giving Sarah her release.

"Logan!" Sarah's body gripped his, moving in

ever greater waves, squeezing around his shaft. She gasped, fighting the impending onslaught.

"Look at me, Sarah. See me. Love me. Let yourself go." He thrust into her as she pushed down on top of him, grinding forward and back. He couldn't hold out much longer. "Let go. I'm begging you," he said, his teeth clenched. "Now." He lifted her hips, increasing her tempo, slamming into her.

Her eyes widened even as her body convulsed around his cock. He ground her hips forward, rubbing her clitoris against him. Her nails cut into him and released, like a cat's claws. His orgasm broke free, a wash of energy that drained every ounce of strength from him and poured it into her in hot, sluicing jets.

When their passion eased, they slumped back to the ground. She buried her face in his neck. And the sobs came. Cleansing her. Brutalizing him. His arms tightened around her. He moved his legs outside hers, cocooning her with his body, his warmth. His love.

Minutes later, he felt Sarah pull a long, ragged breath, bringing an end to her tears. She lifted herself off him, but sat in the space between his thighs. He sat up, watching her. He brushed a tear from her face.

"How will we get through this?"

He smiled, a slow, comforting lift of his lips. "You just said it. We will get through this. Together. One step at a time. One day at a time. One memory at a time. I will not leave you in the darkness. And if it takes you, I will find you."

She stared at him, measuring his words. At last, she nodded. Swiping at the moisture on her cheeks, she buttoned her camisole. He stood up and helped her to her feet. She cupped his face, her thumbs brushing the lingering moisture from his cheeks. Wrapping her arms around him, she pressed her ear to his chest. "I love you, Logan Taggert."

He pulled her even tighter against himself. "That, darlin', is worth everything to me."

They walked hand in hand back to the wagon. The eastern horizon was growing bright, casting enough light around the flat prairie that they could see the Indians crawling through their camp.

Chapter 13

The white canvas covering the wagon jumped and swayed as someone inside rustled through their things. A man stood by the horses, working at loosening them from the corral ties. Another prowled around the wagon. One man knelt on the front seat of the wagon, bent over the back of the bench.

Sarah sucked in a sharp breath, fear making her entire body rigid. Neither she nor Logan had any weapons. They were nearly naked and terribly outnumbered.

They would be killed.

She looked around, wildly searching for a place to hide. They were miles from a creek or river. There was nothing taller than the sweetgrass around them.

She pulled on Logan's hand. "We must run."

He held firm, his eyes never leaving the men who moved through their camp. "They have seen us."

Sarah glanced at their camp. The man on the front bench stood up to get a better look at them walking into certain death at the hands of Sioux warriors.

"Ghosts! Ghosts come!" the warrior shouted, pointing their way. He jumped from the wagon to the ground, hurrying to alert the others. There was much shouting and confusion. An argument broke out. Logan and Sarah continued to approach their camp, arriving with the dawn. Logan knew they presented a frightening spectacle, with their pale skin, white clothes, blond hair—they would appear nearly colorless to the dark warriors. It was the only advantage they had.

"Do not falter. Do not stop."

"Please, Logan. They will kill us."

"There is nowhere to hide. I cannot leave you here. They would steal you away or just cut you down. Stay with me. When we get to the wagon, I will angle you closer to it. Get under it and stay put. Trust me, honey. I've been in worse situations and lived to tell."

Two of the braves jumped on their horses and rode away. That left three. Three were odds he could take.

"Oh, God. Oh, God, Logan. That's Swift Elk," Sarah gasped. Had Logan not been holding her hand so firmly, she would have bolted. "He will kill us. He is ruthless and crazy."

She looked up at Logan and saw him smile. "He is welcome to try. I would enjoy the challenge."

The two other warriors flanked Swift Elk as she and Logan walked into camp. Sarah stepped behind Logan, terrified to face the men who had subjected her to months of abuse. Memories of those days swamped her mind. She'd been beaten for every infraction, for not appearing to enjoy being raped by several men each night, for not rising early enough to begin chores with the women, for not knowing their language, for seeking food. For running when it all became too much.

She recognized each of the men before them, had known them in the most intimate ways. Even with her eyes shut, she could hear their laughter as they forced their way into her body, making it a sport for the others to see.

"Swift Elk. I was not expecting a visit from you," Logan broke the silence, speaking in Sioux. "I sent Cloud Walker to you with a dozen of my best horses. Were they acceptable as a bride price?"

"Yes. I have not come for the woman."

"Why then?"

"To kill the whites who drive this wagon. If it is yours, then you will die this day."

Logan nodded. He glanced at the sky, which promised to be a brilliant, cloudless blue once the sun rose. "It is a good day to die. I have heard many stories of your exploits. You are known among your people as a brave and courageous warrior."

"I am."

"A warrior who follows the path of truth."

"You would use words against me, Shadow Wolf," Swift Elk answered, his eyes narrowing.

"I have bought my wife's freedom. If you kill her or dishonor her, all that you are, all that you have been is a lie."

"I told you I have accepted the bride price."

Logan nodded. "You have said that you come to kill me. I will meet your challenge. But if I lose, my wife is to be given her clothes, supplies, a weapon, and a horse so that she may survive the journey to my people. She is not to be touched by you or your men. Do you accept these terms?"

Swift Elk's men looked at him. He nodded.

"Then let her prepare herself before we begin. Sarah, saddle a horse. Dress. Pack the supplies you need. Go to my father's house."

"I am not leaving you."

Logan did not look away from the men. "You will do as I say."

"Logan—"

"Now, Sarah," Logan ordered, his voice implacable.

She went to the corral line and retrieved the pony Cloud Walker had given her. Logan was pleased with her compliance. He had a plan, but he needed her to do everything he asked as he asked it, without hesitation.

"While my wife prepares to leave, I would ask you to have a meal with me. I am not your enemy, Swift Elk."

"All whites are my enemies." He dismissed that argument with an angry wave of his hand. "Your kind washes over this land, killing my people, poisoning my waters, killing our buffalo. You are a disease. You must be ended."

Logan nodded. "I do not disagree about the damage we have caused, but we can't be ended. There are too many of us and too few of you. You can kill me, but ten more will come, and ten more for each of them."

"I can make you bleed. I can cut out your hearts and turn you away from our lands."

"If you use our women and children to wound us, you harm yourselves. It makes our men angrier than ever."

"We do to your women what your men do to our women. None of us have forgotten what happened at Sand Creek. You tell us to make peace, yet you kill our men, make prostitutes of our women, take our horses and weapons. There is no honor in your people. Your men do not fight to protect your women and families. They fight to make a road to the yellow rocks in our northern rivers. You are soulless demons and must be destroyed."

"I am a man, not a demon, a friend to your people. I love my wife as you love yours. I will fight to protect what is mine even as I have fought to protect your people."

Swift Elk grunted. "I am hungry. You will feed us." He folded his legs and sat by the cold campfire. His two companions did the same. Logan went to the end of the wagon and took down the table. He drew out a sack of coffee beans, some sugar, and mixings for biscuits, keeping an eye on Swift Elk and his men, an ear trained on Sarah as she saddled her horse, and all the rest of his senses focused on the wide prairie behind his back.

His pistol was in the crevice between the mattress and the table board. The Indians who had climbed through the wagon hadn't found it before running off. It was at just an angle that the men seated on the ground could not see it.

Stalling for time, he'd put some flour into a bowl, then dug through the drawers and cabinets for a few ingredients, using the distraction as a cover for withdrawing a couple of knives from the cutlery drawer. The wagon made a small motion. Someone was still inside it. Sarah returned with her mount.

"Tie him to the wheel," Logan directed in English, his focus apparently on his task. "Be ready to get under the wagon," he said, under his breath. "Stay close to this side. There are more inside the wagon. Make an argument with me. Now."

"I'm not leaving you." Sarah spoke in a loud voice, waving her hands as if angry. "I will do the cooking. Look at the mess you're making!" She palmed a knife, keeping her hand where it could not be seen by the three men seated around the cold campfire.

The horse's whicker was the only warning they had. One moment, Sarah was standing next to him, the next she was being pulled back away from the table, a tawny arm about her middle, a hatchet raised over her.

Logan went for his pistol just as the man who'd been hiding in the wagon did the same. Logan stabbed the hand, twisting the knife left and right, pinning the warrior to the mattress frame while he grabbed the pistol.

In a flash, there was no room to fight—the three from across the camp leapt over or ran around the table, screaming war cries that sounded as if the Earth had opened up and released all of hell's demons.

Before they closed in on him, Logan shot a glance toward Sarah. She stabbed blindly into the abdomen of the man holding her. Once. Twice. He screamed at her and shoved her to the ground. Logan whipped his knife at the Sioux, slicing right into his jugular. He fell on top of Sarah in a bloody wash.

Two men grabbed Logan and tried to draw him away from the table. He kicked sideways and down at the knee of one of them, then spun with the other, trying to keep him from the knives. A strange whining sound cut the air. The man he fought grunted, arched his back, and looked at Logan with a shocked expression.

Logan slipped beneath the table. He kicked out the folding table's one supporting leg, letting the wood collapse, offering Sarah a small amount of cover. He shoved his pistol at her and ordered her to shoot the incoming riders—the two warriors who had ridden away when he and Sarah were walking to the camp. As he rolled out from the opposite side of the wagon, two warriors jumped on top of him. One slashed down with his war club, embedding it in the ground, missing Logan's head by a hairbreadth. The other wrapped his hands around Logan's neck and began squeezing.

Logan thumbed the warrior's eye sockets, digging hard until he pulled back. He kicked out at the second man, sweeping his legs out from under him, elbowing his throat as he fell. He rolled over him, grappling for his war club.

For each man he put down, another got up, until it seemed he fought a hundred men, not half a dozen. Logan's hands and body were slick with blood. Gunfire erupted from beneath the wagon. Sarah's pony screamed and bucked. She fired again. Logan shot a glance at Sarah, saw her struggling beneath a dark warrior, pushing at his chin, bucking against him. The man was trying to drag her out from beneath the wagon.

Logan's ribs were being crushed in the deadly hold of an Indian who stood behind him. Logan slammed his head back, connecting with bone. The man staggered back, his arms flying wide. Logan snatched his hatchet from him and crashed it into the man's skull. One of the other warriors, whose knee was broken, drew his arm back to throw his hatchet, but Logan was quicker. He threw the hatchet he held and struck the man dead center in his chest.

The warrior struggling with Sarah now had her most of the way out from under the wagon. Logan grabbed his shoulders. His fingers slipped, fatigue weakening his grip. The man turned around. *Swift Elk.* Logan threaded his fingers together and swung his doubled fist at the man who had destroyed Sarah's life. Following him to the ground, Logan grabbed his hair and banged his head against the hard dirt. Over and over.

"Stop. Logan. Stop." A hand touched his arm. He shrugged free of it. Swift Elk wasn't fighting him anymore.

"Leave him. It's over."

Sarah's words echoed in Logan's battle-hazed mind, made all the louder because of the silence surrounding them, when only moments before there had been gunshots, shouting warriors, screaming horses. Still gripping fistfuls of Swift Elk's hair, Logan ceased trying to bash his head in. He glanced around the campground, littered now with bodies. He drew a ragged breath.

"Finish it," Swift Elk ordered, glaring at Logan.

"No. Don't, Logan. These men have wives, children, elders in Swift Elk's village. They need to know what happened here. His people will make him answer for what his actions have wrought. Leave him alive to take their dead home."

"Kill me," the grizzled warrior demanded.

Logan shook his head and pulled back.

"I will come after Yellow Moon."

"No, you won't."

"My people will."

"I am not an enemy of your people."

"You are now." A breath left his chest on a slow hiss. "We both are." His black gaze was steady, almost gleeful now. "Her first husband still lives. I took ten horses in payment for the raid I made last year."

Logan heard Sarah's gasp. Rage, swift and terrible, blackened Logan's mind. This devil was intent on seeking to harm Sarah any way possible. He pressed a knee to Swift Elk's shoulder and took hold of his head, intending to snap his neck. Sarah grabbed his wrist in a flash of movement.

"No. It is not possible. Eugene would never have put the two of us in such danger. He was greedy, yes, but he wasn't bloodthirsty."

Swift Elk looked at her. "He lives still."

"He died in that raid. Our neighbors buried him," Sarah argued.

"Your husband killed my brother in that raid. For that, I scalped him. It was my brother you buried, not your husband."

"He isn't alive!" Sarah grabbed his arm and shook him.

Swift Elk laughed. "How do you think we knew where you were today?"

Sarah released him as if his skin burned her. She clasped her hands to her ears, blocking out the sound of his terrible laughter. Logan cursed, silencing him with a hard punch to his temple. Sarah stared at him blankly, her features frozen in a look of horror.

He pulled a hand away from her ear, knowing he had to intercept the shock that was rapidly claiming her. "Saddle my horse, then bring the wagon team over. Do it now."

He took a length of rope from a coil hanging on the side of the wagon and tied Swift Elk's hands to his feet, behind his back. There were enough weapons lying scattered around that he knew it wouldn't hold the warrior long once he regained consciousness.

Logan had to get Sarah to safety. He looked around at the battlefield, seeing that none of Swift Elk's men moved. He doubted any survived. It was a terrible waste, a terrible loss for the Sioux people. He feared Swift Elk's prediction that Logan was now an enemy of the Sioux people would in fact prove true.

He climbed into the wagon, making sure no other warriors hid there. The small space looked like a hurricane had come through it. Drawers were opened and empty. The bench trunks were opened, their contents strewn about. The table was overset, the mattress pushed aside.

Very little was thrown out of the wagon—they weren't raiding the wagon's supplies. The men had been looking for something.

The papers Sarah had given Sheriff Declan. Goddamn it. Swift Elk was right. Her bastard husband still lived.

He put away the fold-down table, stowing the broken leg to be fixed later. Sarah brought the horses up in pairs. She secured his pony as he hooked the team to the wagon. They broke camp quickly, heading south. Outside of Defiance, there was a thin trail that led north. He would turn there and make his way up to the Circle Bar. As soon as he had Sarah settled, he would go after Eugene.

Sarah climbed over the wagon bench, intent on retrieving some bandages so that she could at least cover the knife wounds on Logan's arm. She brought back a bowl of water and a cloth and set to work on his injuries.

"Leave it. We'll clean up at the river in a little bit."

"No. You will have a nasty infection starting by then, with all this trail dirt." She washed his arm as best she could, then wound a bandage around it. She would need to stitch it, she was certain. He had bruises all over his chest, jaw, and temple. He looked as if he'd been run over by a wagon. She fetched a shirt for him, insisting he draw it on to cover the rest of his cuts and scrapes.

"Where are we headed?" she asked as she settled next to him once more.

"To my father's ranch."

She focused on the land passing by, listened to the clatter of the horses' swift trot. "Do you believe him? Do you think Eugene's still alive?" she asked. Logan didn't turn to look at her, didn't immediately answer. She caught the tension that washed over his profile.

"I do."

Tension slashed through her. She wrapped her arms about her middle, chilled suddenly. "You don't seem surprised."

"I'm not."

"If it's true, we're not married."

He did look at her then, a long glance, his eyes implacable. "We are married. You are my wife. There is no turning back."

"But if he lives—"

"Then you will divorce him. And I will find him and turn him over to the law. He will answer for his crimes."

"Logan, you have to let me go. He will kill you, kill everyone you love. Please don't take me to your family. I will only endanger them."

He switched the reins to his other hand and drew her close, pulling her in tight against his body. "Honey, my father and brother and his father-in-law have all learned to deal with the hard edge of life. I have every confidence in their ability to keep you—and themselves—safe. If I don't go after Eugene, he will keep hurting people. The best way to make us all safe is to take care of him, and fast."

She folded her legs and leaned her thigh against his as she snuggled in close to him. "I'm sorry, Logan."

"You are my everything. You've got nothing to apologize for. We're gonna be just fine. You'll see." He pressed his face against the top of her head, drawing her scent into his lungs. "You were brave today."

She nodded against his chest. "I wish the nightmare were over."

"It will be soon."

The sun was high overhead when they drew up by the river. While Logan saw to the horses, she collected a change of clothes for them, some medical supplies, soap, and a couple of towels.

He joined her at the river's edge. He shucked his shirt, then unraveled the bandage from his upper arm, leaving both in a pile at the bank. The warm June sun beat down on them. Grasshoppers snapped and jumped in the surrounding field. The horses, tied to a corral line beneath a row of cottonwoods, were quietly enjoying a bit of shade and the rich grass that grew there.

For a moment, neither of them moved, neither spoke. Sarah looked up into Logan's face, struggling to understand how she'd had the good fortune to have him come into her life. His gray eyes watched her, giving away nothing of his thoughts.

"I have cost you everything. Because of me, you've become an enemy of the Sioux."

"You have cost me nothing. We were attacked. The Sioux are a fair people. They know Swift Elk was a liability—every bit as much as he was once a worthy warrior in their fight against white settlers. They will mourn the loss of his men, without a doubt. But we did not provoke him. He took payment from Eugene to attack you yet again. He dishonored his people."

"That isn't what he will tell the others."

"They will hear the truth, Sarah, and will judge me accordingly." He looked at her tattered undergarments. "I am more worried about you. You faced the demons you still hold in your thoughts. You fought them."

Sarah cast her eyes down. She stood silently for a long moment. "It won't take away my scars." She met his eyes. "It won't undo what happened. But at least now I know they can't do to another woman what they did to me. That I like."

Logan reached forward and started unbuttoning her camisole. The cloth wasn't even fit to be a rag. He needn't have taken care removing it, except that he didn't want to traumatize her by ripping it off her. When he reached the last button, he looked at her. "I need to see you. I need to feel your skin. I need to know you are unharmed." She nodded, giving him permission to remove it. The sun on her bare skin felt cleansing. Drawing in a deep breath, she arched her back. Logan untied the drawstring of her drawers and pushed them down her hips.

He stood back and looked at her. Taking her hand, he turned her in a full circle. When she faced him again, he touched the soft side of her neck where bruises were beginning to appear. He drew his hand down, over her collarbone, to the tattoo on her chest. When he pulled away to remove his own drawers, she felt the loss of his touch.

He lifted her chin, forcing her eyes to meet his. "There is one devil left. Only one. I will make an end of him, too."

She nodded. He took her into the river. The water closed over their feet, calves, knees. The current was swift, pulling against them, rushing downstream. They knelt close to the riverbank, sinking to their chests in the water. Logan held her waist. "Lean back. Wet your hair."

She did as he asked. The water rushed between her breasts, swirled past her neck, pulled her hair into the current. He drew her upright. Reaching for the soap, which he'd left on a rock nearby, he rubbed the soap into her scalp, checking her for injuries as he did so.

He wanted to linger with her, here in the cold water with the hot wind and the blazing sun, but they were in danger yet. Not from Swift Elk. But if another party of Sioux came across the battlefield and then ran into the two of them, the warriors would not stop to listen to their side of the confrontation.

He made short work washing off the morning's dirt and blood from her. When she took the soap from him and began returning the favor, it was all he could do not to pull her onto his lap. He watched her hands move over his skin. She paused at each bruise, leaning forward to kiss him. Dozens of scratches and cuts were scattered across his torso, back, and arms. She washed his face gently, moving carefully over the gouge on his forehead.

Logan knelt before her. He moved his hands up her legs, over her hips, to hold her ribs as he drew her body against his. "Have mercy on me, woman."

Sarah wrapped her arms around his neck, pressing her breasts into Logan's broad chest, feeling the water lap at their sides. "I will go get the bandages ready."

He kissed her temple, moving his lips against her skin to the corner of her eye. He took the soap from her hand and set her free.

Chapter 14

Heat radiated in waves off the hard ground, fanned around Sarah and Logan by the hot wind. They were coming down to the Circle Bar from the northeast, riding into the lowering sun. The horses moved slowly, their heads drooping in the blistering temperature. They'd kept up a brisk pace for two days, and now, in the late afternoon of the third day, they were nearly played out.

Logan took off his hat and waved it in response to a distant outrider who was doing the same. Sarah watched his dust trail as he sped off over a ridge. Logan looked at her. "My father's been watching for us."

Their wagon rose up over a ridge of sage and short prairie grass. When they crested the peak, a wide valley opened before them, verdant fields with rich grasses. White, yellow, and red wildflowers dotted the land, glistening in the sun. The dark shapes of grazing cattle spread farther than the eye could see. Far to the west, the foothills of the Medicine Bow

Mountains rose in waves to distant peaks that still held veins of snow cover.

"Logan! This is your home?"

"Nope. It belongs to my father and brother— well, stepfather and stepbrother."

"It's beautiful."

"It is."

They turned onto a well-used road that cut through the pastures. The space was so large, so wide open, that it was difficult to judge how big it was. More than an hour passed before they crested another ridge and overlooked the heart of the ranch. A long, low building sat on the far outskirts of the compound. A wide barn stood next to it, amid several corrals. A few other buildings dotted the area.

In the center of the compound was a large, white house. A deep porch wrapped around the front and one side of the house, shading tall windows. Intricate fretwork softened the corners between the porch roof and the tall columns supporting it. A second story boasted several dormer windows. The grounds surrounding the house were green and edged with lush bushes and flower beds.

The Circle Bar was a paradise. This was the heaven her father had sought. This was her parents' dream.

She sat straighter on the bench. Removing Logan's old hat, she checked her braid, tucking a few errant strands of hair back into the weave. She tucked her shirt in. She was about to stuff her hands back into her gloves, when Logan reached over and took hold of her hand. She flashed him a look.

He shook his head. "You've no need to hide with my family."

"Do I look all right, Logan?"

He smiled at her. The shadows in his eyes had deepened over the last two days, increasing her nerves. "You look beautiful. You look like what you are, honey. My everything."

She swallowed hard. Settling her hat back on her head, she faced forward, ready for what would come.

Logan drew up in front of the house. He wasn't sure what kind of reception to expect. Over the last twelve years, he'd only been home one summer, and that was eight years ago. He helped Sarah down from the bench, and turned to see his brother and stepfather waiting for him on the wide front porch.

Whatever he'd been expecting, it wasn't the wall of tension that met him as he walked up the porch steps. He drew Sarah slightly behind him. Stepping into the shade of the porch, he dropped his hat off the back of his head. He moved forward enough to let Sarah up the last step. But there he waited.

Sid Taggert, his stepfather, gave him a sad smile, volumes in his eyes left unspoken. His brother, Sager, shook his head and muttered a curse. Logan knew what they were seeing. A savage gash in his forehead, scabbed over, the flesh around it swollen and discolored. The purple, fist-sized bruise on his chin. A tear by the side of his lip that he kept from reopening only by not opening his mouth very far. His neck ringed by a dark bruise.

His dad came forward first. He made a tentative

movement with his hands as if to indicate he'd welcome a hug. Sid had rarely been demonstrative in Logan's youth. Logan had always been conscious that he wasn't the real son. He was a poor substitute for Sager, and everyone knew it. Sid hugged him. Logan held still. It was far too little, far too late.

When Sid pulled back, Sager was there. He clasped his shoulder and gave another shake of his head.

"You must be Logan's wife. I'm Sid. Welcome to the Circle Bar." Sid held out his hand to Sarah. Logan couldn't help stepping nearer to her, curving an arm around her shoulders.

Sager shook hands with her after Sid. He noticed the marks on her hand and looked into her eyes. Like that, it seemed, he knew everything there was to know about her. She felt tears well up, blurring her vision.

"What the hell happened to you, little brother?"

"We crossed paths with Swift Elk and his band."

"And you lived?"

"*We* lived. They didn't fare so well." He looked from his brother to his father, bracing himself for their reaction to the request he was about to make. "I need help."

Sid nodded, his lips compressed into a thin line. "I know you do. Your problem got here ahead of you."

A movement behind them by the front door should have caught his attention, but Logan was too focused on what Sid had just said.

"Sarah, darling! At last, I've found you!"

Sarah cried out. Logan caught her up against

himself, worried she'd step back and fall down the stairs.

"That's far enough, Mr. Hawkins." Sager intercepted him. "We asked you to wait inside."

Logan got a good look at the man who had been Sarah's first husband. He was tall and had a hawkish face. Dark sideburns drew Logan's gaze from the patchy blotches of hair at the upper sides of his head. Usually when men went bald, their heads were smooth and bare. Not Eugene's. An uneven texture of scar tissue, pink and knotted, covered the top of his head. His scalping wound.

"What the hell is he doing here?" Logan growled, shifting so that Sarah was now fully behind him.

"I've come for my wife, of course. She left before I could get to Fort Buford. Captain Frasier helpfully suggested I might find her in Defiance. Alas, in Defiance, they told me she'd married you and was headed up this way."

Logan smiled and pushed his way between Sager and Sid, each stalking stride taking him closer and closer to the one remaining demon haunting Sarah. "I'm glad they did. Saves me the trouble of hunting you down."

Eugene backed up. "I don't understand. I'm not here for trouble. I just want to collect my wife and leave."

"Sarah's not going anywhere. When I'm finished with you, if you're still alive, I'll take you to Defiance so that you can end your days at the bottom of a rope. But first, you've got some atoning to do."

"What are you talking about? I have nothing to atone for. My life's been hell since the attack."

Logan laughed. "I'll bet. But not like the hell you put your wife through. The scalping was painful, but not career ending. With Sarah gone, you were still able to close the deal on the illegal land deeds you were processing. You see, Swift Elk got real talkative toward the end of our visit a few days ago. He said you paid him, not once but twice to attack her—first at your homestead, then just this week.

"So here's how it's gonna go. I'm gonna do to you what you had done to your wife. I'm going to strip you naked, then ram a stick up your ass about a hundred times so that you know what it's like being gang-raped by a band of vengeful warriors. Then I'm going to starve you. And beat you. And then I will burn the soles of your feet so that you can't run. By that time, you'll be begging for a bullet. But I won't waste the gunpowder on you. Not when there's a rope with your name on it waitin' in Cheyenne."

Eugene huffed a nervous cough, looking around at the impassive faces of the ranch hands who had gathered in a semicircle around the porch. "I'm not the law breaker here. You're the bigamist. You are the one who will rot in jail."

Logan's hand lashed out fast, catching a fistful of Eugene's Adam's apple, slamming him back against the doorjamb. "The whole world thinks you're dead, Hawkins. No one will mourn your real death."

"I can't argue with that," a new voice spoke up from the crowd gathered below. Sheriff Declan was making his way toward the porch steps. "But it ain't the way this is gonna play out, Taggert."

Logan, still heavily in the grip of rage, turned to

look for the sheriff. The bastard who had destroyed Sarah's life was in his hands. He could end it now. He searched out Sarah. She stood behind Sid and Sager, almost completely blocked by their shoulders. Her hands shielded her face. Logan's heart ripped in half.

He growled a sound of rage from between clenched teeth. Still holding Eugene by the throat, he shoved him over to the railing. He slammed his fist into Eugene's jaw. The force of the blow took him over the railing to land facedown at Declan's feet. "He's all yours, Sheriff."

"Sid, you got a place I can lock him up for the night?" Sheriff Declan asked. "I'll take him down to Cheyenne in the morning."

Sid directed a couple of his men to carry Eugene to the stable, where he could be locked in a stall. Sager and Sid stepped aside so Logan could reach Sarah. She held a hand in front of her mouth. Her face was as white as the clapboard siding.

His brother and father shared a look. "Dinner's in a little bit," Sid said. "Why don't you put your things in your room? I'll send someone to help you unload. You can draw a bath in the bathroom at the end of the hall and freshen up."

When they were alone on the porch, Logan took Sarah into his arms, holding her as if his sanity only existed when she stood next to him. He tightened his hold, curving his shoulders around her, bowing his head over hers. "I will see this ended, honey."

Sarah pulled back. Her face was entirely devoid of emotion, her eyes slightly unfocused. He took her arm and led her inside the house. His room was on the ground floor, at the back of the hall. The far end of the hall had been reconstructed to make space for a full bath. They both paused and looked around the white-tiled space, bewildered by the luxury.

Logan looked down at her, thinking she'd be thrilled with the prospect of a hot bath so easily at hand. There was nothing but shadows in her face. He lifted her chin, bringing her gaze up to his. Her warm, brown eyes swam with tears.

"Don't cry, honey."

"You never should have gotten on that stage."

He grinned. "That was the best decision of my life." He kissed her forehead. "We'll be staying in this room." He pointed to a room one door down from the bathroom. "I'll just go get our things, then I'll leave you to your bath."

Chapter 15

Logan stepped into his father's den a short while later. Sid stood beside the cold fireplace, arms crossed over his chest. Sheriff Declan and Sager stood near him. The men fell silent as he entered.

"Christ, Logan. You look like hell," Declan observed. "What happened?"

"We were ambushed by Swift Elk."

Declan whistled low between his teeth. "How did you get away? Very few white men survive an encounter with him."

"I killed his men."

"And Swift Elk?"

"He lives. Sarah asked me to spare his life." Logan's gaze traveled to his stepfather. His hair was grayer than Logan remembered, his face more careworn. Briefly, guilt attacked Logan. Perhaps, had he been here, he might have lifted some of the load from his dad.

What a useless thought. There'd been room for

only one son. Sager. His stepfather had made his choice.

"You look like you got bad news," Logan said to the sheriff. "How did it happen that you were up here today?"

"I heard Eugene was headed this way." Declan bowed his head and rubbed the back of his neck, then filled them in on what he'd learned about Hawkins. "And, I came for another reason. I did as you asked, Logan. I checked into the forgery warrant posted for Sarah. I haven't been able to get in contact with the law in Yankton. I came up to leave word with your father and to see if you'd arrived yet." He straightened and looked Logan in the eye, his hands braced on his hips. "I think it may be best if I take Sarah into Cheyenne to see if we can get to the bottom of this."

"No." Something cold twisted in Logan's gut. "She's done nothing wrong. She gave you the papers—at considerable danger to herself. Hawkins set this up to discredit her."

Sager snorted. Logan's gaze slashed his way. "What hold has that woman got over you, little brother? You're finding excuses for her. She's playin' you, and you're too goddamned blind to see it."

Logan's gaze narrowed, the only warning he gave. His voice was deceptively calm. "You're talking about the woman I love, big brother. I'd like you to keep a civil tongue in your head."

"Civil? While she works her knife a little deeper in your back? Did you learn nothing from your mother's tricks, from watching her work Sid over all those years? You want the same setup for yourself? I thought you were smarter than that."

Logan felt blood heat his neck, rising to his face. His mother, God rest her soul, had been unbalanced as hell. Her hatred for Sid and Sager had known no bounds. She'd sown poison into the family bonds, seducing a teenage Sager to shame his father. Maybe Logan was just like Sid. But Sarah was nothing like Logan's mother.

"I see we should not have come." He looked at Sid. "My apologies. I won't make that mistake again. Sheriff, I would rather Sarah not be anywhere near Hawkins. If you want her brought to Cheyenne, I'll do that, but I'd like to wait a day after you leave so there's no risk she'll cross paths with her former husband."

"Her current husband," Sager clarified.

Logan stepped closer to Sager, right into his space. They were of an equal height and build, one dark, one light. "What the hell is it, Sager? You've got something on your mind and it isn't Sarah. What do you want from me?"

"I want you home, for good. Helping to run the spread. I want you here, so Sid quits being a lost puppy. I want you to be part of the family."

"That's a rotten taste of your own medicine, isn't it?"

"What I did was wrong. What you're doing is wrong. You belong here. Let the woman go."

Logan glared into his brother's pale amber eyes.

"The 'woman' is my life. I let her go, I die. That's all there is."

"Christ, Logan." Sager turned away, the matter far from settled.

Logan blinked and looked away, catching the sheriff's eye. Declan was watching the three of them with the hard gaze of a lawman, eyes that took everything in and offered little in return. "So what's it gonna be?" Declan asked.

"If my son says he'll bring Sarah down to Cheyenne in a couple of days, he'll do it," Sid vouched for Logan. "I raised him to be a man of his word."

"Well, then, I'll wait for you in Cheyenne. A week. No longer, or I'll put your ass in jail, too."

Logan nodded. He had less than a week of freedom. His gut tightened when he thought of what jail would do to Sarah, after everything she'd been through. She'd only just begun to heal.

"You and Sarah are welcome to join us for supper," Sid offered. "The sheriff's staying. Or I can have a tray sent to your room," his dad offered.

Food. Logan didn't want to eat. He wanted Sarah, alone, for every minute that remained to them. "A tray would be great."

He turned to leave, but Sid stopped him. "Son, I'm glad you're home. No matter what brought you here. No matter how long you can stay."

Logan's gaze switched from Sid to Sager and back. He nodded. "Breakfast at the usual time?"

Sid smiled. "Some things never change."

* * *

Logan closed the door behind him, quietly. Sarah was brushing her wet hair. She wore her simple brown homespun skirt and a calico top with a frilly collar of white lace. He longed to take her to Cheyenne or Denver and have her spend a week with a dressmaker. Let her buy every feminine piece of clothing that she wished to own. Get her out of the ill-fitting hand-me-downs donated by the women at the fort. She never complained, never asked for anything.

Jail would kill her.

She looked at his reflection and smiled. He kept his face blank. He could take her and run north, deep into Sioux country, far, far from the jail in Cheyenne. No one would find them, not even Sager, whose tracking skills were unequaled.

She straightened and crossed the room. Stopping in front of him, she placed her hands on his chest. "There's a hot water tap in the bath. You don't have to do anything at all, just sit and let the hot water fill the bath. I forgot about time, forgot about everything. You should try it."

She laughed, and Logan found he couldn't tell her. Not yet. But it was too late. She caught the shadow in his eyes. "What is it?" she asked, the humor falling from her face.

He took a breath to form the words, but they wouldn't come out. He had failed her. She trusted him, and he had failed her. If they'd never brought the sheriff in on it, none of this would have happened. He wanted to look away, but didn't deserve to be spared the hurt he would see in her eyes.

"I have to take you to Cheyenne."

She didn't speak, didn't move. The apprehension he'd sensed before shifted subtly to a resolute firmness. She stepped closer to him, raising her hand. Briefly, he thought she would slap him, but instead, her hand cupped his cheek.

"I've been in worse situations and lived to tell, Logan Taggert. I have done nothing wrong," she said with utter conviction. "The law is fair and will hear the truth. How can it not with you on my side?"

He brought his hands up to her back, pressing her body against his. This was where she belonged. His hands moved upward to her shoulder blades. He bent forward, burying his face in her neck. She circled her arms around his neck. Her skin was softer than silk. He rubbed his face against her throat. He knew the stubble of his beard probably pricked her. He didn't care. He needed her close. Closer. Her skin against his.

"Love me, Sarah," he whispered when his mouth reached her ear.

"I do."

"I need you now. Right now. Please." *I need you forever.*

She took his head and pulled him down, into a kiss. It was gentle, a soft touching of lips. He pressed against the corners of her jaw with his thumbs, forcing her mouth open, and when it did, he swept his tongue inside, into her moist heat. She tightened her hold on him, accepting him, accepting his hunger. He groaned. His body tightened in anticipation.

He pulled back so that he could remove his vest.

He tossed it on the chair next to them. He watched Sarah as he unfastened the buckle of his gun belt. He draped that over the back of the same chair. He dropped his suspenders, unbuttoned his shirt, and pulled it over his head.

Bare-chested, he pulled her close to start unfastening her shirt buttons. She didn't stop him, didn't pull away, but he could feel the beginnings of her withdrawal—the battle she waged within herself. "Look at me." Her eyes moved to his bare chest and locked there. "Look at my eyes." He tilted her chin up. "I will only bring you pleasure in our joining."

He pulled her shirt from the waist of her skirt. He started on the fasteners of her skirt while she removed her shirt. His hands were trembling. He had to fight his inclination to rip the damned thing off her. Her hands, cool and competent, pushed his aside and made short work of it. She slipped the material down her hips.

He kicked off his boots, pulled off his socks, then dropped his pants and drawers. The air was cool on his bare skin, but did nothing to ease the heat thrumming through his system. She looked at him, her gaze pausing on his erection.

She still wore a chemise, corset, camisole, and drawers. Far too much clothing. "Take off your clothes. All of them." He stood where he was, rooted to the spot, watching her slim hands make quick work of every layer. At last, she stood before him. Naked. Divine.

His eyes swept the length of her. He closed the space between them. Taking her hands, he backed her toward the bed. Nothing in him felt tender or gentle. Her knees hit the mattress. He leaned into her, pushing her back, down on the soft, old quilt. He covered her body with his, feeling the differences in their size and shape. Dominating her. He took her wrists in one of his hands, holding her immobile while his hand and mouth explored, pinned her beneath him. He wanted it rough, rougher than he'd ever had with any woman. He wanted her to know she was his.

He pushed her legs apart with a knee, seating himself in the cradle of her legs, his cock pressed against the sweet folds of her sex. He rubbed against her, aching for entrance, no waiting, no preliminaries. Her breath stroked his ear. Fast. Too fast.

He was scaring the hell out of her.

He cursed silently, reaching for the control that was usually first nature to him. He shoved his hands beneath her body, cupping her back, pressing her up against his face. He was afraid to look into her face, to see the condemnation there. He'd come at her as thoughtlessly as a battering ram. He drew a long breath and released it slowly.

Pushing up on an elbow, he dragged his eyes to hers. Her dark eyes, so unusual with fair coloring like hers, looked huge in the delicate bone structure of her face. Her very white face. Ah, Christ. His cock cared nothing for her fragility. Unable to stop himself, he rubbed against her, hungry to fill her body.

Logan tore his gaze away from her eyes while he struggled to calm his raging desire. He glanced over her body, seeking something to focus on, searching for a distraction. Her hair, which was rapidly drying, flickered in the candlelight, seemed to be coming alive.

"I want to make a memory," he whispered, unfamiliar with the husky rasp of his own voice. He looked into her sultry eyes, dark now like black coffee. "I want to remember tonight for all of our lives. I want to know this night you were mine, that you surrendered your fears and accepted me as I am now. Flaws and all. I want to know you found joy in our coupling. Will you give me tonight, Sarah?"

She nodded, her gaze solemn as it met his. He moved from her to shove the pillows into a mountain at the headboard. Lying back against them, he opened his arms. "Come here."

Sarah looked at Logan resting against the pillows. He was a large man. His erection reached almost to his navel, wide, flaring at the end. A vein was raised along his length. Her insides clenched in anticipation. She was not tied. He did not pull her to him, only beckoned with his eyes. She crawled over to him, not really sure what to do. His gaze dropped to her breasts. She felt her nipples peak.

"Kiss me," he ordered.

She went up on her knees. Bracing her hands on his shoulder and chest, she leaned down and pressed her mouth against his. He did not grab at her, did not force more contact than what she initiated.

"Open your mouth. Put your tongue in mine."

She looked into his pale gray eyes, dilated now with his passion. She bent to him again, her lips opening over his. Her tongue moved timidly into his mouth. He groaned. His hips bucked upward. "Good Christ, yes."

A humming started in her head. She was giving him pleasure. Giving. He accepted what she offered. He did not take. She pulled back, studying him, wanting to give him more pleasure. She kissed his chin, kissed the notch at the base of his neck, kissed the slight indentation of his sternum.

He caught the sides of her face and drew her up. "Honey, that's nice. But I don't think I can take much more." He kissed her, a wide, openmouthed stroke of tongues. "Lie down on top of me." She tried to steel herself against the fear weaving its way from her soul to her body. His eyes were heavy-lidded. She settled over him, feeling the ridge of his penis against her belly. He grinned wolfishly, stricken by the sensations of her skin against his. He cupped the sides of her breasts.

"Turn over."

She did as he asked, unsure of his intent. Her head rested on the pillows next to his. His chest was warm against her back, the hard length of his penis cushioned between her buttocks. He spread her legs open. Lifting her slightly, he adjusted himself so that his penis lay erect between her legs. She held herself stiff, unsure what was expected of her.

"Relax, honey. Lean back. There's nothing you need to do." His hands, large and calloused, stroked her thighs, massaging her tension away. He drew them up, over her hip bones, over her belly to her ribs. He cupped her breasts. She watched his hands work the soft mounds. He kissed her neck, his thumb and forefinger gently squeezing her hardened nipples.

She moaned. His penis stroked her sex, slowly, gently. She turned her head, seeking his mouth. He met her halfway, kissing her even as he grinned a very male smile. He stroked her chest, her arms, her stomach.

She arched herself to press against his upward-stroking penis, wanting more. His legs held hers open, stopping her from grasping him with her thighs. She groaned. One of his hands took hold of her thigh while the other sought out the moist folds of her core, slipping past that spot—there—that made the world disappear and her body come alive. She pushed against his hand as it moved in a circular motion. When his fingers dipped inside her, she cried out.

He curved an arm about her ribs. His hips were rocking harder, faster, driving his penis against her opening. She wanted more. So much more. She ached to have him inside her.

"How does that feel, sweetheart?"

She arched her back, her hands gripping fistfuls of the quilt. She wanted him. She *wanted* him. His fingers were moving inside her, his thumb working that sensitive nub. "Logan—"

"I'm right here, honey. Tell me what you want."

His fingers curved against the sensitive spot inside her. Again and again. Something within her broke, pulled free, burst to life. His penis entered her, at last. Thrusting, drawing back, thrusting, he pumped into her. She wanted more of him, all of him. She sat up, fully impaled on him. Pushing up against his thighs, she lifted herself and lowered back over him, meeting his thrusts, feeling him deep within her core.

He sat up behind her, bringing a hand to hold her breast, pressing his face against her shoulder, his tongue tasting her skin. His fingers worked at the top of her sex, bringing her to an instant climax.

When it eased somewhat, he pushed her forward. Still pumping into her, he moved her to her knees. He held her hips, keeping her still until she could not be held still. His cock pounded into her, stroking the same spot his fingers had earlier, triggering a massive orgasm within her. She bucked and arched, pushing back against him, her inner muscles gripping him like a fist.

Unable to hold out any longer, he surrendered to the passion that blacked out every thought, every emotion. His groin tightened. He pumped again, again, then felt the pulsating release shooting his semen deep within her. He leaned over her, bracing his weight on his fists while the two of them struggled for air. When the aftershocks subsided, he withdrew and dropped to his back beside her as she collapsed onto the bed.

The room was silent, except for the sound of their breathing. He turned to look at her. She was watching him, her eyes wide. She pushed up on her elbows. "What was that?"

He grinned, a very self-satisfied smile, as he folded his hands behind his head. "That, darlin', was how it's supposed to be."

"It was never like that. Never." Not even their first time together, before Swift Elk's attack. She'd been so afraid of what being intimate with him would be like—she'd been too tense to fully enjoy what happened between them.

His humor faded. He smoothed a hand over her cheek. "That's because you've never been in love."

She caught his hand, pressed it to her mouth. "I don't want to go to jail, Logan."

Logan forked a hand through his hair. He got up and moved restlessly around the room. "Hawkins knew you had the papers he lost. I'm willing to bet there is no real warrant out for you. I think he was trying to discredit you on the off chance you were bold enough to take the matter to the law. If you showed up with the papers, he could trot out the fake warrant and claim you were the creator of the forgeries, not him." He came back to the bed. Taking her hands, he drew her to her feet. "We'll get to the bottom of this, Sarah. I promise you that."

He wrapped his arms about her, loving the feel of her skin. "Do you think that tub is big enough for both of us?"

Chapter 16

Logan watched Sarah sleep. He should be as exhausted as she was. They'd made love in the tub, eaten dinner, then made love again, slowly, leisurely. He wanted her again. He couldn't seem to get enough of her. They had only this night with one other before they would have to go back to Cheyenne and face the charges against her. He didn't want to waste a second of it sleeping.

He got up and dressed, then paced around the room. There had to be a resolution to their situation. Maybe he could talk to Eugene, get him to confess, trick him into telling how he'd gotten the Yankton sheriff to write a warrant for Sarah.

Logan opened the door and moved silently down the hall to the last room on this level, the guest room assigned to Declan. He'd no sooner stepped into the sheriff's room than the sound of a pistol being cocked brought him up short.

"Shit, Declan. It's only me."

"What do you want, Taggert?" he snapped as he uncocked his gun and set it on the nightstand.

Logan pushed the door open and leaned against the jamb, his thumbs hooked in his pockets. "Sarah's innocent. This warrant is something Hawkins cooked up. I know it."

Declan cursed. "Couldn't we talk about this in the morning?"

"No. Come talk to Hawkins with me. I want to see if I can get him to confess. I want you to stay out of sight but be a witness."

"Hell, Logan." He threw the covers off and swung his legs over the side. He still wore his denims, but his feet and chest were bare. He sat with his head in his hands for a minute, then straightened and pulled on a shirt.

"Is Sid sending some men to ride shotgun with you tomorrow?" Logan asked, watching the sheriff move about the room, gathering his clothes.

"Yeah." Declan tucked his shirt into his pants and shoved his pistol into his waistband. "Was that you down the hallway screaming earlier tonight?"

Logan grinned. "Didn't know we were so loud."

Declan swiped a hand through his hair. "Well, you were. Had to take a piss outside. Thought you two would never get out of the bathroom."

"I finally got her to not be afraid of me, Cal. I can't send her to jail."

Declan looked at him, assessing him through narrowed eyes. "We're gonna do this within the law. It's the only way she'll ever be able to live free without the worry of what's waitin' ten steps in front of her."

At the front door, the two paused. "How are we going to play this?" Declan asked.

"We'll enter by the side door to the barn—he won't see you come in behind me. You'll keep quiet and out of sight, but come close enough so that you can hear him. I'll get him to talk. We'll see what he says. If he thinks I can get him out of there, he might open up."

The sheriff made a face. "What are you getting me into?"

The stable was dark and empty of animals. Declan removed his boots so that his stockinged feet would make less noise. They moved together into the shadowy space. Logan took the padlock key from the sheriff and opened the sliding door where Hawkins slept. He slammed the door shut, startling Sarah's first husband awake.

Logan sat on a bale of hay across from Hawkins's bed, waiting for him to shake the sleep from his system. The bastard sure slept like a baby.

Hawkins looked around, listening for something beyond the walls of his cell. "What do you want, Taggert?"

Logan crossed his arms and leaned back. "Well, now, that's the stuff of nightmares, isn't it?"

Hawkins swiped a hand over his face. "Why are you here?"

"Besides the fun with a stick I promised you? I figure we both want something. I'm thinking about making a deal with you."

"You want my wife."

"My wife is already mine. You were dead and

buried when I married her, a state I'd be more than willing to return you to. I want information. If it's good enough, I'll walk out of here and leave the door unlocked. What happens to you after that is up to you. I figure they've got enough to lock you up until your dotage. But they don't know half of what I know about you. Like how you stalked emigrant families in St. Louis, searching for an easy mark, rich in seed money, blinded with visions of the future. Mr. and Mrs. Worthington made it easy for you, didn't they?"

"Don't know what you're talking about."

Logan picked up the large, thick stick he'd brought into the stall. Taking his knife from its sheath, he began whittling a smooth surface about a foot long. "That's okay, *Gene*," he said, using another of Hawkins's aliases. "The truth has a funny way of coming out."

He grinned at the pale face of the man lying on the floor a few feet from him. Both were equidistant from the stall door. That in itself was a challenge to Hawkins. Logan made another slice along the end of the stick. "So you killed Sarah's parents."

"A runaway freight team did that to them. I can't be blamed for the hostler's carelessness."

"But you just happened to be the first on-site to wail and decry the accident, to bring their broken, battered bodies to Sarah, to console the young, orphaned woman."

"I was the only one who knew they left behind a daughter."

Another slice. "I asked Sheriff Declan to confirm your story about working on several articles for the

Philadelphia Bulletin with Mr. Worthington. Something young, bereaved Sarah never thought to do." He made another stroke of the knife, long and slow, the sound of the blade shaving the wood loud in the silent stable.

He held up the stick and looked at it critically. "They never heard of you." He grinned at Hawkins. "Ain't that a surprise. And then you married her under false pretenses, using a fake name—which in itself invalidates your marriage. You're wanted in two states and three territories for various felonious activities. That's just what I've been able to uncover so far. This little nonsense with the false land claims is the least of your troubles. I wonder how many times they can hang a man?"

"So what is it you want from me, Taggert?"

Logan shrugged. "Nothing very big. I just want you to fill in the holes. There are bits I don't know. I don't like not having the whole picture. I want the truth. I'm gonna tell you a story. If I get it wrong, you correct me. Do we have a deal?"

"You let me escape?"

"Like I said. I'll leave the stall and stable unlocked."

"It's a setup."

"Maybe it is." Logan shrugged. "Maybe it ain't. It's the only chance you got. It's the only deal I'm making."

Hawkins looked at the door. He cocked his head. He pulled himself up and leaned back against the wooden wall, arms crossed against his chest. He gave the matter little consideration. "Deal. Start talking."

"You tell Sarah that she and her family had been headed where you were headed, that you and she should marry. You convince her. She marries you, giving you her innocence, her parents' money, her entire future."

Hawkins smiled. "And what an innocence it was."

Logan sharpened the stick's pointy end. "You get her to agree that you should go to the Dakotas ahead of her, prepare the homestead, lay in the fields. Then after winter, you promise to return for her. She goes for it. Christ, she was an easy mark. Like a child, she was."

"You have no idea. Worked like a dream."

"You get to Yankton and head farther west, to the Spotted Tail Agency. One of the underagents there is hungry to make a name for himself. He needs money to make a bid to become a full agent. You convince him he can become a bigger power broker by handling the land claims than he could ever be with the responsibilities of an Indian agent."

Even in the moonlight, Logan could see the tension creep into Hawkins's face. "How am I doin' so far?"

"Keep going."

"Everything's going along just jim-dandy. Except you forget about Sarah. Winter ends. Spring is in full swing. She doesn't wait for you to come fetch her. She shows up at the homestead. Rotten luck, that. You give her the song and dance about working on a story about corruption at the agencies and having to use an alias to do that. You ask her to help prepare several fake claim papers you'll use in your investigation."

"She had elegant handwriting. A light hand. She could copy any writing style. A natural. But the bitch wouldn't do it."

"And she started asking questions, questions you didn't have answers for. You decided she was more of a liability than an asset. By this point, you'd met Swift Elk. He had one thing you could use—his hatred of whites. He'd do just about anything to get his hands on horses or guns. You gave him both, and an outlet for his blood vengeance. You sicced him on your wife."

Hawkins lifted a hand to his scalped head. His palm hovered over the raw, scarred skin with lesions that still opened and bled. "I wasn't supposed to be there. He was supposed to wait until I'd left. The bastard."

"And you killed his brother. For that, he scalped you."

"I saw them raping her. Right there in the front yard. Little Miss Goody Two Shoes. They tore her clothes off and threw her over Swift Elk's pony. One of them came back and set the fire. I pretended to be dead. He shot an arrow into my side for good measure. But I got out. I got away. I hid in the trees. Don't know how long I was there. The cry that rose up when the neighbors came roused me. Christ, my head hurt."

His hand dropped to his side. "It wasn't supposed

to go like that, but it worked to my advantage. I lived. I had a new disguise. No wife to worry about."

"There was just one problem. Your whole deal burned in the fire."

"Almost all of it. I got a fever from the wounds. I wandered off, mindless, lost. I came upon some men panning for gold. I was with them for weeks. When the fever left and I'd healed some, I remembered Sarah had come home that night with the hand cart. What was she doing with that? She said she'd been to a neighbor's. Only I didn't know which neighbor.

"Goddamn her. I had to search three homes for the damned trunk. Never did find it. Thought it was gone. A year of work. Gone."

He lapsed into silence. When he didn't seem inclined to continue, Logan prompted him. "Then Sarah showed up at Fort Buford."

"Can you believe it? Who could survive a year with Swift Elk? I sent a man to watch her. He told me a trunk arrived there one day, and I knew she still had the papers."

"What about the warrant for forgery?"

"I had nothing to do with that."

"Come on. We were having such a nice discussion. You promised the truth."

"I had nothing to do with that."

"You think you're better at this game than I am?" Logan leaned forward, bracing his arms on his knees, his knife in one hand, his sharp stick in the other. "You're running from the law. I don't give a good goddamn about the law. Killing you in a slow and painful way will give me joy to the end of my days."

"I told Pete—Pete Bederman—that Sarah was back. He thought up the warrant."

"That it? That all of it, Hawkins?"

"That's it."

Logan nodded. He sheathed his knife. "Stand up."

"What for?"

"'Cause I'm gonna beat the shit out of you now."

Hawkins scrambled to his feet. "That ain't fair. I did what you said—"

Logan dragged him forward and cut off his complaints with an upper cut to his jaw that sent him flying backward against the stall wall. Logan fingered the stick he'd been whittling, seriously contemplating ending the man's days right then.

"Logan. It's enough. I'll write the Yankton sheriff, tell him what happened. He may want Sarah to be a witness against Bederman. Let's get this statement written up. I'll have Hawkins sign it in the morning—but he's got to be alive to do it."

Logan's shoulders dropped with a long exhalation. Sarah was free. Free. It was done. He walked out into the night while Declan locked the cell back up. Looking up at the brilliant stars, he drew a deep breath. Cool fresh air filled his lungs. He laughed, filled with the joy of his wife's freedom.

Declan drew even with him. Logan gave him back the key. He took it and clapped Logan on the shoulder. "I had my doubts. I was trying to keep an open mind. I've seen it go the other way around too many times. I'm happy for you, Logan. Christ, your woman has been through hell. You'll have to get her divorced from Hawkins and redo your vows."

"Yep. But that's the easy part. She's safe now, Cal. You have no idea what that means to us."

Chapter 17

Logan felt like roaring. He was rangy and restless, too wild to be cooped up inside the house, waiting for Sarah to rise. In their room, he dug out a breechclout, a pair of leggings for him, a deerskin tunic, leggings for her, and both of their moccasins. If ever he needed a night run, he did this night. He changed into the Sioux clothes and slipped his knife sheath over the thick tie of the breechclout.

"Sarah," he whispered, bent over her. "Honey, wake up."

She looked up. A warm, sleepy smile welcomed him. But it was chased far too quickly by fear. "Is it time? Do we have to leave now?"

"No." Logan sat on the bed. "It's over. You're free. It's done."

She drew herself up to a sitting position. "How?"

"I got Hawkins to talk. Sheriff Declan heard his confession. He absolved you. Declan's going to write it up and have him sign it."

Sarah wrapped her arms around his chest, pressing her face flat against his heart. "It's done. Logan, I can't believe it. I really don't have to go to jail?"

He wrapped his arms around her. "No, sweetheart. Not to jail. You may have to be a witness in court against the men who were in this with Hawkins." He felt the hot moisture of her tears on his chest. He drew back, swiping his thumbs against the wet streaks on her cheeks. "Let's go for a run."

She nodded, laughing. She reached for her nightgown, but Logan stopped her. He pointed to the dress and leggings. "Wear these. We aren't alone here at the ranch. I don't want the men to get an eyeful of my wife in her underclothes."

Sarah drew the tunic onto her lap. It was made of soft deerskin, still a natural color. The neckline was sliced open in front, bordered by a thick panel of intricate beadwork, as were the cuffs and hem. The sides of the tunic were open, allowing the wearer free movement.

Sarah had helped prepare deerskin hides for this sort of clothing. It was intense and time-consuming work. She'd been allowed to make herself a plain tunic while she'd been Swift Elk's wife, but it had none of the elegance or decoration this one had.

"This is far too fine, Logan. I will ruin it running."

"It is far less elegant than you, believe me. It is what I want you to wear. Please."

"I won't want to take it off."

"I'll be able to get you out of it." He drew her to her feet. "Are you familiar with these?" he asked, holding up the leggings.

"I wore them while I was with Swift Elk." She looked around for the breechclout to go with the leggings. He gave her a slow smile and shook his head. Pulling her over to a chair, he tied the hide around her hips that would have supported the breechclout, if he were letting her wear one. He held one legging for her to step into, then tied it to the ribbon of hide, then did the same with the other leg.

She stood before him naked except for the leggings. He took hold of her waist, mostly to keep himself from touching her in other places. He pulled her slim body forward, burying his face in her soft stomach. He looked up at her. "I love you."

She smiled and brushed his hair from his face. "I love you."

He lifted her tunic and drew it down over her arms. It fell to her knees, the sleeves covering her arms to just past her elbows. She moaned as the suede went from cold to warm, taking on her body's heat. "I feel naked in this."

"Mm-hmm. A state we'll make use of right after our run."

Outside, they moved silently down the drive, walking hand in hand. "Where shall we run?" Sarah asked.

"East. Always to the east."

She grinned and turned in that direction. There was a faint lightening of the eastern sky, a hint that dawn was not too far away. They stepped off the drive onto the prairie and moved into the night wind. The Circle Bar was surrounded by gently rolling hills. They ran down the first hill and up the second, sometimes racing, sometimes just simply moving next to each other.

Sarah's laughter spilled out into the night, quickening something deep inside him. She looked back at him. In the slowly brightening light, he saw her eyes widen as she looked at him. She gave a little shriek and took off running hard. He gave chase. About a half mile east was a clutch of boulders on the crest of a hill. He let her keep her lead until he'd cornered her in the rocks.

She turned and faced him, laughing. Catching sight of his intense look, she held up a hand, clearly realizing she'd become his quarry. "Logan Taggert," she warned, struggling to catch her breath.

"Turn around," he ordered.

"I don't trust you," she laughed.

"You shouldn't. Turn around." Slowly, she did as he ordered. "You are mine. Only mine, Sarah Taggert," he said against her ear, his hand circling to the softness of her belly. He moved her back a few steps so that she was up against the lower boulders. "Bend over."

"Here?"

"Here." He pushed her forward, moving her hands to brace against the rocks. He loosened his breechclout and lifted her skirt. The leggings framed her soft cheeks. He almost came just looking at her. He slid into her, seating himself to his balls. She was wet, slick, ready for him. He held her hips and pulled out of her, slowly, slowly, knowing she felt the long stroke of him. In again, just as slowly. He found a rhythm that made her body react, clasping and releasing him.

The sky was growing ever brighter. He could see the slickness of her when he drew out, feel the heat of her when he pushed in. He stroked her mound, pressing against her sensitive nub in time with the way he was pumping into her. He could feel her body's reaction. She started arching back, taking him as he took her, whimpering little sounds of pleasure.

"Say my name, Sarah," he growled. "Say it."

"Oh—"

"Say it."

"Logan. Logan!" she cried out as her body convulsed over his cock, milking him like a soft, wet fist. He slammed into her hard, pumping fast, wanting more of what her body was doing to him, more until ecstasy broke free within him. He cried out as he spilled himself inside her, his body releasing in an orgasm that eased into a dozen little aftershocks.

He pulled free and straightened their clothes. Leaning his back against a boulder, he pulled her against his body. "That, darlin', is why you will always wear this when we run."

She slipped her arms around his waist. "Only if you always wear the getup you have on now, too."

"Do you want to head back?"

She shook her head. "Let's sit and watch the sunrise first."

They moved around the clump of boulders and sat on the far side of the hill. It was the most peaceful moment of Logan's life. He put an arm around

Sarah's shoulders. Behind them, to the north and west, a low rumble of thunder sounded.

Logan looked back, disappointed that a storm would intrude on their morning. The boulders blocked his line of sight. He supposed they should head back rather than be caught out in the open in a lightning storm. "We'd better get back. We'll have to catch another sunrise," he said, giving Sarah help rising.

No sooner was she on her feet than a horse cleared the boulders and landed just inches from Logan. He barely had time to register the look of rage and hatred on the Indian's face as the flat of his war club struck him against the temple.

Swift Elk.

He screamed a fierce war cry as the blow he'd struck Logan knocked him off his feet and sent him tumbling down the hill like a rag doll. Sarah flew down the hill after him as another horse came around the boulders.

Eugene.

She had almost made it to Logan's side when she stumbled and fell. Swift Elk let loose an arrow that screamed by her ear on its way to the ground where Logan lay. Sarah dragged herself to her hands and knees and scrambled for Logan's prone body. She draped herself over his torso, her hands testing his head for the wound Swift Elk had caused. Her fingers came away bloody, but his skull was intact.

The ground shuddered as Swift Elk turned his pony and came back at them. He leapt from the saddle, withdrawing his knife. Sarah turned and faced him, keeping herself between him and Logan. "Don't you dare touch him. He spared your life. You owe him." She didn't know whether she spoke in English or Sioux. It didn't matter. Her words gave him pause.

"What the hell are you doing, you crazy devil?" Eugene asked as he pulled up next to them. "It's bad enough you knocked him out. If you kill him, there will be no avoiding the hell that will rain down on us. Let's just get away, before the rest of the ranch wakes up."

"You have the heart of viper and the brain of polecat. You have no words I wish to hear," Swift Elk cursed Eugene in Sioux. He turned and came toward Sarah. She did not flinch, did not surrender her position over Logan's body.

He stepped toward her, grabbed a fistful of her tunic, stroked the knife over the soft flesh beneath her chin. Sarah had no doubt her life was about to end in a bloody wash of hatred. She lifted her chin, daring him to do as he threatened.

"Dammit, man, I'm not waiting around. Leave her and let's go!" Eugene shouted. He took up the reins of Swift Elk's spare horse, then kicked it into a fast trot down the slope of the hill.

Swift Elk grabbed Sarah's arm and jerked her forward.

"No. No, I won't go. I won't do this again. I am not married to you any longer. You are taking me from my husband." She dug in her heels and tried to jerk herself free. Swift Elk backhanded her, effectively silencing her.

"You come with me, or I will kill him. It is your only choice."

Sarah looked back at Logan. He'd once vowed to find her if she were ever taken again. He'd told her to live, to believe. She looked at Swift Elk and didn't fight when he tossed her up on the back of his horse and turned his mount after Eugene.

Sid, Sager, and Sheriff Declan sat at the kitchen table, enjoying a second cup of coffee. Declan was filling them in on his and Logan's visit with Hawkins. Hearing the details of Sarah's ordeal, both Taggerts fell silent.

Sager stared down at his coffee. How would he have felt if it were his wife, Rachel, who'd gone to hell and back? He looked at Sid, seeing he wrestled with the same thoughts.

"I want him home for good, Sager."

"I do, too. We need him."

"Sheriff!" a man shouted as he ran toward the kitchen door outside. "Sheriff!"

Declan lurched to his feet as the man stumbled into the kitchen. "He's gone. Hawkins is gone and the guard's dead. His throat cut."

Sager and Declan hurried out to the stable. So many of Sid's men were in and around the area that it was useless trying to distinguish footprints in the dirt floor.

Sager called Sid's foreman over. "Get horses ready for me and the sheriff. And get a couple of men ready to escort Sid over to the Crippled Horse.

Tell Old Jack to double the guard and keep Rachel and the boys inside. Do it now!"

He pulled another man aside. "Tell me how many horses are missing."

Declan was examining the lock. Someone had used a crowbar to pop the lock open. Sager knelt by the door, searching for something, anything that seemed out of place or notable. "Cal—look." He nodded to a soft moccasin print, partially obliterated by several boot prints.

They looked at each other. "Swift Elk."

Sager checked inside the stall. Between the straw on the ground and the many footprints in the space, he was only able to distinguish one other impression.

"Sager—there are just two horses missing," the man reported. "Sid's sorrel and the sheriff's palomino. No saddles are gone. They rode bareback. There were three horses making tracks outta here though."

"Swift Elk took a fresh horse and is leading his old one." Sager went back to the house to gather his gear. Sid met him at the door. "Logan and Sarah are gone."

Sager went down the hall and into Logan's room. The bed was unmade. Sarah's nightclothes were in a pile on the bed. Another outfit of Sarah's was on the floor. Logan's shirt and trousers hung over the arm of a chair, along with his gun belt. A trunk of Indian clothes was open and several pieces had been pulled out. A pile of clothes sat near the trunk, still packed. He couldn't tell what was missing, other than the occupants themselves. "Maybe they just went for a walk."

"Without their clothes—or shoes?" Sid asked, nodding toward Logan's boots.

"What's wrong?" Declan asked as he joined the other two in the room.

Sager shook his head. "They're gone."

Declan looked around the room, seeing no signs of a struggle. "Gone as in out for a stroll or gone as in taken?"

Sager met his look. "Maybe when we find Hawkins, we'll find them. Let's go." He paused on his way to the door. "Dad, I want you to go over to Old Jack's. Stay there with Rachel. Take your gun and a couple of men with you."

Sager and Declan headed down the hall. "If someone came in and attacked them, I would have heard. I was up, in the kitchen writing out his confession. I didn't hear a thing."

"Shadow Wolf. Shadow Wolf! Do you live?" Logan came awake fast. Without moving, he met the gaze of a pair of dark brown eyes. Cloud Walker. His cheek hurt. His head felt like a son-of-a-bitch. Sarah!

He pushed up fast, looking around for her. The Earth spun and vibrated. He clasped his head between the heels of his hands. Christ, he wanted to be sick.

"Do not move fast. You still bleed."

He sat up, catching sight of Cloud Walker's

braves astride their horses, staring impassively at him. He held his head and looked around them, terrified he'd see Sarah's body.

"What are you doing here?"

"We are looking for Swift Elk."

"You're too late. He's already gone."

"Did he do this to you?"

Logan nodded. "Where is Yellow Moon?"

Cloud Walker shook his head. Logan stood up. The world wavered beneath his feet. He tried to breathe his way through the nausea, the pain hammering at his head. He checked the level of the sun, gauging how long he'd been out cold. An hour at most.

"I need to go after her."

Cloud Walker shook his head again. "You will come to my camp. You have killed five Sioux. You must answer for those deaths."

Cloud Walker pulled Logan's arm over his shoulder and led him over to the warriors. "Put him with me," Many Deer said.

Logan looked at his hard, impassive face. He nodded, a gesture of gratitude. Taking hold of the warrior's arm, he swung himself up behind him. The men turned as one and rode fast down the hill. The hard stride of the horse jostled his head, blurring his vision.

"Shadow Wolf, take the rope. Tie yourself to me. We cannot slow down."

Logan looked down at the rope tied loosely around Many Deer's waist. He smiled to himself, but left the rope where it was. "I'm fine. I'm fine, Many Deer. Do you know how to use that yet?"

"I can tangle a man in eight moves."

"So, that would be no."

"Not much. But I will get it."

"I will show you. But first, we have to find Swift Elk and save Yellow Moon. She is my heart, my everything."

"It is foolish to love a woman so. It gives them too much power. They think to rule you in the tepee and out. I care nothing for your wife. We have come to stop Swift Elk from making more trouble for our people."

"Good. Go faster." Logan focused on relaxing into the horse's stride. Slowly, his mental faculties realigned themselves. He still had a wretched headache, but it was nothing compared to the pain he'd felt earlier.

At midday, they rode into Cloud Walker's camp. Children shouted and ran to greet them. Dogs barked. Several campfires were smoking, tended by women busily preparing meals. He'd never been to Cloud Walker's village before, but it was like so many others he'd visited, it felt like home to him. Logan's gaze swept the women as he searched futilely for Sarah. He had to get Cloud Walker to lend him a horse so that he could go after Hawkins and Swift Elk. This time, he would show no mercy.

Women hurried to take the warriors' horses. A young woman hurried to Many Deer, touching his face, chattering at him. He looked entirely smitten. Logan laughed and looked away, knowing full well who ran Many Deer's tepee.

"Logan!"

Impossible. That was Sarah's voice. Logan's head shot up as he tried to locate where her shout had come from. He turned and she launched herself at him, crying, laughing. He picked her up, holding her tightly. "Are you hurt?" he asked, his voice gruff.

"No. I'm fine. Swift Elk tried to claim me as his prize, but when he brought me to this camp Cloud Walker's men said I belonged to you and that they would not dishonor their friendship with you." She pushed away to get a better look at him. "Swift Elk has become an enemy of his people. He is held in a tepee apart from the others, awaiting judgment. Eugene, too."

She looked at him critically, gently testing the wound at his temple. "The way he hit you, the way you went down, I was afraid he'd killed you."

Logan pulled her into his arms. "When I woke and you were gone, I thought I would never see you again. I promised to keep you safe, and I failed you."

"You didn't fail me. You thought Swift Elk was finished. And Eugene was under guard in a locked stall."

He curved his hand around her neck, slipping his fingers back beneath her hair. Her skin was warm. Her heartbeat steady. "No matter what, Sarah, it ends here."

"What happens to us now?"

"There will be a trial. I killed five of Swift Elk's men."

Sarah shot a glance around at the large Sioux village. "No. How will you ever get a fair judgment here?"

"The Sioux are a proud and fair people, Sarah. They will hear the truth, and they will make a fair decision. I would rather be tried by a Sioux council than a white court."

One of Cloud Walker's wives came and took Sarah's hand. "You must come with me now," she ordered quietly, never once looking at Logan.

A path cleared in front of Logan, leading directly to Cloud Walker. Silence blanketed the village. Many Deer, his second in command, spoke in a loud voice that carried across the camp. "This man who stands before you is Shadow Walker. He has been a friend of our people for many years."

Many Deer looked around at the faces of the people. "But this week, he killed five of Swift Elk's warriors."

Hushed conversations started up as all eyes turned his way. Logan looked neither to the left, nor the right, but kept his eyes fixed on Cloud Walker, as if he were the one speaking.

"There has been much trouble all across our lands. Some of the trouble has come from the man Yellow Moon first called husband, a man so cowardly and evil that Swift Elk took his scalp so that all would know him for the bad man he is. Some of the trouble has come from Swift Elk himself and some from our new friend, Shadow Wolf.

"The council will meet tonight to discuss the trouble and to determine a judgment. Tomorrow, the judgment will be carried out."

Riders approached, coming in fast. Logan turned to see who appeared. Two men. Sager and Declan. They pulled up on the slope near the village, a respectful distance away. Many Deer conferred furiously with Cloud Walker. Logan could just make out what they were saying. It was well known that Logan's brother had been raised by the Shoshone. Shoshones often acted as scouts and guides for the white soldiers, helping them track Sioux warriors who had stepped outside the treaties. That Sager had brought a lawman with him to the village was proof of his hostile intentions, Many Deer felt.

"Cloud Walker," Logan said, holding up a hand to stop the discussion before it went too far. "Sager is my brother. He does not come to you with a bad heart."

"He has brought a lawman with him. He is a scout for our enemies," Many Deer said angrily.

"The man who was Yellow Moon's first husband was under Sheriff Declan's custody. The sheriff was taking him to Cheyenne to be tried for his crimes. Swift Elk released him from us and brought him to you." Logan looked at the men gathered around, noticing they had edged the women, children, and elders back farther in the crowd. "Swift Elk's heart has blackened with hatred for his enemies and with sorrow for his people. He has brought to your people a man whose heart has never been good. My brother and the lawman come not as your enemies, but to take evil back with them. They will aid you in the justice you seek."

Cloud Walker spoke, choosing his words carefully, speaking quietly, forcing the crowd to settle so that they could hear him. "Yellow Moon's first husband, whose name will not be spoken, has been captured by us. He will meet our justice first. The rest will be determined by the council."

"Will you permit my brother and my friend to stay here to await the justice you promise?"

"If they will surrender their weapons to me, I will allow this."

Logan nodded to him. He turned and raised a hand, inviting Sager and Declan to come into the village. As they neared the path into the village, one by one, people began to turn their backs to the newcomers. Logan watched the motion, fury building deep within him at the insult.

Cloud Walker and Many Deer turned to leave the gathering. "Cloud Walker!" Logan's roar stopped him. "What have I done to be given such an insult?"

"It is not you they object to."

"I am insulted nonetheless. I asked you to welcome my friend and my brother. And this is the welcome they receive?"

"You asked us to admit enemies into our homes. It is you who offer us insult."

"My brother has taught me everything I know about the greatness of the people of this land on which we stand. He seeks only to know that his brother is well treated. The sheriff is a great warrior and a great keeper of the peace. He seeks only to know that justice is served. They are not your enemies." He looked at Cloud Walker. "Unless I am also your enemy."

Cloud Walker stared at Logan, his weathered face set in hard lines. He called to two of his wives to see to the ponies of Logan's family, indicating that the two were to be treated as his guests.

The women hurried forward and took hold of

the reins, but did not take the horses away. Declan frowned at them, uncertain what was expected.

"Leave your weapons with your saddles. If you have a knife, you may keep it," Logan explained. "It is a condition of your visit."

The men slung their bedrolls and saddlebags over their shoulders, then unbuckled their gun belts and draped them over their saddle horns.

Sager eyed Logan critically. "That was some powerful talking."

"What happened to you two? Where is Sarah?" Declan asked.

"She's here. We went for a run this morning. Swift Elk broke Hawkins out and crossed paths with us. They took Sarah and came here. But they did not find the asylum they'd hoped for." He told them what he had learned from Many Deer on their ride to the village. "One of Swift Elk's men survived the battle and brought word of Swift Elk's treachery to the village. Cloud Walker and his men came looking for Swift Elk and found me." He looked at both men. "There will be a council meeting tonight. Hawkins, Swift Elk, and I will all be judged and sentenced."

Sager's brows lowered. "Why you?"

"Because five of Swift Elk's warriors died when they fought me."

"We have to get you out of here," Declan said, low so no one could hear.

"I do not fear their justice. I have lived among the Sioux much of the time since I left the Circle Bar. I trained and hunted with them. I built trading posts near the agencies to help them. I will not leave.

And if you try to go, you'll be killed. The council decision will be what it will be. Just promise me that you will take Sarah back with you if I'm unable to go with you."

Sager gave him a hard stare. "If it comes to a fight tomorrow, let me stand in for you."

Logan studied his brother's pale eyes. "What kind of man would I be if I let my brother fight my battles for me?"

"Jesus, Logan. You're beat all the hell up. Let me do this for you. I couldn't stand to think how Sid would react if I let anything happen to you."

Logan sighed, feeling the same way about Sager. "You do me a great honor. But if it goes as I expect it will, I'll face the two devils who destroyed Sarah's life. I will not turn aside from that challenge."

Declan clapped his hands once, then rubbed them together as if he were looking forward to the coming fight. "Then let's get our boy fed, watered, and rested so he can do what he has to do when the challenge comes." He slapped a hand on the backs of both men as he turned them toward the woman who was waiting to show them to the chief's tepee.

Chapter 18

Sager and Declan flanked Logan's woman in the fringes of the outer ring of observers as the council session began. The sun was dropping behind the distant ridge of mountains, casting long shadows over the prairie. The circle of men was so thick that Sager could only see Logan's features by the light from the small fire.

Three men sat in the innermost area, closest to the fire—Logan, who faced Chief Cloud Walker sitting at the head of the main ring of men, and down from him, Eugene and Swift Elk, who faced each other. The next circle was comprised of the village's elders and main councilmen. The ring beyond that was of young men who would soon become full warriors or hunters. All around the outer circle stood women and children and others, including Sager and Declan.

The silence was so thick in the tight gathering that the snap and crackle of the fire seemed loud. He looked down at Sarah, standing next to him.

One hand was wrapped around the other in a white-knuckled hold. Her eyes were locked on Logan. While he watched her, she spared not a single glance for her first husband, or for the devil who'd abused her so terribly for the year she was his captive. She took up little space, holding herself utterly silent while Cloud Walker spoke.

Declan bent close to her. "What is he saying?"

Sager was adept at reading the sign language that accompanied the chief's speech, so he had a fair understanding of what was being said. Still, he found himself listening to Sarah's soft recital of her first husband's damning crimes against Cloud Walker's people. Most important of the complaints was the fact that Hawkins had caused Sioux warriors to act against the rules of their people as well as the white man's treaties in exchange for money, horses, and whiskey.

Listening to her whispered recital, Sager felt his rage build. What kind of damned fool woman took up with a man like Hawkins? She deserved what she'd gotten. And damn her eyes for bringing Logan into her hell.

He crossed his arms and glared at his brother, on his knees in a circle of some of the fiercest warriors the Sioux people had ever produced. He hoped his fun with Sarah had been worth it, because it was entirely likely Logan would be giving his life for the woman.

Hawkins was allowed to speak to defend himself. He looked around the gathering, his eyes a little white-rimmed. He spoke in English, offering riches in money and horses to Cloud Walker's band if they would release him. No one met his look. No one spoke or in any way indicated they heard his words. After a time, two warriors pushed him back to a seat on the ground.

Cloud Walker asked if anyone would speak in defense of Hawkins, "the man whose name would not be spoken." No one did.

The council deliberated. Hawkins's punishment was told to Cloud Walker, who announced it to the gathering: Hawkins was to face a warrior in a fight to the death tomorrow.

The next man to face an accounting of his crimes was Swift Elk. Sarah began to tremble. The edge of her sleeve rippled with the tension in her body. She held her hands higher against her chest as she translated.

Cloud Walker told of the many great deeds Swift Elk had done for his people, battles won and lost, wounds received in gallant acts of bravery, about how his anger at those who would make peace with the white men and move to the agencies led him to form his own band of warriors, his own village. How his band had broken with the tribe in taking white women captive and causing the soldiers to come hunt all the Sioux. How they had done this and other acts of men with bad hearts, all for money. How he had allowed great warriors who held him in high regard to sell themselves as slaves to the one whose name would not be spoken in exchange for whiskey. How he had caused the deaths of all of his men in service to their white owner at a time when the Sioux needed all their warriors whole of heart, focused on the purpose of saving their people.

Sager looked at Sarah. Twin paths of tears streaked her cheeks. Her eyes were unfocused, as if she looked inward at untold atrocities. She held her head high, her shoulders back, but he could tell she bore a weight that would break a much stronger person.

His gaze shifted back to Logan. He saw his brother look at Sarah, then glare at him. His gaze was unblinking, demanding. Sager fought the command in his brother's look. Because of the woman who stood so solemnly next to him, Logan was on trial for his life. He'd be goddamned if he offered her support. By God, she would stand as he stood and watch the results of her choices condemn Logan.

Logan did not blink and did not look away. Sager cursed silently, his resolve wavering. Right or wrong, this was probably the only aid he could offer his brother.

He reached an arm out to Sarah and pulled her against his side. She shook like a frightened bird and was just about as fragile. She did not lean into him, did not accept his strength. Something in Sager bent.

Snapped right in half.

How would he feel if it were his wife, Rachel, here instead, watching Sager take a punishment he didn't deserve? Who the hell was he to judge his brother or the woman he loved? Sager himself was living proof that love made no sense. It came when it wished, changing everything in its path, and lasting forever.

Or at least, for as long as either lover lived.

He pulled Sarah closer, holding her with both arms. He kissed her forehead. "Be calm, little sister. I bet Logan's been in worse situations and lived to tell," he whispered against her temple. At that, a sob did break free. She pushed her face into his chest and cried softly.

He watched while Cloud Walker received Swift Elk's judgment from the council. He announced to the gathering that the proud warrior was to leave and never return to the people of this village, or any Sioux village, for the rest of his life.

At last, the focus turned to Logan. Sarah straightened and resumed translating for them.

Sager smiled. They called Logan "Shadow Wolf." It was a strong name. The chief said that while Shadow Wolf was a new friend to him and the village, he had been a friend of their people for many years, teaching them the language of the white man, making generous trades with their artisans, many of whom were women who had lost their husbands and sons and had no way of contributing to their people other than through the work of their art. He listed a few very harsh winters when different villages were camped near the agencies but were not fed. Logan's trading posts had provided food in exchange for furs that were to be taken the next season. Often Logan had acted as translator and defender, standing between a village and soldiers who came to kill. Shadow Wolf was a friend of all the Sioux people.

Sager looked at Declan and shook his head,

stunned by the list of Logan's deeds. He looked back at his brother, wondering who the hell he had become. He was proud of the man he saw kneeling in the council ring, watching the chief without fear, without any emotion whatsoever.

Cloud Walker continued telling about the crimes Logan was accused of, saying that Shadow Wolf had killed five warriors of Swift Elk's band when they broke the peace and attacked his camp, that he had committed the ultimate treachery of scalping the defeated warriors of a people Logan said he loved.

This last crime was so heinous that whispers broke out in the assemblage.

"It's not true!" Sarah hissed. Sager laid a restraining arm on her to keep her from interrupting the proceedings.

When asked if he had anything to say in his defense, Logan stood and glanced once around the entire ring. He took his time with his words, as befitted such a solemn occasion.

"In many of the Sioux villages I have visited, the people have opened their homes to me, shared the stories of their families, fed me when I was hungry, healed me when I was injured. If I have helped them in any small way, my heart feels joy. I regret having to take the lives of such brave men as Swift Elk's warriors, but I do not regret protecting my wife. When Swift Elk's men stopped fighting me, I stopped fighting them. I left Swift Elk to see to their wounds or to carry their bodies home. I did not scalp any of them."

Swift Elk jumped to his feet and waved his hand

toward Logan. "He is a white man. He lies like all of them do. Lies are all they can say. I fought him bravely. I knew he would bring trouble to the people. He has brought a Shoshone spy and a lawman. He is as false as any white man!"

Cloud Walker gestured and two warriors pushed Swift Elk to sit again. He asked if anyone would speak in Shadow Wolf's defense. Silence blanketed the assembly. At last, one man stood. Swift Elk saw the reaction of the council members. He turned to see who defended Shadow Wolf.

Sarah sent Declan and Sager a worried look. "That is Red Tail. He's one of Swift Elk's men." She looked at Sager. "There was a survivor that day." He told the story of the battle, including how Swift Elk had told them they were to find papers in Shadow Wolf's wagon, and that if they met Shadow Wolf or Yellow Moon, they were to kill them. When Yellow Moon and Shadow Wolf had walked toward the camp, he and another warrior had fled, thinking they were ghosts. When they realized the others had not followed them, they returned, but still watched from a distance. Seeing there was only talking and that Shadow Wolf had started to prepare food, they started to rejoin their party. Swift Elk and his men attacked Shadow Wolf suddenly, all of them coming at him. He and his friend had ridden hard to join the battle. Yellow Moon fired at them from under the wagon. His friend was killed, but Red Tail had his horse shot out from under him, pinning him, his gun thrown away from his grip. He pretended to be dead so that Shadow Wolf and Yellow Moon would not see he was defenseless. When the battle ended, Shadow Wolf took his own horses only and pulled his wagon out. The warrior watched as Swift Elk checked each man. Stabbing and scalping the ones who lived, scalping the ones who were already dead. By that time, Red Tail had freed himself from his horse's body. He hid so that Swift Elk would not find him. He watched while Swift Elk built a fire and burned their scalps, then left their bodies there to rot in the sun. Red Tail was the one who returned their bodies to their village.

Silence met this terrible news. No warrior would have levied so terrible a complaint and risked his own death by judgment of the council if it were not the truth.

Cloud Walker looked at Swift Elk. "Did you do this to your men?"

Swift Elk lowered his head, the gesture his only answer.

The men of the council began quiet discussions. Eventually, one approached Cloud Walker with their findings.

Sarah sent Sager a worried look. He and Declan moved a little closer to her.

"Swift Elk," Cloud Walker announced. "The council has determined that you cannot be released into the world. You will pay for your crimes tomorrow. You will face a challenger in a fight to the death.

"Shadow Wolf," he addressed Logan. "Tomorrow, you will challenge these two who have become enemies to our people."

Animated discussion broke out among those gathered. Sarah concentrated on breathing in and out. A curious numbness was starting up her body. Logan's brother still had an arm around her shoulders. As if she'd sobbed aloud, he drew her into his arms. One hand patted her back in a conspicuous show of support.

"It's going to be fine, honey, just fine." He bent his head to her and whispered into her ear, in a voice meant not to be overheard. "You're a Taggert now, and we take care of our own. I'm not gonna let anything happen to you or Logan. If things go bad, we'll get you both outta here. When the fighting begins tomorrow, bring our horses, including the ones Hawkins stole, out near the fight, saddled and ready."

"With our guns, if you can get them," Declan leaned near to add.

Sarah straightened. She swiped the tears from her face and brushed her hair back. She wasn't alone. Logan wasn't alone. He faced a Herculean challenge, and he was still so terribly injured, but Plan B was in place. And no matter what, the two men who had done so much harm to her would never be able to harm another person after tomorrow. She didn't regret that.

The crowd thinned out now that the council meeting was concluded. Swift Elk and Eugene were taken to different tepees.

Logan approached Sarah as Cloud Walker and the rest of the council moved away. Her heart caught in her throat. He looked weary, bruised, and utterly determined to see his task through. He crossed the field toward them, stopping when he was merely a few feet from her.

"I did not want this, Logan. It is too much to ask of anyone," she said, heedless of his brother and the sheriff, who stood so near.

"When I claimed you, I claimed your troubles, too. I knew what I did."

"It was wrong of me to get you into this mess. This is not your burden."

He moved closer. "No matter what, you gotta put the mad dogs down, honey, whether they're your devils, mine, or anyone else's. It is a just sentence. I would not have accepted anyone but me being their challenger. Tomorrow, they will pay for what they did to you. No one will ever lay a hand on you again. Ever." He opened his arms as he gave her a look that told her exactly where he wanted her to be. She closed the distance between them, wrapping her arms around his waist, careful with his bruised ribs.

Sheriff Declan looked at Sager. "You realize that wily bastard just got your brother to take out the trash."

Logan looked over Sarah's head at Sager and the sheriff. His brother met his gaze. "Declan and I will be ready should you need us tomorrow."

"I only need you to watch out for Sarah."

Sager's expression hardened. "I do not need to be asked to guard my sister."

Logan smiled at him. He moved Sarah to one side so that he could reach a hand out to his brother.

Many Deer walked by him just then. Logan called to him. "Many Deer, this is my brother, Sager. He was the one who taught me the rope trick. If you like, he will teach it to you."

Many Deer stared at Sager for a long moment, animosity simmering in his hard gaze. Sager grinned. "Tell him if he is afraid, then I will not teach him," he said in English to Logan, making the hand signals for a coward as he spoke.

Many Deer untied the rope from his waist and handed it to Sager. "Tell him he will not sleep this night until he has taught it to me."

Logan translated the challenge. "Since you will be busy, hand me your bedrolls. I am going to sleep with my wife a short ways outside the village."

Chapter 19

Logan watched Sarah step from the river. Twilight lingered in the western sky, but already a full moon was rising, low and orange and enormous on the eastern horizon. Its pale light glistened on Sarah's damp skin and in the water rivulets still streaming from her wet hair.

She stepped into her leggings and was reaching for her tunic, but Logan stopped her. "Just your moccasins." He moved his hand from her soft stomach up to cup a breast. The evening was warm and the breeze barely stirred. He wanted to drink in the sight of her nudity, covered only by the night.

He took up his clothing and the bedrolls his brother and the sheriff had lent them. He knelt to roll out the blankets on the eastern side of the hill so that they could watch the moonrise.

The bedrolls had been heavier than expected and he soon discovered why. In addition to routine foodstuffs in each, Sager's had a knife, a Colt, and a loaded gun belt. Declan's had a Colt, a sawed-off shotgun, a loaded gun belt, and cartridge belt. He hid the weapons under the edge of a bedroll, hoping they wouldn't be needed tomorrow.

"Good heavens! They brought an arsenal. And the sheriff was worried about the weapons they left with their horses when the women put them up."

"Sager's not one to go tracking without some firepower. Guess the sheriff's the same way."

Logan sat on the bedroll and looked up at her. Warmth pooled low between her hips as she watched his hungry gaze sweep over her. He hooked his fingers in the wide tie around her hips that her leggings were tied to. She stepped onto the bedroll, her feet on either side of his hips.

He kissed the area of her belly just above the tie. The stubble of his beard rasped against her soft skin. He bit the string and smiled up at her with it in his teeth as he pulled her a few inches farther over him.

"Logan?"

"Hm-mmm?"

"What are you doing?"

"Making love to my wife."

"I've never done it this way."

He made an unintelligible sound as he moved a finger between the folds of her sex. He kissed her belly button, then the soft skin of the lower part of her belly, down to her mound. Sarah sucked in a breath. Resting her hands on the crown of his head, she felt him move lower so that his tongue stroked where his fingers had just been. Warm and wet, pressing against and around the most sensitive area above her opening until she thought she might scream.

Two long fingers entered her body, stretching her, stroking inside as his tongue stroked outside. He caught her clitoris in his mouth and sucked. She bucked against his hand. His fingers were slipping in and out, in and out, in long, slow slides. She was slick. His fingers moved differently, pressing up against the upper wall of her vagina, tapping, tapping. Something thick and warm began to uncoil. Her legs felt like rubber.

"Logan, I can't stand."

He pulled back enough to answer her. "Yes, you can, honey." She missed his tongue. But something was happening, something terrible. Wonderful. His fingers rapped again and again at the same spot until she broke. She cried out as her body convulsed, her inner muscles clenching around his fingers. He pulled her down over his lap, impaling her with his erection, sending her flying into a second and third release while he pumped into her, sinking to his balls in her flesh. Holding her, he turned them so that she was on her back. He covered her with his body. He twined his fingers with hers as his cock moved inside her. There was no fear in her face. She watched him with her great, dark eyes. Passion tightened her features. He could feel her passion start to crest again. He cupped a breast, pressing it upward so that he could suckle her. She cried out his name as she flew over the edge, taking him with her. He ground her hips against his body, holding her tightly to him as he spilled himself inside her.

She wrapped her arms around his shoulders, felt him tighten his hold on her. There were no words she could find to express the depth of her love. He'd found her, protected her, cherished her. He was always true, always kind. And she stood to lose him tomorrow.

"Logan," she said in a broken whisper against his neck, her arms and legs still wrapped around him. "Let's run away. Let's go far and fast and never stop."

He stroked her back, his hand warm and calloused. "What's this? Run like cowards?"

"I cannot live without you."

He pulled back. Her hair was nearly dry. He smoothed it from her cheek, held it still beneath his palms as he gripped her face. "Nor I you." He studied her face. "You have nothing to fear about tomorrow. It is just a fight. I will not take careless chances."

"You are already so injured from Swift Elk's attack."

"I will not fail tomorrow. I will not lose. Believe in me, even if you believe in nothing else." Still embedded in her warmth, he moved inside her. "I want you again. A hundred more times tonight." He wanted to drive every memory of every other man out of her mind so that when she saw the two who had nearly destroyed her life tomorrow, she would have no room in her mind or her soul to think of any man but him.

Cloud Walker's warriors stood in a wide circle, forming a natural arena. The sun was directly overhead; it beat down on the three men with blistering heat. Swift Elk paced toward Logan, who stood in place, watching him come near. None of the three had a weapon, nor

did any in the first circle of observers. This was a fight
to the death in straight hand-to-hand combat.

Each man was dressed in a breechclout, nothing
else. No moccasins covered their feet. Hawkins,
being unfamiliar with the attire, was the most dis-
advantaged. Logan kept his eyes fixed on Swift Elk
but monitored Hawkins with his peripheral vision.
The former chief did not speak to Hawkins. Didn't
look at him or signal in any way that he could per-
ceive, but it felt as if they moved in sync, both focusing on Logan as the first target.

Swift Elk charged toward him. Logan jumped to
the side at the last moment, shoving an elbow into
his ribs as he went past. Hawkins grabbed him,
trying to trip him. Logan rolled to his back, taking
Hawkins with him, using the fast motion to flip
Sarah's first husband. Logan bounded to his feet as
Swift Elk grabbed his wounded arm, digging his fingers into the bandage until blood darkened the
white linen. Logan gripped his shoulder, pulling
him forward, banging his forehead against Swift
Elk's. They staggered apart.

Hawkins was on his feet. He slammed a fist against
a dark bruise on Logan's back. Logan arched in
pain, but turned to face his attacker, grabbing his fist
before he could land another blow, spinning him
around in front of him. Just as they turned, Swift Elk
landed a punch that was intended for Logan. If he'd
hit Logan's cracked rib, he would have driven it into
his lung. Instead, the punch landed in the middle of
Hawkins's chest.

Seeing his botched hit, Swift Elk grabbed both

men and tripped Logan, dropping them to the ground. Logan still held a sputtering Hawkins in his arms. He wrapped an arm around Hawkins's chest and another around his jaw. "This is for Sarah," he said before snapping the man's neck.

Swift Elk tried to kick Logan's head, but he rolled to the side and jumped to his feet. The two men circled each other within the ring of warriors. The cut on Logan's temple began throbbing. The blood on his cheek told him the cut had opened up again. He swiped the blood from his face just as Swift Elk jumped him, landing a fist in his stomach, a hard cross to his nose.

Logan kicked Swift Elk's knee, bending it sideways, snapping the kneecap. He followed with a kick to the groin. Swift Elk rolled to the side and tried to drag himself away. Logan stared down at him, heard him begging for death. An image flashed in Logan's mind of what Swift Elk had done to Sarah when he'd captured her, what he'd allowed his men to do for weeks until he'd married her. She'd begged for mercy and never received it.

He had no stomach for killing, but he hadn't lied when he'd told Sarah that mad dogs had to die. Swift Elk had dragged himself over to the nearest warrior. He begged him to kill him. The man stood as if unaware of Swift Elk. Logan looked around the ring of people, desperate to see Sarah. He found Sager and Declan watching him, their faces somber. Sager turned away. Logan swayed. Then he saw Sarah. Sager had lifted her to one of their horses. She was fine. She was safe. If Cloud

Walker had him killed after he ended Swift Elk's life, Sager and Declan would get her out of there.

He walked over to Swift Elk, who clung to the legs of one of the warriors. He gripped his head and twisted fast, ending his life. When he straightened, he looked around the circle of warriors. No one moved or spoke, but the whole assembly seemed to spin and dance. He fell to one knee, coughing on the blood from his broken nose.

A loud cry went up among the men. Cloud Walker shouted to the Great Spirit, thanking him for sending the two bad-hearted men to their demise. One of the warriors gave Logan a knife, told him to take Swift Elk's scalp so that he couldn't enter the great hunting grounds of the afterlife.

Logan shook his head, refusing to take the knife. Let someone else deal the final insult. He would do no more. Then Sager and Declan were there, standing over him. Sager knelt before him. He was saying something, but the words made no sense to Logan, couldn't get through the humming in his ears. His brother held the back of Logan's head and cracked his nose back into place. Logan bent over and vomited from the pain and the blood and the tension of the fight.

Sager and Declan helped him to his feet. Sarah pushed her way through the crowd, rushing to Logan's side. He crushed her to him, heedless of the dirt and blood covering him. The humming receded. He was still unsteady on his feet, but the world began to right itself very slowly.

When he looked up, Cloud Walker was there.

His face was filled with resignation, relief. He reached for Logan's forearm. Logan clasped his arm. "You have said you would not kill a friend. I am glad to see you could kill an enemy."

"It is done."

Cloud Walker nodded. "It is done," he repeated, making the hand signal for the end of a transaction.

"What happens now?"

"Tonight, we will feast. We will dance and celebrate the people we once were, our great heroes who are no longer among us, and the heroes who will help us in our new path.

"Tomorrow, we will begin our move to the agencies. We cannot live peacefully in our own lands. Your people have seen to that. We will be a long time recovering from the wounds your people have caused."

Logan knew no words could lessen the pain Cloud Walker and his people faced in leaving their lands and giving themselves over to the agencies in the Dakotas. Logan was glad for the pain from his broken nose, for it explained the water in his eyes. "If you have need of me, send word through my posts or to the ranch near where you found me yesterday. I will come if you summon me."

Cloud Walker nodded. "It is good to know that we have one friend among our enemy's people." The chief walked away, keeping his head raised, his shoulders square, his broken heart hidden from his people.

The four began making their way through the

crowd to their horses. Declan helped Sarah to mount, while Sager got Logan into his saddle. Logan forced himself to straighten. He looked across the proud faces of Cloud Walker's people. He hoped he would see them again, though he knew something had changed that day, something that would never again be the same. He looked at Sarah, who watched him with a steady, intense regard, then at his brother and the sheriff, who were likewise watchful.

He nodded. "Let's go—" He stopped himself from saying "home." The Circle Bar wasn't his home. Maybe it never really had been. He'd grown up there, but he'd long known he was just a place-holder for Sid's only blood son. He couldn't blame Sid for that, and he no longer blamed Sager. It just was, that's all. He'd made a life outside the Circle Bar, one he was proud of, one that had helped many people.

Sarah was his home now. Wherever she was, he would be, and he would be complete.

Chapter 20

A half hour from the Circle Bar, Logan began to sway in his saddle. His eyes were swollen shut, he could no longer direct his horse, instead depending on his mount to follow the others in the group. His head was throbbing, the pain and movement making him nauseous. He couldn't even grind his teeth, because that sent more pain shearing through his skull. All he could do was breathe, but even that hurt—his cracked rib felt as if a steel trap had clamped down on his side.

Sager and Declan flanked him closely. He forced himself to straighten again. "Logan, give me your reins," Sager ordered. "Declan, put Sarah up there behind him."

"Bad idea, Sager," Logan growled as they came to a stop. "If I fall backward, I will crush her, and we'll still both fall off the horse."

"Don't bet on it, Logan. I'm stronger than you think," Sarah said, gripping fistfuls of Logan's leggings. "Lean back against me."

"You're as big as a minute, woman. Not even that, maybe just a half minute." He felt her nod against his shoulder toward Sager. They moved into a trot. Logan cursed and took hold of Sarah's hands, holding her to him even as he leaned back against her.

At the house, people erupted from the front door, including Sid, a beautiful blond woman, and several young boys, their voices raised in a cacophony of excitement. Sarah felt Logan stiffen. His tension slipped into her. She couldn't help staring at the woman who had to be Rachel. The woman who'd rejected Logan. She felt an unwelcome wash of jealousy slip through her. Did he still have feelings for her?

Rachel smiled at her. Sarah nodded in response to the tentative greeting. She'd never been jealous a minute in her life and didn't like the feel of it now.

Sager dismounted, catching Rachel as she launched herself at him. He knelt and hugged each of the three boys, his sons, Sarah realized. He looked at Sid. "Why are you here? I wanted you to wait at Old Jack's."

"Your wife wanted us here so that we could help when you got back. Maybe you haven't noticed, but when she gets the bit between her teeth, there ain't much a person can do. Boys, stand aside, let your dad and the sheriff get Uncle Logan down." He waved the children back.

Sager helped Sarah down; then he and Declan got Logan off. Declan took his head, Sager his feet, and they carried him up the front porch.

"God Almighty, Logan. What happened, son?" Sid whispered.

Logan tried to smile but wasn't sure the gesture made it to his lips. "It's a long story."

"And it starts with a woman," Declan scoffed.

"Of course," Sager added, giving Sarah a quick wink.

"Don't pay them any heed, Sarah," Rachel said, taking her arm. "They'll only be worse if they think they can get to you."

"Rachel?" Logan held up a hand.

She took it quickly, pressing a quick kiss on his scraped and bruised knuckles. "Hi, Logan. We thought you'd never come home again."

"Honey, think you could scold him when we get him to his room?" Sager asked. "He ain't exactly a lightweight."

Sarah pulled free of Rachel's hand and hurried down the hallway to turn down the covers on the bed in Logan's room. She settled the pillows behind Logan. When she straightened, the room was filled with people. His father, Rachel, Sager, the sheriff, a couple of the ranch hands, the housekeeper, and three boys jostling for position in front of the adults. All of them wore faces filled with love, worry, and fatigue. These weren't people who hated Logan. Not a one of them. Why had he left them?

"Out. All of you. Out. He needs to rest," she insisted.

Sager grinned at Sarah. "Looks like you got yourself a little she-bear after all, brother." He went over to her and pulled her into a hug. "I told you he'd live to tell." He kissed her forehead, then took Rachel's hand and headed for the door.

"Shout if you need anything, Sarah," Rachel called as Sager pulled her from the room. "I'll bring bandages and a medical kit."

The room fell silent. She listened to the noise grow distant down the hallway.

"Sarah, honey, you still here?"

"Yes."

"Come over here."

She sat on the edge of the bed. His eyes were swollen shut; red vied with black, blue, and purple for the primary color of his face. She choked back a sob.

"That good, huh? This is nothing, sweetheart. Well, it's a little worse than usual—"

"Logan Taggert, don't you dare tell me you're often in fights. I won't have it. I just won't."

He lifted a hand to her cheek. "I want to get something straight right now, honey. You're my wife, Sarah Taggert." He must have felt her brace for an argument, for his thumb quickly covered her lips. "We were married in the way of the Great Spirit and before God. I have grave doubts about your first marriage's validity. We know Hawkins used several aliases. There might have been several other women he married and cheated just like you. In a couple of weeks, when I'm allowed to get up and about, we'll redo our vows, here, in front of friends and family. Until then, you are my wife. You will sleep here in my room, in this bed, with me."

"What about your family? What will they think?"

He pulled her onto the bed, into the crook of his arm, against his side. "Sager has already accepted you. Rachel will be happy to have another female so nearby. And Sid will love you because I do. They are your family now." Logan threaded his fingers through hers. "What is it, honey? You're wound tight enough to break."

Sarah sighed. This was not the time to be fretting about her petty worries.

"Out with it."

"Do you still have feelings for Rachel?"

"I do. Very strong feelings." She started to pull away, but his arm tightened around her. "They are exactly the same type of feelings I have for Sager or Sid. Hell, even Rachel's dad, Old Jack. They're family. I would give my life for any of them, as they would for me or you." He kissed the top of Sarah's head. "But I am not in love with her. I never was. I love you. And only you." He nuzzled her forehead. "It's kinda fun having you jealous. Tell me about it again."

"Logan Taggert!" She pushed herself up so that she could lean over and kiss him, ever so gently, on the mouth. He pulled her up against him and used a knee to spread her legs over him.

"Honey, there's only one part of me that doesn't hurt right now." He ground her hips over his erection, which had begun to rise ever since he knew he was alone with her.

"You can't want that now! You're injured. You need rest."

"It is exactly what I want. Right now." She pulled him free of his breechclout and lowered herself over him. He let out a long, low groan. "Yes." She was slick and tight. Magnificent. "I fought for you. I killed your devils, Sarah. I won you. I'm keeping you. God, I love you."

He slipped a hand up her thigh, moving his thumb to her mound, lower to the sensitive spot above her entrance. He worked his thumb in a slow, circular motion. Heat filled Sarah, radiating from her hips outward. She took most of her weight on her knees, careful to jostle Logan as little as possible. She reached back and fingered his sac, gently massaging as she pulled herself up and slipped back down the hard length of him.

Logan cursed. "Sarah! Sarah, now! Please. Now!" He slammed his hips up, seating himself to the balls. He felt her inner muscles contract, grabbing and releasing. He thrust against those spasms, pounded into her. The orgasm ripping through her took him along with it. She braced her weight on her knees until the last little aftershocks rippled through them. He pulled her down for his kiss, hooking a hand around the back of her neck. "Don't ever leave me."

She wrapped her arms around his neck and smiled against his mouth. "I never could, Logan. I don't know where I end and you begin. You're my everything." She pulled free of his hold, disengaging their bodies. Logan sucked in a breath at the loss of her body.

"And that, Mr. Taggert, is the last loving you're going to get until you're better."

"The hell it is."

"I'm going to give you a sponge bath, then I'll see what food there might be in the kitchen." She untied his moccasins and pulled them off, then set to work on the strap holding his leggings and breech-clout up.

"I don't need a sponge bath. My legs aren't broken. There's a perfectly good tub in the other room." He stood up, wincing at the pain from his sore rib. She slipped the leathers off his hips and down his legs so that he could step out of them. When she straightened, he cupped her cheeks. His eyes were still closed, but he felt the rigid tightening of her jaw. He was hard again and he knew she'd seen him. He grinned at her. "Maybe you should take a bath with me."

"No. Sit here for a minute while I draw the water." She helped him to the edge of the bed.

"You're a bossy little thing."

"Yes I am, Mr. Taggert."

Sarah stood at the kitchen doorway. Logan's family was seated around the table. She felt like such an outsider. If Logan didn't need bandages and something to eat, she would have turned and run. Sager saw her first. He stood up and motioned her forward. "Come in, Sarah."

Sid and Declan stood as she settled herself. Rachel patted a seat next to her. "How is he?" she asked.

"Sleeping now, but getting grumpier by the minute." Sarah looked at Logan's father. "Mr. Taggert, has a doctor been summoned?"

"Yep, as soon as you got here. And I'm 'Sid' or 'Dad,' Sarah—anything but 'Mr. Taggert.'"

Rachel squeezed her hand. "You must be starving." She started to rise, but Maria, the housekeeper, was already bringing a bowl of soup over.

"You sit, Miss Rachel. I have Miss Sarah's food right here."

Sarah pushed her bowl away. "I should feed Logan first."

"Eat," Sid ordered. "You look ready to drop. You've been through one hell of an ordeal yourself. You'll be no good to Logan if you're not well yourself."

Maria brought two more bowls of soup over for the sheriff and Sager, following that with a platter of sandwiches. Rachel retrieved the coffeepot from the stove and filled coffee cups.

She set the pot back, then settled in her seat with a great sigh as she looked at Sarah. "I, for one, am dying to hear everything! Logan keeps so much to himself, I worried he'd be alone the rest of his life. And here you've brought him home to us, Sarah. You're a miracle worker."

Sarah looked at the faces of Logan's family. Her family, he'd said. "We met at Fort Buford. He'd come in to change mounts and ended up riding in the stagecoach instead," she began, giving Rachel a quick smile. Rachel smiled back.

Home. She was home. It felt good. It felt wonderful. Over the next hour, through two bowls of soup, Sarah related the whole story.

Sid sat at the head of the table, white-faced and drawn. "I can't imagine the peril you two were in."

"He was never afraid," Sarah told him. "Never once. It helped me to see the Sioux as he does. He trades with many villages each year. He is well known among the different tribes." She looked at Rachel. "He bought some beautiful pieces of bead and leatherwork. When he wakes, you should come select something for yourself. I know he'd like you to have a gift."

"I'd like that." Rachel smiled.

The sheriff leaned back in his seat. "I heard Hawkins admit that the wanted poster we found for you was itself a forgery. He never did sign that confession, but I'll get the word out around here and make sure those posters are taken down."

"Thank you, Sheriff," Sarah said.

A week later, Logan was up and about. The doctor had been to see him a couple of times. The swelling was receding around his nose and eyes. The doctor said his broken nose would heal cleanly, thanks to Sager's setting it so efficiently. Logan was getting edgy to complete his tour of his posts. He'd just finished grooming his and Sarah's horses, his first physical activity in days. The doctor had said no riding for another couple of weeks, but Logan was thinking of breaking that edict.

"Logan!" Sid stepped out to the porch and hollered for him.

Wagons had been coming and going with increasing frequency as the household prepared for the wedding. Invitations had been sent out, supplies were arriving every day.

The dining room had been turned into a milliner's shop. Yards of fabric were bunched and piled throughout the room and half a dozen women, including Sarah, Rachel, and her friends Leah and Audrey, were gathered there, sewing a trousseau for Sarah. Audrey had brought a sewing machine and all of her children with her. Her oldest two girls sat in the dining room stitching away. His nephews and Leah and Audrey's children ran like hellions around the ranch, thrilled to have each other's company.

Logan paused in the foyer, watching the women work. They chattered and laughed. Sarah looked up and saw him. The smile she gave made his mind go blank. He started for her, intending to take her down to their room, but Sid called again from his office.

Logan kissed Sarah's forehead and followed his father's summons. In the den, Sager closed the door after him. Logan looked from his brother to his father. "What is it?"

Sid motioned to the chairs in front of his desk. "It's time we had a talk about a few things."

"What things?"

"What are your plans after the wedding?"

"What are you fishing for, Dad?"

"I want to know if you're home for good."

Logan looked at his father, read in his carefully blank expression the truth that Logan's answer mattered. "No, I'm not. I've built a life outside the Circle Bar. I need to get back to it."

"Logan, we want you to stay," Sager said, filling the silence that followed Logan's announcement.

"You want me to stay to work your ranch, Sager? I'm not interested."

Sid tossed a folded piece of paper to the edge of his desk. Neither he nor Sager said a word. Logan picked it up. It was Sid's will. "What is this? Have you been ill?"

"Read it," Sid said.

The will was short. There were provisions for Sid's long-term household staff and ranch hands, and Sager got a generous financial settlement. But Logan had been willed the house and all the Circle Bar land. He read it twice, then checked the signatures. Sid's and his lawyer's—dated nearly eight years ago.

"What is this?" he asked his father.

"I've been a damned fool, Logan. Sager convinced me to change my will shortly after he married Rachel. I thought what I had originally provided was fair, but Sager made me see things from a different perspective."

Logan looked at Sager. The will was exactly the opposite of what it had been all those years ago, with the financial settlement originally going to Logan and the land to Sager.

"So you see, little brother, I've been working your land for you all these years." Sager grinned at him. "We want you home."

"If there's not enough room in the house for your family and your old man, we can build an apartment for me over the bunkhouse."

Logan got out of his seat and paced once around the room. He looked at Sid and Sager, then shoved a hand through his hair. "Why would you do this?"

"Because you're part of this family. This is your legacy. And you belong here with us." Sid got up and came around to lean against the front of his desk. "You're my son, Logan Taggert. I raised you. I sent you to college. I want you home."

"I don't know what to say. I've built a business I need to continue to oversee."

"I don't see why you can't do both," Sid suggested. "Put a strong manager in charge of your trading posts. Step back a bit. Spend some time up here."

"There's room for an alliance between our ranches and your posts. We can supply all the beef your posts can sell. And with the agencies filling up, we could use your help getting contracts for beef," Sager added. "What do you say?"

"Let me talk it over with Sarah. I need to give it some thought."

Logan leaned against the archway leading to the dining room. Sarah looked up. Their eyes connected. Seeing the tension in him, the color washed from her face.

"Ladies, mind if I borrow Sarah for a bit?" he asked.

"Of course not. You two do what you need to do. I think we're close to a stopping point for today anyway," Rachel told him.

He held the front door open for Sarah. They walked across the porch and out into the afternoon sun. She looked up at him as he looked down at her. Their gazes held for a moment.

"You're scaring me, Logan."

They walked down the road a ways to the shade of an old cottonwood. He turned and drew Sarah's back against him. From where they stood, they had an excellent view of Sid's house.

Logan rested his chin on her head.

"Honey, how would you feel about staying here?"

"Staying here? Where are you going?"

"Nowhere. I'll be here, too. That was the deal, remember?"

She turned and looked up at him. "Live here?"

He watched her face, hoping beyond hope that her heart felt what his did. "Could you be happy here?"

"Yes. Could you?"

He nodded. "Sid and Sager want me to join their ranching operation. They want us to make our home here. I'm not closing the trading posts, so we'll still need to do some traveling, but this would be our main home."

Tears welled in Sarah's eyes. She turned and looked at the house. "My home. Our home." She swiped the tears from her cheeks. "I thought you said this would belong to your brother one day."

"Sager had Sid change his will. It will be ours one day—hopefully a very long time from now. They made room for us. I want to be here, Sarah, but only if you do, too."

She nodded, words having simply failed her. He laughed and swung her around.

"Logan, be careful! Your ribs haven't healed yet."

"I'm healed enough, honey." He let her down slowly, keeping her body close to his. He bent his head, his gaze locked on hers. She tightened her arms around his neck, rising to meet him halfway. The kiss they shared was gentle, full of promise, full of joy.

They didn't immediately hear the distant rumble of a rider coming in fast. It was the sudden flurry of men hurrying toward them that triggered Logan's attention. A horse was thundering down the valley, charging toward them.

Sarah tensed. Even from this distance she could see it was an Indian. She straightened and sent a frenzied look around, caught up by the instinct to flee. Logan took hold of her arm. "Steady there. It's just Chayton."

As their friend approached, they saw he rode with White Bird in front of him. Sarah looked to see if Laughs-Like-Water was following with their son, but didn't see any others. Hearing the rider, Sid came out of the house and several men from the bunkhouse approached with guns, standing across the drive, putting themselves between the Indian and where Logan stood with Sarah.

"He is a friend. Stand down." Logan shouldered his way through the men as Chayton drew up in the drive. Sarah moved to stand beside Logan. For a moment, neither man spoke.

Chayton looked at Logan, then looked away. Pain ravaged his face. "Shadow Wolf, you have been like a brother to me," he said in English, his gaze swinging back to Logan.

"As you have been to me."

"I ask a favor."

"Anything."

Again, Chayton paused before speaking. "The scalp taker and his men attacked my village while we men were out hunting. They killed many, took many scalps. He killed Laughs-Like-Water and Little Hawk."

Sarah gasped. "No, Chayton. No." Sarah thought of them as they'd been at the camp a few weeks earlier. Little Hawk and White Bird playing chase with the younger apprentices, manning the spit over the roasting pit, holding a chocolate bar in their hands until it melted. She remembered the love Laughs-Like-Water had in her eyes when she looked at any of her family members. She'd been a force of nature.

"I am taking my people to Red Cloud's agency. When I go there, they will take my gun and my horse. In two years' time, they will take my daughter and send her to a school far away. I have lost everything. My home. My wife. My children."

Logan put his hand on Chayton's knee. "Stay here with us."

"I cannot leave my people. The favor I ask is that you continue to trade with my wife's apprentices. More than ever, they will need your support. It is her legacy I would have you honor."

"Of course. I will come in the autumn with the materials they need to work through the winter."

"Chayton—" Sarah came forward. "Chayton, leave White Bird with us. We will foster her. She will have the education the agency demands, but in the home of people who love her. And you can visit her anytime you like."

Chayton's dark eyes studied her. He looked at Logan. "You would do this?"

"Gladly, my friend."

"I don't know when I will be able to come back."

"She will be safe with us. Come when you can."

A muscle worked at the edge of Chayton's jaw. He picked up his daughter, standing her on his thigh, facing him. He lifted a necklace from his neck and draped it over hers.

"You are my heart, White Bird," he said in Sioux. She put a tiny hand on his face as she frowned at him, her brows drawn together in tiny wrinkles. His nostrils flared with the effort of not weeping before strangers. He kissed her and hugged her tightly until she began to squirm, then he handed her down to Sarah. He and Logan exchanged a look.

Putting his heels to his horse, he rode away.

Epilogue

Logan watched White Bird come toward him, moving slowly, silently, between the rows of chairs. He gave her an encouraging smile, dropping to a crouch and motioning her forward. Her big, dark eyes monitored the assembly of white adults as if expecting them to transform at any moment into flesh-eating monsters. Every few steps, she stood still and sprinkled rose petals over the grass, checking the adults before stepping forward again. When she reached Logan's side, he gave her a big hug and told her in Sioux how proud he was of her before sending her to stand next to Rachel.

The women had transformed the side yard of the main house. Half of the space was arranged with several long tables, one for family and friends, one for the gaggle of children who had come with the adults, and the last for the ranch hands, all of whom were longtime workers at the Circle Bar or Sager's spread, the Crippled Horse. The other half of the area was given over to rows of chairs that led up to where Logan stood with Sager and the Reverend Adamson.

When Logan looked up after getting White Bird settled, Sarah was there, starting down the aisle on Sid's arm. She wore a beautiful gown of white brocade that hung in simple lines from her slim hips down. It hugged her ribs and curved enticingly up over her breasts. At the edge of the deep neckline, he could just make out part of her tattoo. He was glad she hadn't hidden it. He knew she'd done that for him.

Her hair was coiled and tucked in tiny braids over the crown of her head. A veil was draped over her hair and reached down to her shoulders, leaving her face uncovered. Her warm, brown eyes were shining with happiness. It was hard to reconcile the woman coming toward him with the woman he'd first met just a few months earlier.

Logan looked at his dad, who was bursting with pride as if she were his own daughter. In the month since their return, in addition to caring for Logan, sewing a new wardrobe, and dealing with frantic wedding preparations, she'd made time to oversee the arrangement of a suite of rooms for Sid on the ground floor of the house, ensuring he had his own drawing room off his bedroom. She'd ordered new furniture for him, making his space masculine and comfortable—something Logan's mother had never allowed and Sid hadn't sought for himself after her death. Sarah had given him a place where he could retreat should he want a little solitude.

She had also rearranged their quarters upstairs, switching out furniture from some of the other rooms, giving the space her own personal touch. She had revived a house that had long been dormant, waiting to be made a home.

Logan smiled at Sarah as Sid kissed her cheek and handed her over. She gave Rachel, her matron of honor, her bouquet to hold. This time, when the reverend asked her to place her hands in Logan's, she did not hesitate. The shade from the cotton-wood trees overhead shifted. Light and shadows danced over her. She smiled up at him, her eyes filled with love. Heedless of the ceremony, Logan touched her cheek, stroking her skin with his thumb. He leaned forward and kissed her forehead, then forced himself to listen to the reverend as he and Sarah were married for the third time.

Logan was unsure how he made it through the ceremony and the feast that followed. He couldn't take his eyes from his wife. She laughed with his friends, danced with his brother and father, and charmed everyone who had gathered.

"Hard to believe Sarah's transformation, Logan," Leah said as she brought him a cup of punch. "She was so broken when she first came to Defiance. Just look at her now. I think you may have saved her life."

Logan smiled. "Maybe. But I know for sure she saved mine."

Jace came over and clapped him on the shoulder. "I think you should get married at least once a year, Logan. I'm enjoying these celebrations."

"Or we could just have a shindig at one of our ranches each year, once Audrey and Julian come in for the summer," Leah suggested.

Jace smiled down at his wife, his warm gaze sweeping the new dress the ladies had made for Leah, a pale, lavender chiffon that complemented her dark coloring and violet eyes. "Would you do me the honor of giving me this dance, Mrs. Gage?"

"Yes, I believe I will, Mr. Gage." Leah took his arm and let him lead her into the dance. Seeing them join the waltz, Audrey waved her fingers. Her husband, Julian, nodded to Jace before sweeping her away.

"Look at all of you. Grown and beautiful and settled," Maddie sighed as she paused by Logan's side. "Your father says you'll be staying here. I'm happy about that." They watched Sarah take a turn on the temporary dance platform with the sheriff. "Now there's a man who needs a wife," Maddie said, tapping her chin pensively.

Logan laughed and shook his head. "Good luck with that!"

When the dance ended, Declan escorted Sarah back to Logan. He lifted his hat to thank her for the dance, then offered Maddie his arm and led her back toward the dance floor.

"Watch out for that one, Cal. She's making plans for you," Logan warned.

The sheriff laughed. "Hold on there, Maddie. I got my life arranged just the way I like it."

Maddie sent Logan and Sarah a wink. "Do you, now . . . ?" Her voice faded as she and the sheriff walked away.

Logan drew Sarah into a hug. "I love you," he said as he looked into her eyes.

"I love you." She smiled and tightened her arms around his neck. "This has been a wonderful day. A big memory that's filling all the empty spaces inside me. Thank you."

"Honey, I'm going to spend the rest of my life giving you big memories, so you better keep making room for more."

Did you miss the other titles in the
Men of Defiance series?
Start from the beginning!

Rachel and the
Hired Gun

When Rachel Douglas left her aunt's house in Virginia for the wilds of the Dakota Territory, she knew the journey would be long and arduous. But she didn't realize that she has been summoned west to be used as a pawn in a ranch war with her father's neighbor—or that her fierce, sudden attraction to Sager, her father's hired gun, would put her heart and her life in jeopardy. Seducing Rachel and feeding a bitter feud between the two ranches was Sager's plan of vengeance against those who slaughtered his foster Shoshone family. Instead, Rachel's guileless mix of courage and vulnerability touches the conscience he thought he'd buried long ago, and draws them both into a passion without rules, without limits—one that will change their destinies forever . . .

AUDREY AND THE MAVERICK

In Elaine Levine's stunning novel of the American West, a proud rancher and a determined young woman are drawn together in the lawless town of Defiance.

Virginia financier Julian McCaid has put his troubled past behind him. His plans for the future don't include Audrey Sheridan, the extraordinary frontier woman he met just once. But it's because of her that he's come to the Dakota Territory to investigate problems at his ranch. And it's all the more surprising when he discovers she isn't the innocent he believed. Now nothing but her complete surrender will purge her from his soul.

If it weren't for the children she cares for in her makeshift orphanage, Audrey would have left Defiance long ago. Now the sheriff is blackmailing her to distract the man who might derail his corrupt schemes—a man who can offer Audrey not just protection, but a passion bold enough to make them claim their place in this harsh and beautiful land . . .

LEAH AND THE
BOUNTY HUNTER

They are brash, they are brave, and when they see a chance to be a hero, they take it. They are the Men of Defiance, and they are not easily tamed . . .

To Leah Morgan's mind, the last thing her hometown of Defiance needs is another gunman stalking its dusty streets—especially one as sweet-talking and fine-looking as Jace Gage. Despite her warnings, the infuriating man seems determined to meddle in her life and risk his own, all for a town that can't be saved and a heart she locked away long ago.

Professional bounty hunter Jace Gage has cleaned up plenty of corrupt towns in his lifetime, and he knows he can handle whatever Defiance's thugs have to offer. But the town's most lawful citizen is another story. Beautiful, willful and exasperating at every turn, Leah is the one person capable of bringing the ruthless gunslinger to his knees—and capturing his desire with a single kiss . . .